WHY
SHE
RAN

BOOKS BY GERALDINE HOGAN

Her Sister's Bones

WHY SHE RAN

GERALDINE HOGAN

bookouture

Published by Bookouture in 2019

An imprint of Storyfire Ltd.
Carmelite House
50 Victoria Embankment
London EC4Y 0DZ

www.bookouture.com

ISBN: 978-1-78681-912-3
eBook ISBN: 978-1-78681-911-6

For Bernadine Cafferkey

PROLOGUE
Ten Years Earlier...

She was drowning. Her eyes were open to the darkness, bulging from their sockets. The water stung at first, but now the filmy softness of it was like a balm and maybe if she stared hard into it, there might be some reprieve. Of course, she knew the only way *it* would really stop was when she was dead. Maybe not this time, but Eleanor understood the hatred had to end somewhere. The last of her breath gasped desperately, hiccupping strange sounds that ran far beyond her. This wouldn't kill her, but still she struggled, a fighting furious force, thrusting and lashing with arms that never met their target. She was trapped, strong hands over her head, a forearm tight across her shoulder blades, a knee digging into her – she would have bruises, but that was nothing new. Her belly, aching and hungry, weighed her further down and she knew that hatred would never go away.

'*Eleanor.*' She heard her mother's voice a long way off, as if it had surfaced, and then she was pulled out of the water, a shivering, shaking rag, almost dead, but not quite yet. 'This can't go on...' the words were uttered quietly. 'Oh, my darling, this can't go on...'

CHAPTER 1

Eleanor Marshall sighed, blowing out an almost perfect smoke ring from the last cigarette in the packet. Friday night and this was all she had, an empty packet of cigarettes and an early night in a bed that might as well have been in a cell. It hadn't always been like this. Far from it: before her father had insisted she come to this happy-clappy, lovey-dovey crazy house, Eleanor had lived a privileged existence. The daughter of one of Ireland's wealthiest men, with designer clothes in her wardrobe and more freedom than perhaps was good for her, she'd rebelled early and with the trademark style of one keen to set an example for the sister coming behind. That was before they'd sent her here to Curlew Hall.

Such a stupid name to call this place. For one thing, they were miles from the seaside and so the chance of having curlews anywhere near were slim to nil. For another, the hall had been razed to the ground almost a hundred years ago. There was no hall here now – only a fancy counselling centre, built for kids with parents rich enough to pass on their responsibilities to someone else. Well, not for much longer. In a few months' time, she'd be sixteen and old enough to sign herself out of here and do whatever she wanted, and there wasn't a damn thing anyone could do about it.

She looked across the courtyard, the light fading fast behind clouds too domineering to reveal what sunshine remained with any great vigour. There were two units, one of them empty for now, the other housed four girls. She spotted one of them pass by a window. Bitch. Suz Mullins – a hard nut, here only because the state couldn't find anywhere else to take her, so the tax man coughed up the exorbitant fees to keep her in luxury that was far too good for her in Eleanor's opinion.

Jealousy, that was Suz's problem, even if – in Eleanor's opinion, again – she didn't have that much to be jealous of at all. True, Eleanor's father owned a quarter of county Limerick – the good quarter. She had a family, for what that was worth. She'd had a home before… this. Although, sometimes it felt as if home was moving further away, blurred with time and antidepressants; perhaps she was better off here, even if she'd never actually belong.

Tonight, she was tired. One of the hippy counsellors, a woman called Ava, considered it her personal mission to run their addictions out of them. Eleanor figured it wouldn't matter if you were here with an eating disorder or a case of schizophrenia, Ava would have you trotting through the woods to clear your head and sort out all of your worries. Ten miles today – and her feet hurt like hell. It wasn't the distance, the problem was she'd stuck to her guns and refused to wear her proper shoes, so now the expensive boots she'd bought in Harvey Nicks a year earlier were ruined and she had the blisters to prove she'd walked every single mile.

'You ready for bed, love?' Rachel asked as she put her head around the door and smiled kindly. It was that kind of place – you got to move around, but you were never really alone; with Eleanor's history of self-harm and damage to property, there was always someone close by. Rachel was lovely. She probably wouldn't last much longer. They never did. 'You can stay out a little more, if you'd like, just don't get cold.' She walked over with a large faded blanket and placed it over Eleanor's shoulders like a tarpaulin. Eleanor was barely five-feet tall, so it covered her skeletal frame in a fabric-softener infused whirl of well-washed cotton. Rachel reached across and pulled the hair from Eleanor's eyes, then she looked at her, perhaps they were both tired. It had been a very long day.

'Good evening, Princess.' Nate Hegarty was standing at the door, filling up the height of the frame, his skinny arm stretched across the opening. He smelled of cigarettes and cheap aftershave and something much too dark for Eleanor to put a name on. He was wearing his usual uniform of hoodie and tracksuit bottoms, with trainers that had to be a couple of sizes too large. His dark and greasy hair fell across one eye and he shoved it back with the heel of his hand to reveal cruel eyes and a taunting mouth. How long had he been there? She knew he was not watching her. He was watching Rachel – he always did, as if it was some game they played.

Eleanor wondered if they'd *done it*. She couldn't imagine anyone sleeping with Nate Hegarty, but then Rachel was a funny sort of girl. She'd started at Curlew Hall only months earlier. She was the kindest of all the staff, but there was something about her, as if she had been apologising all her life. And there was no reason – she was that elusive blend of all good qualities as far as Eleanor could see, smart, funny, thoughtful and, yes, even pretty. Eleanor could never quite put her finger on it, but it was almost as if Rachel was grateful to Nate. And that just made no sense to Eleanor. Nate Hegarty never did anything for anyone that didn't involve some return for himself. Eleanor had thought idly once, if they were *doing it* – having sex – here, she could get him sacked. The only problem was it would also mean getting Rachel sacked and Eleanor wouldn't want that for the world.

'How's my girl tonight? It's me, you and Rachel here.' He waited for some sign of recognition from Rachel. Nothing doing, and Eleanor smirked, only because she saw how much it unnerved him, as if she knew all his secrets even though she didn't. 'Hi, Rachel.' He smiled with yellow teeth and eyes that didn't crease.

'You're not meant to be hanging about here, Nate, you know that. Go and get a cup of coffee for yourself and we'll join you in a while,' Rachel said icily. Nate was meant to be working security – this was an all-girls rehab centre, no need for male staff here.

'God, get a grip will you?' He sniffed. 'It's not like *she* cares.' He turned on his heel, heading off to the kitchen.

'Sorry, love, don't be heeding him – when he's finished his tea, we'll snuggle down with a movie, how's that?' Rachel said softly. It meant something, Eleanor figured, the fact that she counted her as something more than just a case number. 'Now, you just pop into your jammies and we'll see about a nice hot drink for both of us.'

Eleanor shuffled into her pyjamas. Then hot chocolate before bed, her favourite time of the day. Hot chocolate alone was a panacea in a world lacking any real joy. Sleep arrived easily. With epilepsy there is no need for extreme sports, with her heavy medication there's no need for anything stronger than warm milk. She'd be asleep within minutes – usually.

When she arrived in the day room, Nate was spread over two hard chairs, his head bent forward. Eleanor sat on the couch and burrowed beneath a fleecy throw.

'She's quiet tonight – ye give her something?' He slurped coffee, blowing before each noisy mouthful.

'She's had a good day. Her appointment with the psychiatrist went well and then we had a game of rounders in the courtyard, the kids versus the staff.' Rachel was removing the keys from the fastening attached to her belt.

'Very nice,' he said sarcastically.

'Hmm.' She began to count out the meds for handover, a low whisper of Irish numbers following her fingers, which moved each pill across the table as it was counted.

'Any changes to her tablets?' Nate had always been interested in the medication cabinet. Eleanor had noticed it and she was sure everyone else must have too.

'Give it a rest, will you?' Rachel handed him the stock book to sign, confirming that he had witnessed the count. It was the same each night, every single tablet counted out and then locked away until the following day. Nate signed slowly, making her wait.

'Suppose she's wrecked now?' He didn't sound like he cared either way. Wrecked or not, it was all the same to Nate.

'Aye, she'll sleep tonight.' Rachel's voice was soft. Perhaps she was tired too.

Eleanor got up from the sofa, pulling the fleece throw with her. It was good to see Nate flinch as he reacted to the sudden movement. The few steps to the kitchen were enough. She stood with her back to the door. Nate, if he was looking, could see nothing. It was all too easy. She had done it before; she'd do it properly this time. Didn't they ever learn? The tablets were there for the taking. She gathered them quickly, slid them silently into her pyjama pocket, and left the rest. It was done in seconds. She heard a noise behind her, but saw no one. She placed her cup in the dishwasher. Someone was coming.

'Almost nine o'clock, Eleanor,' Rachel said softly. She took down the small container with two tablets, one to lessen the effects of her epilepsy, the other an antidepressant. Rachel handed them to her and waited while she swallowed them.

There was still the hint of light behind the now fast-moving clouds when Eleanor looked out her window that night and something on the air – if not promise, certainly the feeling of change. She was tempted to stand there a little longer, consider the day just gone, but her eyes were heavy and the alarm clock would ring at the usual hour the following morning regardless of what time she turned in. She slid between the bed covers, which were cool and freshly laundered – perfect. She turned towards the window, glad she'd left the curtains open. Clouds skidded across a velvet sky.

Soon there was the click of the heating thermostat, kicking into a lower temperature for the night; it hummed noisily, rattling out its age along the cooling pipes. The pipes were ancient, thick copper, running the length of this unit and off into the others, until they arrived back, eventually, where they began. These bungalows (as they called them) were probably as old as the house that once stood here; a square of adjoining stables that had been converted into self-contained units facing onto a courtyard. Eleanor snorted; basically, her father had paid a small fortune for her to stay in a horse shed. At least she didn't have to share. Suz Mullins had seen to that when she set the other girls against her so now Eleanor looked across at them from her single-occupancy expensive jail. Sometimes she imagined what life was like in the unit opposite, with four girls who couldn't be more different to each other, and it reminded her of how much she missed having Karena nearby, if only for company.

Next was the sound of Rachel. She would start preparing tomorrow's dinner, and then disinfect the bathroom and long corridor, heaving the mop over and back, crashing into the bedroom doors and muttering her apologies to no one in particular. Then she'd sit and drink some juice and maybe leaf through a magazine or waste an hour on her phone, but by then, Eleanor would be fast asleep.

Later, Eleanor woke to the sound of voices. Familiar, loud, in the kitchen, their words were indistinct, but there was no mistaking their intent – an argument. She listened for a short time, then, just as she was about to go and investigate, she heard a noise that caught her breath. A crash, something had been thrown. She jumped from the bed and opened her door a fraction, enough to catch the conversation that had been muffled noise before.

Now there was no mistaking what had happened. There was a small thud, insubstantial for someone so important. She hadn't even washed the floor, Eleanor found herself thinking foolishly. Then, she remembered, she was alone here now, she needed to get away, before it was too late. It was now or never. Eleanor pulled on trousers up to the hem of a faded sweatshirt and rifled for shoes, picking up wellingtons instead. She cursed silently as the door creaked, then, coast clear, she pulled it back. It would close slowly behind her. Eleanor picked up a can of air freshener from the hall table – it was as close as she could see to a weapon – she was ready for flight or fight.

Rachel was lying in the kitchen, awkwardly; her head angled between sweeping brush and oven, unseeing eyes bulging in that once so pretty face. She was dead and Eleanor had a feeling if she didn't move quickly, the same fate could befall her.

Eleanor couldn't halt. She wouldn't stop, not now. The door code was easy. She'd watched them, every time, wondering if they really thought she didn't know it. Survival had made her an opportunist. Part of her had wanted to get away since the day she arrived, but she couldn't just walk out the door. She'd had all the time in the world to watch and wait. She punched in the numbers easily, her hands steady, her mind thinking only as far as getting through the door then onto what would happen next.

Never look back. Simple, easy. She was out. Eleanor Marshall was free at last. She moved slowly, carefully, her newly awakened senses gluttonously drinking in the night. No one was going to miss her yet. It didn't matter where she went. Her haul of tablets slid silently into the pocket of her soft trousers – she had enough to keep her epilepsy at bay for a few days, and if she took some when it got bright she'd have quite a few hours to roam at liberty.

Then they could bring her back and do their worst.

CHAPTER 2

Iris Locke woke with a start. It was the same nightmare, over and over – how many times can you dream the same thing and still wake up shivering with fear? She wasn't sure which she hated more: understanding that it was a bad dream or the slow, cold recognition that the reality was even worse. She lay in the darkness, listening to the sounds of the boarding house whispering its own night-time code. It was a tuneless, grating melody of creaking wood, weary pipes and a constant background fizzle of electrics emitted by residents' overcharged phones and an emergency system that lit up the endless narrow corridors with green night lights and a low buzz of irritation.

It was a stopgap, this place. Mrs Leddy ran a clean, if somewhat shabby, boarding house – three square meals a day, if you wanted feeding, and walls so flimsy they might fold if you leaned against them. It was somewhere to stay while she tried to get a grip on life; she was nowhere near ready to put her world back together, she wasn't sure if she ever could. Her apartment – on the other side of town, the better side of Limerick – had finally yielded all it could to the crime-scene boys. A week ago they'd handed her over a set of keys, as if she could just trot back to that other world of white sofas, exposed stone and reclaimed-oak floors. If only it was that simple.

At least she *was* here. In Limerick. Iris knew that while she had craved the big smoke of Dublin, this was where she now belonged. It was where she'd grown up and even if it was Ireland's most dangerous city, it was also, in her opinion, its best. There was nowhere like it, with King John's Castle crouching on the mouth of the Shannon, holding back centuries of disquiet, rumblings, wars and treaties. This city of clans and tribes, of history and modernity was home – and Corbally station, and the Murder Team were where she belonged, she could see that now.

It was shocking what a couple of weeks could do to a person – what a couple of hours could do. Iris had spent a lifetime believing her whole future had been dictated by the detective blood inherited from her father, a lifetime longing to be on the Murder Team, and it turned out that none of it had been what she believed. Coleman Grady had persuaded her to return to Corbally station; he had been her inspector when she joined the Murder Team. Now he had gone – shipped off on secondment for the foreseeable – and she was left, and while she felt emptied out of emotions, she recognised, occasionally, a sliver of aching sadness that he'd had to go.

And so she lay, in this uncomfortable bed, surrounded by furniture picked out long ago by Mrs Leddy in auction rooms all about the city. It was a medium-size room that would never grow into the heavy furniture squeezed into it. The ensuite, tiny and dated, was a faded apricot room with mildew that had stuck in stubbornly. None of it mattered anymore – not to Iris. She was operating in a kind of middle world, as if stepping forward was too much to contemplate and there was no going back.

Theodora Locke, the woman Iris had called mother, had been discharged to a convalescent home a week ago. Smoke inhalation – that was what her medical records would say. The truth was, the results of the fire that had killed her husband and destroyed the family home went far deeper than smoke inhalation. Iris tried not to think of it at night-time, but some things are impossible to block out. Iris hadn't told her about the boarding house. She couldn't face the idea of Theodora just turning up, transferring a lifetime of neediness that her husband had kept in safe harbour over to Iris.

Five bells. They rang out, jeering at her across the rooftops. Funny, she had lived most of her life in Limerick and until these past few weeks she'd never noticed church bells during the night. The two possible offenders sat snugly on the other side of the river, the distance protecting them from any possible insane attempt to silence them with the Sig Sauer semi-automatic she kept locked in her dressing table when she wasn't on duty. Either St Mary's cathedral or St John the Baptist's church could be to blame for the melodious company she'd been keeping of late. *Please stop the clocks.* That wasn't right either. There was no turning back time, she knew, as she twisted awkwardly in the too-narrow bed.

When had she gone off the sound of chiming clocks? She had loved them before. She wasn't sure if it was because they managed to keep her awake now, like just about everything else in life. She suspected it was the clamour of time that they balefully announced. It was no longer just the ticking of minutes, the background music of her life – suddenly it was a booming orchestra. Her whole world had changed utterly, and every second was taking her further away from everything that had been familiar and the tantalising whisper of a connection that might have made a difference, if only she had known the truth before it was too late.

Damn it anyway, there would be no sleep tonight. She threw back the covers, walked to the window. Limerick brooded in the moonlight. Far off, she knew there would be sirens, Gardai walking the streets, the sound of their shoe leather imposing some sense of security in a city that was driven apart by gangs and held together by tribalism. She turned back to the room. She was on duty in three hours, but in the meantime, all she had was this space.

She'd booked into Mrs Leddy's boarding house after her apartment had become a crime scene. She couldn't face going back there again and so she was living like a first-year college student: room and board and no access to the kitchen or the garden. Sometimes, she thought of Woodburn, the generous Georgian country house she'd grown up in – it was only a dozen miles away, but it was a million years from the way her life had turned out. It was no good thinking of that life now.

She walked into the small ensuite and splashed cold water on her face. These days, catching her reflection in the mirror always made her start. It seemed she was looking at a faded version of herself: gone was the confident smile, the full cheeks, the clever green eyes. Now she wore her hair neat; there was no need to style it when you just scraped it back in a ponytail. Her eyes, once dancing, held a grim determination. Slattery would have said 'haunted' – but then, that was the poetic licence of a drinker for you. Ben Slattery. She smiled now as she thought of the rumpled grouching sergeant that she'd warmed to in spite of herself. She had a suspicion the feeling was mutual; they were oil and water and yet somehow their weaknesses bonded them in a way that defied her explanation.

Her skin was bare of make-up – she just scrubbed it clean these days – and she wouldn't know where to put her hand on a dangly earring if lives depended on it. She was smaller too, everything in her wardrobe looked as if it had been handed down to her from an older sister, or maybe a well-fed aunt. The expensive suits and perfumes were left behind in her old apartment; they were part of a life that was no longer hers, it seemed. She'd have to sort through all of it, but she wasn't ready for that yet. She had three T-shirts and a couple of blouses on strict rotation. She was on first-name terms with Alesha in the nearby launderette, and couldn't remember the last time she'd stepped inside the dry cleaner's.

She pulled on her running gear, then let herself out of the boarding house as silently as she could. Soon she was running along Athlunkard Street, her breathing the only sound in her ears, elevated to a universal rhythm in the darkness of her thoughts.

*

Iris knew that no matter how hard she ran, there was no getting away from the reality of it all, but still, the pain in her chest, the burning up of her muscles, even the hunger pangs in her stomach distracted her from the memories that lingered always at the back of her mind.

She turned into the People's Park. This was a nice part of the city, overlooked by grand houses that nodded to times long gone. Because the weather had not yet turned too cold, one or two of Limerick's poorest had chosen to spend their nights sprawled across the benches and she made every effort to sprint as noiselessly as she could past them. There was no justice in this city; she had learned that the hard way. It was dispiriting, having spent her life wanting to be a detective, to realise that maybe, no matter what you did, it might not make any difference in the end. She drew herself up at that thought, her feet in harmony with her soul, pulled to a stop and then walked slowly towards one of the old trees, leaned against it while she doubled over. She wanted to cast it out of her – this despair needed somewhere else to be and she knew it. It could not reside within her for much longer before causing her some real sickness.

Overhead, ominous clouds were rolling into each other, giving off some hint of light beyond them. Perhaps, if she walked slowly back to the boarding house there might be a hint of dawn to redeem this unsociable hour. Mrs Leddy had stopped asking her how she'd slept – perhaps she feared it reflected badly on her hospitality. Instead, she looked at her with an assessing eye, as if she could tell one way or the other how the night had gone.

Just as she walked through the North Gate, her phone rang.

'You in the scratcher?' It was Slattery, sounding rough. Slattery was an old-fashioned Irish garda through and through, the notion of being a cop or even a detective sat unevenly in his cynical eyes. Pick any time, day or night, and his voice was gravelly, his stare unnerving and his brown eyes inscrutable in that clear face.

'I should be so lucky. No, I'm not sleeping much these nights.' Time was, she'd have taken his grumpy tone personally. Now she wondered if perhaps he was just irritated by the whole world or if he used it to cover up his own self-loathing. Jack Locke had said the drink does that to every alcoholic. It wasn't much helped by the guilt Slattery was carrying about now he could blame himself for one more cross his wife had to carry. After her last and only case with him, she knew the sharpness was just raw appetite.

'Right.' He had no interest really in how she was sleeping; he was more likely asking about the spectres they probably shared, if either of them ever opened up enough to admit it. 'We have a case; I thought you'd like to be in on it?'

Maybe he knew she needed something to sink her teeth into also.

'Of course I'm in, Slattery, I'm still a detective.' As if there was a choice and she was going to sit on the sidelines at this stage. It was bad enough that it seemed as if Coleman Grady had wanted to wrap her up in cotton wool, it didn't mean she had to let Slattery try to do it too.

'Good, I'll swing round and pick you up in about twenty minutes, okay?'

'What's up?'

'It sounds like murder. I'll tell you when I get there…' His voice was distant, competing with radio static in the background. When he hung up, she knew she'd have to move as fast as she could.

Sometimes she thought investigative work was like a progressive illness. There was no shaking it off, there was no antidote, only retirement or death. She tiptoed back upstairs and slipped into the shower, then she pulled out jeans, boots and a heavy fleece – hardly her usual office attire, but these last few weeks had seen more than just her wardrobe slide. The main criteria at this hour of the morning were warmth and comfort; 'fitting' and 'matching' had managed to fall way down her list of priorities recently.

She was standing on the street steps when Slattery swung by in a dark unmarked police car.

'Hungry, are we?' He handed her a paper bag which told of his stopover at the garage on the way, probably for fags or coffee strong enough to push aside the hangover before it landed. The bag had been scrunched down tightly. Inside were two slightly squashed doughnuts.

'Thanks, but I think I'll pass,' she said as she threw them onto the back seat. He was volleying along the empty road as she struggled between sitting down, placing her bag in the footwell and fastening her seatbelt. 'What have we got?'

'We have one dead body out at Curlew Hall and a missing girl who looks like our suspect, that's what we've got.'

'Curlew Hall?' she asked trying to place the name.

'Yep, it's a fancy detox centre, Limerick's answer to the Priory, only for kids. It was on the news recently. It's the kind of place rich people send their kids to get them back on track.' Slattery stared ahead; his face inscrutable.

'One of the residents?' Iris asked, faintly. She hoped it wasn't some kid that never stood a chance. She wasn't sure either of them could take a murdered child again, not so soon, not yet.

'No, the victim was a young woman called Rachel McDermott, early twenties, from what I can gather, she was working there.'

'And the suspect?'

'Well, now that's where it gets a bit tricky. McDermott was on night duty with just one kid – Eleanor Marshall…' Slattery let the name hang between them for a second.

'And that should mean something to me?' Iris asked eventually.

'It should, her father is Kit Marshall.' Slattery didn't need to say anymore. Everyone knew Kit Marshall – he owned half the city and then some.

Slattery turned the car through tall pillars. On one side a hand-painted sign pointed you towards Curlew Hall. From the long, winding avenue, it could be a country club or top hotel for all you knew. 'The thing is, it's not going to be straightforward.' Slattery slid a look towards her as if gauging her readiness. 'All that money, he's going to be torn between finding that daughter of his quietly and making sure we don't hang a murder charge on her.'

'Who's the officer in charge or do we not have one?'

'Well, with a bit of luck they'll send Grady back to us. In the meantime, Byrne has asked for both of us to get to the scene and set the ball rolling, no doubt he'll have managed to get Grady back in time to take over.'

'Good.' Iris meant it. She enjoyed working as part of the Corbally Murder Team and even if that team was in place long before she arrived, their first case together had been enough to cement her to its centre. Coleman Grady had convinced her to return to Corbally after the unthinkable, she hoped he'd be here for this case, if there was one to work on.

Iris sank deeper into the passenger seat, admiring the sweeping drive winding through dense woods for almost a quarter of a mile. Through the thicket, she spotted a range of native oaks, ash and rowan, swaying like a drunken chorus line against the approaching morning, their near naked branches eerie in opposition to the darkness of the evergreen foliage around them. The road veered onto a gravel driveway, down a small incline onto the forecourt of the ruins of what had been an impressive four-storey house. The remains of Curlew Hall stood surveying the surrounding countryside forlornly. It had probably been impressive before it was pulled down and razed by land agitators – she thought of the saying, baby and bathwater – now a monument to what was lost in the land struggles.

'It's around the back here.' Slattery swung the steering wheel sharply, narrowly missing stone chunks of old walls that had once surrounded a garden. He parked away from the yellow tape marking out where the crime-scene people were gathering every particle that might help illuminate their search for answers. Several officers were visible moving across open pastures. Their bright-yellow jackets bobbed occasionally in the distance as if to announce to anyone interested, even if it was only the dairy herd, that they were police.

'Anything?' Slattery nodded at Joe Kenny. The younger man was down on all fours combing methodically through grass on one side of a small path leading into the woods and from there into acres of mountain lands.

'Too early to say. It's difficult yet to know what we have, but it looks like lots of people come through this place every day so…'

'What's the story with the other residents?' Slattery asked.

'It's okay – it's just the one here. There are kids in one of the other units.' Kenny was standing now, arching his back like a great ginger cat, probably just thankful of the excuse to be upright for a few moments. He waved his hand around the courtyard. 'Each unit is separate, they call them bungalows – there's no access between them, other than via the courtyard – and everything, so far as we can tell, was locked up securely for the night. It's a sad do all the same,' he said almost to himself. 'Looking at that place, it's a sad do.' He shook his head balefully.

'How do you mean?' Iris asked.

'Ah, ye'll see for yourselves…for a kid that came from so much money, she didn't have much of a life there all on her own.'

'No one wants to think of a kid ending up here, but let's face it, there has to be a reason, doesn't there?' Slattery took out a packet of cigarettes.

'I'm sure we'll find out, soon enough,' Iris said, mentally thanking Slattery for not smoking in the car. She looked around again; a place like this would have so many people coming and going: staff, deliveries, maintenance. Iris thought it must be like sifting through Piccadilly. 'So, we think there was a break in?'

'Hmm, it looks more like someone broke out,' Kenny said, savouring the opportunity away from searching on all fours.

'Eleanor Marshall?' Iris asked.

'Yeah, the one and only daughter of our very own local mogul.' Slattery had turned now to look directly at Iris while he continued. 'The man who gives to foundations and charity, a real crusading do-gooder. Butter wouldn't melt.

'Yeah, well, there's tax breaks for everything these days,' Kenny cut in sarcastically.

They walked around the perimeter of what had surely once been a very impressive garden and orchard. Two tall doors broke up the bulwark, the first facing east, the second facing north, both wooden. They reached to over nine feet in height, four foot in width, and the second swung open with relative ease. A squat building, once a series of generous stables, sat at the end of the concreted garden; there was a claustrophobic feel about the place. Perhaps, a long time ago, when it had been bursting with life, it might have been idyllic, but now it had been moulded into a long, low construction of mean modern windows and a door on either end with keypads instead of bells or knockers. It was the kind of building that would be dark even on the sunniest days, with eighteen-inch-thick walls and windows too small to let in anything more than meagre light.

Iris looked around the deserted courtyard. A cold shiver ripped through her, reminding her to pull close the light jacket that encased her shoulders. She puffed out warm air, but she knew that the icy fingers working their way around her heart had as much to do with the loneliness of the place as its temperature. Suddenly, the chilly air bit in between the folds of her clothes so that she felt perished right to her core. The small bungalow might have been a shed, so functional was its exterior. Iris had never seen a building so devoid of character. The buildings stood crouched and bare, without the adornment of moulding or dash, ridge tile or chimney pot, there was neither a flower nor curtain in sight. The only nod to personality, a solar-powered dancing fish, which sat on a windowsill, in what from outside looked like the kitchen.

'Aye, safe as houses all right.' Slattery sighed. It was hard to miss the sarcasm.

Yellow tape sealed off the kitchen and a young garda stood at the entrance. Beyond, the accommodation ran via a long narrow corridor, small windows in deep walls permitting minimal daylight to knock aside the gloom. 'Is this really the best that we can offer to keep kids from going completely off the rails?' Iris whispered to Slattery as she took in the austerity of the place. He didn't answer, Iris supposed he probably couldn't. Along the hall, she could hear sobs, low and determined, echoing against the emptiness of the cold walls. Shock.

Slattery nodded at Iris and she walked in the direction of the sound. Inside, the building was a series of rooms leading into each other and in the second from what she presumed was the end, an interminable murmur of grief cancelled out the low buzz of a crime scene crawling with a life of its own. Her feet made no noise beyond the pinching cushion of leather on the rubber floor covering, and when she turned into what looked like a sparsely furnished sitting room, the crying girl flinched.

'Hi,' Iris said in her gentlest voice. She nodded towards Detective Jo Pardy who was guarding a packet of chocolate digestives. There was just something so wrong about munching your way through tragedy on this scale. For a second, Iris wanted to grab the biscuits and tell Pardy to clear out immediately, but of course she didn't. Pardy was here to make up numbers, she'd never worked Murder before and she was no substitute for Grady, no matter how the bums on seats fitted. 'I'm Detective Sergeant Locke.' She held out a cold hand towards the white-faced girl.

'Morning, Iris.' Pardy cleared her throat and popped the remainder of a well- nibbled biscuit into her mouth. Even the way

Pardy pecked her way around her food got right under Iris's skin. *Never trust a woman who doesn't enjoy her food, or a woman who wants sergeant stripes so badly she'd walk over anyone to get them.* Jo Pardy ate like a mouse, rationing it out in tiny bites, a speck here, a crumb there; at times almost bovine-like back chewing went on, and sometimes it was all Iris could do to stop herself force-feeding the girl a half a dozen biscuits at once just to get it over with. Iris wondered if her new-found obsession with the flaws of others might be an undocumented side effect of her own despair; it was certainly making her consider terrible acts of vandalism to church clocks and unsuspecting colleagues. Iris looked at Pardy now: short, broad and badly dyed blonde. She managed to make her way slowly, but determinedly, through almost a full packet of biscuits a day, as if sugar was going out of fashion.

The sobbing girl on the chair fell silent, her face damp and blotchy from salty tears that had been left to sit, save the odd rub with an overlong woollen sleeve.

'This is Julia Stenson– she was due to come on shift this morning with Eleanor Marshall and take over from Rachel McDermott.' The girl returned her stare to the middle distance, abandoned mugs of unctuous cold tea littering the floor at her feet. She shivered, her whole body wracking a half sob and caught breath as Iris sat next to her.

'Will you get her a blanket, Detective?' Iris said quickly. Julia Stenson was a bird of a thing, surely too young to be working in a place like this. Her shoulder blades were as thin as slates and if her face was hardened by life, everything about her eyes was vulnerable and childlike.

'Sure.' Pardy headed off towards what Iris assumed was a bedroom.

'I'm sorry about your colleague,' she said gently, but Julia was lost in the nightmare of the last few hours. No one had managed to get a formal statement from the girl yet, just rough notes taken down by Pardy since she arrived on the scene. Discovering a murder victim shook most people to the core, harder again when you knew the person. Iris could hear the police investigators next door, soft murmurs, the dead still warm. So far, beyond a shocked outline, it was all supposition. This girl might be essential to piecing together the night's events, and Iris knew they needed to get any information she had sooner rather than later. She bent forward to gather some of the cups and put herself directly in front of the girl. 'I'm afraid we're going to have to ask you some questions, do you think you're able for that?'

'I'll try.' Julia hiccupped and then wiped her eyes viciously to get rid of the tears that still sat there.

'Can you tell us about last night? Really we're interested in hearing everything that happened and if there was anything you noticed that was unusual or different.'

'Oh God, I'm not sure I can tell you much. It seemed the same as any morning coming on shift. Even the door had been closed, there was nothing to say that this was...' Julia began to cry once more.

'So, you just walked in to find Rachel had already died?'

'Yep.' Julia shuddered at the memory. 'I can't really remember what I did when I saw her.' She shook her head now, as if the memory might free itself. 'I know I went to check on Eleanor, but in that moment... I don't know... I...'

'You assumed she'd be there, sleeping soundly through it all?' Iris asked gently.

'I suppose I did. I'd never have thought anyone would...' Huge tears began to cascade down Julia's cheeks now. Shock. It was grief too, but mostly shock, Iris had seen it before, but still, she knew, she needed to press on.

'No one would want to kill Rachel?'

'Well, that too, but...' She looked at Iris now. 'You think someone came here to kill her? Oh my God...' She began to retch, the enormity of what had happened just hitting her anew. 'Oh my God… and Eleanor, do you think she's…'

'We don't know yet.'

'She's a good girl, I know. You'd think that because she's here, but really, she's a good girl, she'd *never*…' Julia said emphatically, shaking her head. Iris wasn't sure if Julia was trying to convince Iris or herself with the words. Julia reached up and rubbed her earlobe, a habit perhaps, or just time to let her think.

'But she was housed on her own? Not with the other girls in a shared bungalow?' Iris asked.

'That's not because she was any more trouble than the others, if anything it was because she was easier.' She left her ear alone for a second. 'The others here, well, they're different to Eleanor. Harder. Once they realised who she was, who her family were, well, they gave her an awful time. A couple of months ago it all came to a head and it was decided that it would be for the best if she was moved here for the remainder of her time.'

'What happened exactly?'

'Oh, it was typical bullying – probably jealousy and, of course, there's always that thing with these girls, any reason to single one out, well…it's pack mentality, isn't it? She was in bungalow four, the girls there are older, real worldly – or at least that's what they're pretending to be. They'd been picking on her for ages and then one night, after lights out, they set on her, cut off her hair and the message was clear, they could have cut something a lot worse if they'd wanted to.' Julia shook her head. She reached up to her earlobe, taking out an earring that looked as if it might already be the cause of a nasty infection.

'I see.' Iris tried to ignore the earring Julia was now inspecting, picking pieces of scab from it thoughtfully. 'And no one heard a sound through all of this happening?'

'The walls here are as thick as Fort Knox – you probably wouldn't hear a tank charging through until it arrived on your lap.'

'But an incident like that, surely there must have been scream-ing…' Iris played it out in her mind, the terror the girl must have experienced while she was being attacked so violently.

'It's likely, but the sad fact is there's no one you could ask now.'

'Why is that?' Iris already had a feeling she knew the answer.

'Because the staff member on that night isn't going to be able to help you…' Again the tears put a halt to any words for a long while. 'It was Rachel…' she said eventually. 'Rachel, she felt so badly afterwards, I think, well, we all thought it was why she was so extra nice to Eleanor from then on.'

Outside in the narrow corridor, heavy footsteps cushioned by scene-of-crime shoe covers moved about, but it was hard to make out any sounds beyond the anonymous movements. 'Next door is Eleanor's room. Your men will need the code to get in there.' Julia sighed. 'It's the same code the whole way through, all the nines…'

'Would Eleanor have needed that to get out of her room?'

'She has a buzzer inside, it means she can come and go, but it sounds in the kitchen if she's left the room.' She placed the earring in the pocket of her tracksuit bottoms. 'The thing is…' Her eyes began to water again. 'The thing is, even if Eleanor had woken during the night, I don't think she's ever left her room – why would she? She has everything she needs there, bathroom, music, magazines. The management have been trying to do away with the security person on duty at night because of it, saying that there's no need for two staff here when she never even needs the one.'

'Are you suggesting that she may have been taken from her room on purpose?'

'I'm not sure what I'm saying. Eleanor isn't like anyone else here, is she? Her father is Kit Marshall – I mean, she'd be worth a decent ransom if someone kidnapped her, wouldn't she? It's just a funny coincidence that she decides to leave her room the night Rachel is… well, when something like this happens.' She sat back in her chair a little then, staring off into space with her thoughts playing out silently behind her eyes, until Jo Pardy arrived back in the room with a cheap fleece blanket and to collect the half-drunk cups of tea that stood at her feet on the floor. Iris darted a glance at her that silently conveyed the message that she was not required at the moment.

'There's no need, I can take them out and wash them now.' Julia's accent was Limerick, with a little something else thrown in, but it was hard to make out exactly what that might be. Julia reached down, her movements quick and sparse with nothing wasted, and she began to gather the cups from the floor. 'Not a great tea drinker at the moment, but they said it might help.' She placed the four cups in a neat line. The room was empty bar the sofa they were sitting on and a single chair. The television, a music system and a signal box were all high tech, the best and most expensive brands available, but hardly visible in the gloom save for a small red power light blinking determinedly. To the side an old black-and-white teddy bear sat forlornly, perhaps abandoned. The room was kitted out like a trendy student flat – one with lots of money spent on it. Julia must have spotted her taking in the room.

'Mrs Marshall is very generous. She came here with a cheque and told the supervisor to have free rein – the only stipulation being that it was spent entirely on Eleanor's accommodation.' She shook her head again, dolefully. 'That was just after she was moved across here, after the…incident,' she finished off. Julia was thoughtful for a moment. Small green eyes focussed somewhere far away, perhaps somewhere in the unforgiving wood encroaching on these hollow quarters. 'It doesn't make you happy, you know, all that money. It certainly didn't do a lot for Eleanor – having twinkly Habitat lights at Christmas, it never made up for not having a proper family, people who make you feel loved and wanted.' She sighed. 'Not that out there is going to be good for her, if she did run into the night. I mean, one big seizure and that could be it.' Again, the sobbing took over.

'She has epilepsy?'

Julia Stenson nodded, perhaps she had told her enough, it was time to let her get over this for a while. Iris waited until she wiped the tears harshly from her eyes.

'What's the story with the teddy bear?' Iris asked lightly. It seemed to be the only item in the room with any personality attached to it. She walked across to the glass doors to take it out.

'That's Jeremy. Eleanor has had that teddy since like forever, he's even more precious than her phone. She's always kept him safe, takes him to bed with her every night.' She sat back on the chair.

'But she didn't take him with her,' Iris said softly.

'She would have, I'm sure she would have, if she had a choice,' Julia said quickly.

'So, nobody ever touches Jeremy?' Iris looked at the bear, one ear missing, his head falling tragically to one side.

'No, Eleanor hates anyone near him.' Julia sighed. 'I can't see her lasting five minutes out there, I really can't, poor wee mite.'

'Could she have killed Rachel McDermott?' Part of Iris didn't want to ask, but it was the only thing that really counted now, that and finding Eleanor.

'That's the question, isn't it? We'll all be wondering that from now on.' Julia Stenson took a deep breath and ran pale hands through her mousy-brown hair.

'Really, how do you mean?' Iris kept her voice neutral, her eyes never leaving Julia's.

'Oh, I don't know, don't mind me, I don't know what I'm saying.' The girl shifted in her seat, her hand moving towards her ear, which even in this shaded light made Iris wince – it was badly infected. Julia made a face as if she'd said too much, and not half enough at the same time. She inspected her hands again, as though divine inspiration might well up from the dry skin before her. 'Have you spoken to Nate yet?'

'Nate?'

'Nate Hegarty, he was on security last night, he's probably going to be able to help you far more than I can.'

'Not yet, but we will.' There was something Iris couldn't quite put her finger on, something about the way Julia said the name. 'What's he like?'

'Like? Oh, I don't know – he's just Nate, really. Sorry, I just can't think at the moment.' She stopped and Iris watched as a storm of conflicting thoughts rumbled across those quick eyes. Iris had seen it before: shock, it shook you so you hardly knew what was right and what was not. Now large, salty tears were flowing down her cheeks again. Shock and loss, no doubt in various degrees of capacity, Iris recognised it too well.

'Her phone? Can I get Eleanor's number?' Iris asked, at least they could track her if she had it switched on.

'I can do better than that,' Julia said softly and she slipped a key from her pocket to open the locked cupboard beneath the TV. 'Here,' she said, handing it over to Iris. 'She's only allowed to use it for short times at the weekends, it's all part of a reward system we have in place.'

'Great,' Iris said, but of course it wasn't really, because lacking a mobile phone made Eleanor Marshall much harder to track down.

Iris left the girl with Pardy; she was still in shock and the information they had was enough to get started with. Pardy handed Iris a set of neatly handwritten notes – prepared no doubt over the four neglected mugs of tea – outlining the usual run of a night's events in the unit, according to Julia. Unsigned, it wouldn't do as an official statement, but it was enough to set up a timeline. Iris skimmed through the notes. It was lights out before ten o'clock and, generally, Eleanor would have been happy to go to bed at around nine. Julia had found Rachel when she arrived for her shift at six thirty and had rung the police almost immediately. There was no sign of Eleanor, no sign of a break-in, and Iris found herself praying in equal measure for the safe return of Eleanor and just the slightest scent of a suspect other than the missing girl.

Slattery was standing in the hall when she closed the door gently behind her to let the girl get on with her grief in peace.

'Nate Hegarty?' Iris asked.

'Got him, had a few words, it's all written down.' He tapped his breast pocket and turned towards the kitchen. It was unlikely, Iris knew, that Slattery had so much as taken out a pencil, but probably one of the uniforms had been happy enough to commit to notes what had passed between them.

In the kitchen, two technical officers were methodically bagging and tagging, and Rafiq Ahmed – the pathologist – was waiting to have the body removed.

'We're missing Rachel's laptop,' one of the techies, a heavy-set woman called Aine, said. 'The girl' – she nodded towards the door leading to the sitting room, trying to find the name from somewhere in the recesses of her early morning, pre-coffee brain – 'Julia said she always brought it to work, but there's no sign of it now.'

'So, Eleanor Marshall took it?' Iris did her best to sound like a laptop would be just the thing to bring if you planned on running off into the woods in the dead of night, *like fun it was*.

'Possibly, or maybe someone else was here…' Aine went over to the keypad lock-up system. 'Anyone could have made their way in here overnight without our being any the wiser. All they needed was the combination to this…' She pointed at the basic device. 'These things are as old as the ark, and the codes are rarely changed. I'll bet there are well over fifty people who know the access code here, probably more.'

'That opens it up a bit, doesn't it?' Iris sighed, thankful for the prospect of more than just one real suspect.

'Oh aye, like we need forty-nine more possibilities at this stage,' Slattery grunted before returning his attention to the pathologist. 'Cause of death? Any notions yet?' Slattery was being sarcastic. Rachel McDermott had a huge wound to the back of her head, open and bloody; she'd been bludgeoned with a force and violence that spoke of blind panic as much as rage. Her attacker had been prepared because there was no weapon in this kitchen that could have inflicted the damage caused by the repeated beating she had been subjected to.

Slattery bent over the body, the scent of death filling the room: a mixture of stale air, loss of bowel control and the acrid smell of vomit mixed with a wasp of saliva dried up as foam at the victim's mouth. 'Poor cow, you'd hardly recognise her now, but she was pretty.' Slattery held up Rachel's phone and pressed the power button. It shot up the screen saver, an image of Rachel and an oversized sheep dog. Rachel McDermott had been exquisite in life, a delicate, shiny-haired, even-toothed smiling girl – with, it seemed, everything to live for.

Ahmed peeled off latex gloves. 'Well, I think we can say she didn't just slip.'

'Can we make a guess at time of death?' Iris whispered from somewhere beneath the bile that threatened to rise in her throat if she looked down on the contorted face for much longer.

'I'd say she's been here six, perhaps seven hours, going on the degree of clotting and temperatures of both the victim and the room… but obviously, I'll confirm that in the official report.'

Slattery stood over the body. 'Anything else?'

'I don't need to tell you it was a very brutal attack. Whoever did this wasn't taking any chances on her surviving… some of the marks, you can see here' – he bent down pointing to the victim's face – 'I'd say he used a large hammer, maybe a sledgehammer.'

'Jesus, what kind of sicko takes a sledgehammer to someone?' one of the techies murmured from the other side of the room.

'You up to it?' Slattery looked at Iris.

'Try and stop me,' she managed, the ticking of the dead girl's watch ringing in her ears, pounding out in time with a slow-burn throb that had begun to pulse along her spine. Each minute from here on counted, on so many levels.

CHAPTER 3

Day 1

Slattery caught sight of his reflection in the rear-view mirror. He looked like hell, but then, beside him, Locke didn't look a whole lot better. It was unbelievable what a couple of weeks could do to a person. Not to him. Obviously, the way he looked was a direct reflection of the way he lived – well, mostly anyway. It might be that his rounded shoulders were a result of his drinking posture and some might say that his surly temperament had as much to do with a lifetime of cynical thinking as it had with the fact that he'd probably seen the worst there was to see in human beings and still come back for more. He was as broad as he was long; as one of his drinking buddies once said, taller standing like a dog sitting. He walked tall – well, as tall as his shortening height would allow – and he still managed to retain a bearing that would make the meanest bastard think twice before crossing him. He had hooded eyes and a narrow gaze, but he missed very little and anything he did, wasn't worth noticing. No, Locke was the one who had gone so rapidly downhill. Only months earlier she'd arrived on the Murder Team, chipper and hungry, on the outside she'd been polished and probably the most glamorous detective they'd ever had in Corbally. A chocolate bunny of a woman, all curves and glossy tumbling hair – now she was skin and bone and her hair looked as if it had been scraped up into the tightest knot she could manage.

One case. That was all it took, but Christ, it was some case. Her whole world turned upside down – she was only here now because Grady managed to cajole and bully her relentlessly to return. At least here, they could keep an eye on her. There was no telling what that kind of loss could make a person do. In one case they'd managed to pull apart everything Iris thought of as her world, leaving only a woman she couldn't look at in a nursing home and her family home razed to the ground. The family she'd never known were buried just a stone's throw from the man she'd called her father – tragedies of that magnitude were bound to leave a mark. Even if he wouldn't admit that he felt any real connection, whether Slattery liked it or not, he didn't hold any truck with people doing themselves in for the likes of old Jack Locke. Grady had lured her back with a mixture of begging and ordering. They all knew she had the makings of a great detective, if only she could sort out the jumble of her past.

'Come on,' Slattery called to her now. 'Time to get back to Corbally.' He was glad to get into the car and turn the heat up high. There was a time when he'd never felt the cold, but too much booze – well, it tempered his body's thermostat, so now he was either shivering or sweating, there was no middle ground. *Be the death of you yet*, Maureen's warning hung in his ears.

Maureen. Well, that was a worry that he'd have to shelve for a few more hours. Their only hope was that his wife's decline into dementia would be slow – at least that's what the doctors said. She was in good hands, getting the right medication and even if she wouldn't entertain Slattery dropping by, at least Angela seemed to be able to boss her about with the efficiency that Maureen had taught their daughter from an early age. Now when he visited, it felt as if he was stepping into a fragile no man's land. As if, with the wrong word or a look, he could feel its potential disintegration around him. So he walked on eggshells, tried not to say too much, tried not to rise to the bait. She had started to mention Una, since they'd gotten her diagnoses. It was unsettling, hearing his sister's name fall between them in a conversation. They'd avoided it steadfastly for years. Maureen had been Una's best friend. Her only friend, it turned out, after she was murdered and it was that one bond that had thrown them together, as if a marriage in a state of permanent loss had any chance of happiness.

Slattery sighed. It was funny, well, maybe not funny, but odd, all the same, how every time he thought of Maureen now, somehow, Una managed to slip into his memories too. There was nothing more he could do, for now, just get on with things. He'd managed to get one of the neighbours to call into Maureen in the mornings. Slattery offered to pay the woman a few quid but she wouldn't entertain it. He knew that one day he'd have to get professional help to care for her, but at least for now he was happy Maureen would just believe she was having a friendly visit from a caring neighbour. At least it meant that there was someone watching out for her. Slattery swung by the little house five or six times a day, more if he thought she might be a little off with him. It wasn't love. The love had long disappeared from Slattery if it had ever been there to begin with. Maureen didn't expect anything from him, probably, more than anyone, knew there was no point. If you can't love your own… he sometimes wondered what that made him.

'Nate Hegarty?' Iris said and from her expression she knew she'd intruded on his thoughts, but being Iris, she didn't much care.

'Yeah? Scumbag,' Slattery answered her question before she had a chance to ask, keeping his eyes on the horizon. A granite sky was pushing out indifferently over the Atlantic; soon they would have an inkling of the day ahead, even if they wouldn't be in much of a position to enjoy it.

'You have history?'

'Not exactly, but when you've been around as long as I have, well, you can spot the signs easily enough.' Slattery glanced towards his packet of fags on the dash.

'That doesn't make him guilty, Slattery, not the same thing at all.'

'Yeah, well, when you look at that girl, her brains spilled across the floor, it makes me suspicious of anyone that messes with my gut.'

She smiled, because Slattery had never been ambitious – he was all about the job, but not about the rank, the idea of a career ladder was something Slattery never entertained. 'I'm not sure I should share this with you, but I think Julia felt there was something off about him too, especially when it came to Rachel and Eleanor.'

Chief Superintendent Byrne was waiting for them when they returned to the incident room. There was no love lost between Slattery and Byrne – it might be that there was mutual respect, but Slattery knew it was, at best, grudging. Slattery had solved more cases and slid off more hooks than Byrne would ever see and that got up his boss's nose no end. And Byrne had a rather large hooked nose; it was probably the biggest part of him. He was a narrow, neat man, hair soft and thinning, his hooked nose and small eyes made it seem as if he was always on the lookout for something, owl-like. Slattery often thought it was a bit of a waste, really, because undercover he'd have passed for anything from bus conductor to gay waiter... but there you have it, sometimes a book cover can surprise you. From Byrne's stony expression now, Slattery had a feeling that whatever he wanted, his visit would cost rather than credit them.

'You two!' he called them and headed for Grady's office.

Slattery thought he'd never noticed how small a space it really was. Byrne stood uncomfortably behind the desk and Iris hovered by the door. 'Right, you were both out at Curlew Hall this morning so, what are we looking at here? Accident, suicide or... manslaughter?' He turned his stare towards Iris, as if she could somehow give him a more palatable form of the truth.

'It's early days, but we're looking at murder.'

'Nonsense! How can a girl like that possibly be capable of murder?' He shot the words out, but there was no mistaking the anger beneath them. Then he looked at Slattery, 'Ben?'

'Like Iris says, early days, but it's not a suicide and as for accident?' He shook his head. 'Rachel McDermott was battered to death, probably with a sledgehammer – it's unlikely she did that to herself.'

'I suppose we'll have to wait until the pathologist comes back with more. In the meantime, you're both well aware that Grady has been seconded to a case over in Cork and there's no getting him back yet.' He held up his hands to halt Slattery in the verbal onslaught he knew would ensue. 'The thing is, we need to get a team up and running and while I'm aware that you're both at senior rank…' He picked a stray hair from his otherwise pristine uniform. 'Ben, let's call a spade a spade, you've never wanted any sort of responsibility, not for a team or even for an investigation, we both know that your *strengths*' – he leaned on the word as though it caused him pain – 'lie more in digging holes in a case than building one up.'

'Thank you, sir,' Slattery said flatly, 'although, I'm not sure for what.'

'You can thank me in a minute.' He glanced at Slattery then turned his full attention on Iris. 'Now, Sergeant Locke, I know you've been through a terrible time, but you've come back on duty, you feel well enough to be here and, to be honest, from what Grady has told me, I think you have the makings of a good detective…'

'Oh.' Slattery tried not to grin, seeing now why they'd been dragged in here. Byrne wanted someone to take on the case and he didn't need two sergeants, so making one of them up to team leader wouldn't do his budget a lot of harm, now the year end was looming close.

'So, I'm happy to let you have an opportunity on this case…
see how you'd like to lead it out…' Byrne stood watching Iris; if
he'd been expecting her to jump at the opportunity, it was a disap-
pointing response. 'It's an important case, even if it's not a murder
case. It'll need delicate handling.' His eyes slid towards Slattery
who everyone acknowledged had the diplomacy of a bulldozer.
'Kit Marshall is not a man to be trifled with and regardless of what
has happened out in Curlew Hall he will want answers quickly
and quietly, do you both understand?'

'Ben, you're the most senior here.' Iris turned to Slattery,
sounding him out.

Regardless of the fact that they all knew he was probably the
least appropriate person in Limerick for the job, he appreciated
it. 'Maybe, but you're the most suitable.' Slattery managed to
drift half a smile into his words, enough for her to catch but not
enough to reach towards Byrne.

'I could do a little moving about, there is another sergeant
interested in applying for Grady's job, should it become available,'
Byrne said slyly, perhaps he had expected Iris to bite his hand off
in her gratitude for the *opportunity* he was handing her, but of
course, she'd been around long enough to know that being Officer
in Charge meant more than just running a team. 'The thing is, this
is a chance to make a name for yourself, but this case – with the
Kit Marshall connection – well, it's going to have to be handled
sensitively and by the book. If there's a question of anything being
missed or a corner being cut, it won't just be the inspector's neck
on the line. Mind you, Tony Ahearn is chomping at the bit so…'

'That won't be necessary, Superintendent, I think that as a
team we can handle this case until Grady gets back to us,' Iris said
steadily and she looked towards Grady's desk, as if checking with
him that it would be okay to take this on.

*

A few minutes later, they walked back out to the incident room together. Iris walked a little taller, though it seemed to Slattery that over the last few weeks she'd shrunk by about half a foot – still, she threw her shoulders back to prepare to take her first morning briefing as the senior officer on the team. Byrne planned to make the announcement that she would be, for now, the new inspector – or the *cigire* in Irish, as she would be called behind her back. She went to her desk to gather up some clean sheets of paper, make some notes and pull herself together for the day ahead.

'You did the right thing,' Slattery said at her elbow.

'I know, it just seems a lot to take on at the moment.'

'Byrne wouldn't have asked you if he didn't think you could do it.'

'Wouldn't he? Come on, Slattery, we both know I'm the easy way out for him. He doesn't need two of us here at sergeant grade, but he can't get rid of you and it'll look bad if he throws me out now.'

'You belong here and don't you forget it. You've earned your place as much, if not more, than anyone in this room.' He said the words quietly. 'Anyway, you don't have much of an option…' He nodded over towards a couple of detectives making their way in the door.

'Tony Ahearn?'

'Yep. He's been looking to get into Murder for ages now and he'd be as popular with the team as early closing on Christmas Eve down the Ship Inn. Grady doesn't like him, but an opportunity to slip into his shoes while he's away…' It was the truth. Ahearn had his cronies and none of them were in Murder. He was a guard that liked to saunter and snigger, with a reputation for the ladies and an aversion to any real work, he'd delegate his way around the team and take credit for everyone else's results in the absence of his own.

'Well, it's a good thing I said yes, so.' Iris picked up a sheaf of papers and then turned towards Slattery. 'You'd better have my back, Ben,' she said quietly, but her eyes dug into his and he felt the weight of so much more owed to Iris than this whole station could ever repay.

Iris divvied out the day's tasks as if she was born to it and wisely set Tony Ahearn with full responsibility for the search party that was combing the woods around Curlew Hall. Most of the uniforms were put on grunt work, checking out properties where people might have noticed something or indeed where Eleanor might be hiding.

'Ben, you and I should visit Rachel McDermott's mother and we'll do it before she has a chance to hear it from anyone else.' She glanced up at the clock. Imelda McDermott wouldn't even have got out of bed yet. This was, apart from the post mortem, probably one of the shortest straws at the beginning of an investigation. Mrs McDermott should be able to tell them more about their victim than anyone else, however – this made breaking the news to her as valuable for learning as it was awful beyond words.

'Right,' Slattery said as he reached for his fags and stuck them deep in his pocket; thinking to himself, at least it was better than the PM.

'And then, we'll head over to the pathology lab and sit in on the post mortem,' she said, avoiding his eyes, knowing that it was the last place Slattery would want to go this morning.

CHAPTER 4

As Imelda McDermott opened her front door slowly, Slattery reached for his identity card, but she told him not to bother, knew who he was anyway, and maybe when she looked at her watch, well, maybe she knew why he was here too. Iris introduced them both; she suspected the names would not infect this woman's understanding, not with everything else she was going to have to take in. She backed away from them, holding the door open so they could take some shelter in the cold and dreary hallway.

'It's Rachel, isn't it? 'The words were out before she had even closed the door behind them. 'It's that car, there's been an accident, hasn't there?'

'We are truly sorry, Mrs McDermott. Can we come in?' Iris gestured towards the kitchen door beyond. Imelda turned from the detectives and made her way towards the kitchen. In the background, the presenters on *Morning Ireland* were doling out their daily quota of doom and gloom. She switched them off. Now only the gentle tick of a clock long since gone out of fashion, high above their heads, would distract from whatever tidings they brought.

'Are you here alone, Mrs McDermott?' Slattery asked. He leaned towards her, his eyes sympathetic; there was no hiding that their news was not good, it was a gesture, for all the good it would do her now. 'Do you have any family nearby we can call for you?'

'What are you saying? 'Her voice trembled and she looked as if she was steeling herself, bringing up a strength perhaps she hadn't realised was deep within her. 'Tell me what's happened?' She put out a hand towards Slattery, blindly reaching for something, anything, to anchor herself in these unfamiliar emotional waters. His arm was strong, and he guided her towards a kitchen chair. She sat, gathered up her cardigan around her body, hugging her weary arms to her.

'Are you okay?' Slattery's stoutness and quick eyes spoke of too much time at a bar counter, but still something about him made you feel he would always know the right thing to do. An old-fashioned policeman, the kind you could trust.

'I'm fine, really.' She sat up straight in the chair. 'Now, you came to tell me about my daughter, please.' She looked him in the eye, perhaps bracing herself against the pity she saw lurking there.

'I'm sorry. Rachel died earlier this morning.' Iris moved towards her, taking the chair opposite. 'Is there anyone we can call for you?'

'Rachel. That can't be! No, I'd have known, a mother would know?' It was as much a question as a reassurance. 'They must have made a mistake. That's it. No, no, Rachel couldn't be dead. She is too young; she's only twenty last July, for heaven's sake. Surely, it should be the oldest to go first. Doesn't every mother expect that?' She was talking as much to herself as to them, letting her thoughts pour into the emptiness of the kitchen until the words petered out. In a small voice she said pathetically, 'She was going to go to college, she told me so herself, even been in there looking about one day.' Her words tapered off, pathetic in their innocence as much as their unassuming tone.

Imelda sat then for some time, saying nothing, trying to take it in. 'I can't feel anything,' she said softly. She began to shiver, her limbs and neck letting her down just when she needed them to sustain her. She rocked gently back and forth, the motion making her look as if she was a huge child, seeking solace in such a simple gesture. When at last the right words came to her, they sounded colder than her daughter's perishing body and they sent a shiver through Iris. 'Thank you, Sergeant, but you haven't come here

to offer your condolences. You've come to tell me how she died.'
Imelda McDermott's voice clipped through the small talk; she
wasn't a woman with time for wasting. Slattery had told Iris on
the way over that she'd been a district nurse. She'd tended to her
patients, washed and scrubbed them, and made sure they were as
comfortable as possible. She hadn't entertained them, nor had she
been one for hand-holding or unnecessary chitchat. She would
expect the same professional approach, now, that she'd given to
so many of her patients over the years. 'Can you tell me yet how
she died?'

'All we can say is that we believe it warrants Gardai investigation,' Iris began softly.

'*Not natural causes, so,*' Imelda said darkly. Iris figured she could
be Slattery's age, she might be even younger, but when she spoke,
there was an old-fashioned ring to her words, so it sounded as if
she could be eighty if she was a day. So many questions swirled
between them. Mrs McDermott was in shock so Iris knew it would
be hard for her to form one question from the maelstrom of words
– the tempest of who, when, where and most hauntingly of all,
why – for now, all the questions would have to come from them.

'Mrs McDermott, Rachel was killed as a result of trauma to
her head. She sustained an injury after being hit with something
that may have been taken into Curlew Hall with the intention
of doing her harm,' Slattery said, perhaps knowing the woman
needed to hear the plain truth. 'We're looking into the death of
your daughter along with the disappearance of a young woman.'
Slattery's voice penetrated the overhanging despair, his accent was
surprisingly gentle, his words almost the soothing antithesis of the
message carried within them. County Limerick soft, he hadn't
grown up in the city.

'A girl disappeared? I hadn't realised. I'm sorry.' She twisted
nervous hands in her lap now, the cotton tissue breaking under
the pressure. Her voice had changed. It was understandable in this

strange world that had somehow managed to slip off its familiar axis overnight. She took a deep breath. 'And this girl? Had she anything to do with...I don't know...I suppose...' She moved towards the heavy sideboard and rubbed a worn hand along it, trying to drag herself into this awful reality. The cabinet was like everything else, too large and outdated, with a character of its own that frowned on a house that had never been quite good enough for it.

'Was there anything strange, Mrs McDermott, in the last while, did you notice anything queer?' Slattery asked.

'Queer about what?' She couldn't quite get a grip on the conversation. Her eyes had drifted off into memories or perhaps longing. She pushed herself away from the heavy sideboard, knuckles white against the polished wood. Standing straight-backed, she cleared her throat a little. She was silent, waiting a second, perhaps hoping they'd repeat the question. 'I'm sorry, I didn't quite catch what you said.'

'Don't worry, Mrs McDermott, it's the worst news and impossible to take it in. I wondered if there was anything unusual in your daughter's behaviour over the last number of days, if she said anything, maybe she had a run-in with someone.'

'You think someone meant to kill her?' The words came high-pitched, startling them all. 'You didn't know her at all, did you? She was a good girl, kind and generous to a fault.'

'We don't think anything yet. We just want to build up a picture of Rachel.' Iris's voice was gentle. 'Look, Mrs McDermott, I'm sorry we have to ask, but we're only trying to figure out why your daughter has died, and anything that would help us find the missing girl.'

'Little girl.' She misheard them, repeating the wrong words. 'A little girl has gone missing...but you said...' Her voice trailed off. She clasped her hands tight, hot tears were welling in the corners of her eyes once more.

'I said a girl was missing, that was all I said. Please, Mrs McDermott, was there anything troubling your daughter of late?'

'Nothing. What can I say? Look, it's just... I'm not myself. Rachel is a good girl, she is just a normal girl.'

'Can we get a list of some of her friends, Mrs McDermott?' Iris had her pencil poised.

'You'll have to ask Tim, I'm afraid. I'd be no good and I get them confused. Of course, she had friends, why can't I think?' She began to cry again, great big sobs that wracked her body as if they might empty her out. Iris found herself looking away. It was too heartbreaking to watch what a mother felt when they lost their own child. 'Sorry. You might talk to Nate Hegarty, they've been friends, he might know if... or Tim, of course...'

'And Tim is?'

'Tim is my son, Rachel's older brother.'

'Of course.' Iris went back through her notebook again. 'He lives with you too?'

'That's right. He's not here at the moment though.'

'At work?'

'Em, no, he'll be back in a little while, you might catch him before you leave.'

'Where does he work, Mrs McDermott?'

'He's a musician, so he's... Well, here, for now.' Imelda McDermott smoothed downy hair into place needlessly. 'Oh God, I only have Tim left now.' She shuddered, a pathetic tremble that shook her whole body.

'Please, take your time, Mrs McDermott.' Iris looked at Slattery. They should offer to make tea, but neither wanted to break the tension of her thoughts. Perhaps, too, they knew that Imelda McDermott wouldn't want anyone making tea in her kitchen and with that she rose from her seat and filled the kettle with water.

'Where...where is Rachel now?' she half whispered. She placed the kettle on top of a gas ring, lit it and blew out the long match.

'She's out at Curlew Hall. The county coroner will arrange for her remains to be brought to Limerick hospital later today. You'll be able to see her tomorrow if you'd like,' Iris said kindly, moving a strand of burnished-copper hair from across her forehead.

'Tea, I think, would be good now. Tea is fine for both of you?' After murmurs of agreement, she took down a large cream earthenware teapot, patterned over in bright burgundy and orange flowers. Her stubborn, slightly arthritic fingers worked their way across the lid and down the raised flower pattern. It was a handshake of sorts with an old ally, providing not just tea but comfort too. On the first whistle from the kettle, she scalded the inside of the pot, returning the water to continue boiling until a chorus of shrieks filled the air. The ritual of making a simple pot of tea seemed to calm Imelda. Waiting for it to brew, Slattery took the opportunity to look over the various framed photographs on her walls.

'Sugar?' she asked as she poured the tea through a weary metal strainer.

'Ta.' Slattery reached across for a deep brown mug in the centre of the table. 'I'll help myself. Long time since I've had proper tea.' He nodded towards the pot.

'Wouldn't have anything else inside the door. The kids give out sometimes, tell me I should join the modern world, but, well, it's old dogs and new tricks, I'm afraid.' She looked like a woman who always preferred the old to the new. The new was much too complicated.

'Thanks, best cup of tea I've had in months.' Iris sank back into the carver chair, notebook neglected for a moment. They sat in silence for a few minutes, the only punctuation coming from the Swiss carriage clock counting out the seconds with a loud tick-tock. The sound of the approaching hour was heralded by a tightening of springs and coils before it bellowed out loud gongs. The euphonious tones, echoed somewhere in the distance by church bells, brought them back to the present. Iris exhaled loudly in the silence, the marking of time struck her much more forcefully than it ever had before.

'Mrs McDermott, can you tell us if Rachel went straight to work yesterday evening, or do you know if she was due to meet anyone beforehand?'

'I really wouldn't know. Why? What difference does it make now, if she went straight to work or if she was doing something beforehand?' She could see the young detective had already moved on.

'Was Rachel on any medication – did she take anything on prescription or otherwise?' The pencil was poised once more.

'Why do you want to know something like that?'

'I'm sorry, Mrs Dermott,' – it was Slattery again – 'but it's just for the autopsy, you know, to make sure we have everything accounted for.'

'Of course, forgive me. These things…if it was anybody else…I'm just not thinking clearly.' She glanced across at Locke who appeared to understand the muddle her head had become. 'Of course, I'll get you anything that she might have taken over the last few days. She's had a touch of a head cold, so she's been taking some kind of herbal remedy.'

'She wouldn't have taken anything else?' The sergeant's probing eyes searched her face and Imelda felt herself colour slightly under the scrutiny.

'You mean was she taking drugs, Detective? The answer is no, not to my knowledge, but then these are modern times. I'm probably not the right person to ask.' The tea, so recently hot and inviting, was now beginning to cool. Soon the heavy milk would make it cling greasily against the side of the cup and then form tidemarks, which would prove difficult to remove. A lot like life, Iris thought to herself.

'Did she leave her computer here yesterday?'

'Her computer? That laptop thing, is it?' She looked across at their nodding heads. 'No, she took it with her. She always took it with her, that and her mobile phone, never without either of them. Why?'

'It's not at Curlew Hall and we just wondered if maybe it was here.'

'I can check for you, of course, but I'm sure she took it. If she hadn't I'd have got a call to take it out to her, keeps her going, she does night shift, so…'

'Of course, Mrs McDermott. I suppose our only other question really is if there was anyone else close to her, a boyfriend perhaps, someone she might have talked to if she was worried about something.'

'There was no one. At least not as far as I knew, but there were boys in the past. No one I heard about, but a mother knows these things.' She tried to stall them as they were getting up to leave. 'The missing girl, do you think she might have…?'

'No, we certainly hope not. She's one of the kids living out there in Curlew Hall.'

'Oh.' Suddenly it seemed she couldn't wait to get the two detectives out the door. 'Can you see yourselves out? I'm very tired, you understand?'

'I'm afraid we'll have to take a look at her room.' Slattery managed to make this request sound like an apology. She motioned to the stairs and muttered directions. She had enough to take in for now, but there would be more questions; they didn't need to tell her that.

Rachel McDermott's room was the first at the top of a narrow dog-legged staircase. Upstairs did not disappoint in terms of being as stuck in the last century as the rest of the house. If anything, it looked and felt as if time had begun to stammer somewhere around the 1970s and hadn't much progressed since apart from rewiring and a potted plant. The carpet was brown with a highlight of faded orange and on the walls a patterned paper that had to date back to long before Rachel was born. But still, everything was pristine and Iris wondered if Mrs McDermott patrolled up here on an hourly basis to defend against dust and cobwebs. Rachel's room was far tidier than she'd have expected. Aren't twenty-year-old girls, for the most part, meant to have mountains of cosmetics and clothes piled up on the floor? The bed covers had been screwed down with military tightness. Apart from a few photographs on top of a chest of drawers, there was little here at first glance to mark it out as Rachel's room at all. Of course, her clothes hung in the old-fashioned wardrobe and tidied away in a drawer was a bag of toiletries that included expensive perfume, nail polish and a glut of mascara bottles, opened once and then discarded. The products belonged to a young woman, even if it appeared the room may not.

'Well, you could warm me up with an ice cube,' Slattery whistled, stretching blue examination gloves over his large hands. 'If I'd ever given any thought to what Rachel's room would look like, it wouldn't have been this. The only thing here that seems to belong to her is that make-up bag – not so much as a fairy light or a scented candle in sight.'

'God, Slattery, you have a very narrow imagination when it comes to women's boudoirs.' Iris tried to make light of the moment. 'Still, it's a bit creepy, isn't it? It's almost as if she was expecting someone to come in and check things over.' Iris ran a finger along the rim of the window. 'I mean, it's like she's ghosted herself in and out of here, she's certainly neat.' She shook her head.

'I wonder if Imelda came up here when she went to work and gave this place a going over with her feather duster?' Slattery jerked his head towards the stairs and by extension Imelda.

'Hopefully not, although…' Iris wasn't sure which would be worse for them, if not so much as a stray hair could be found in the place because Rachel was organised enough to go about her business leaving no trace behind her *or* if she'd tidied things away because she wanted to hide things from her *interested* mother. Either way, there seemed to be little here that would point to a motive for her death. Slattery pulled out a drawer, sifting through matched socks and folded underwear, before checking the drawer beneath it.

'Pockets are probably our best bet now.' Iris dug into the wardrobe and began to check the pockets of the clothes hanging there. 'Nothing,' she said, moving towards an old framed picture of the holy trinity that might have been a wedding gift to her grandparents. It was hung with that same neatness as everything else in the room, perfectly level as if it had been measured at all corners to make sure it was straight; it was the only picture to adorn the walls. Iris examined it for a moment; it was old, but hardly worth a lot, the frame was plain, the print faded. As she moved past it something caught her eye – there was a tiny inconsistency between the lower corners, perhaps something at its back. She examined it again, tracing her finger along the side, then she lifted the frame out, just a fraction, and the movement was enough to dislodge a small card.

'Well done,' Slattery said, but his voice held no enthusiasm, as if he'd just been on his way to check it out himself. 'What is it?'

'It's a note, just numbers.' Iris examined it. 'Could be anything really. We'll run it through the system back at the station and see what it throws up.' She placed it gingerly in a plastic evidence bag. At least it was something.

CHAPTER 5

Iris needed coffee and sugar to dispel the light-headedness that was making her ears buzz and sapping her eyes so they felt as if they'd receded about six inches into her fatigued brain. She'd gone through the timeline a thousand times in her mind. Now it felt as though she'd actually been in that small kitchen all night and watched the clock insistently passing each minute above Rachel McDermott's head.

Tony Ahearn was running the search party. She should have been pleased, another sergeant on board to take some of the flak. The truth was, she wasn't sure whether she'd prefer him far away from the incident room where he couldn't cause her any grief or right here, under her nose, where she could keep a close eye on him. They'd never hit it off, he'd always been a smarmy wanker as far as Iris was concerned. Too much talk and not enough work. He'd been tipped as a potential highflyer from the day he left Templemore, didn't mean he was any better at his job than anyone else. *Sell his granny for a promotion,* Slattery had said, and Iris knew he was spot on the money there. From day one, Tony Ahearn had been welcomed into the clandestine 'boys' club' that runs the guards. Iris, on the other hand, had to slog her way through, work for every stripe despite the fact that her colleagues believed she'd be fast-tracked thanks to her father Nessie Locke. In some ways, their relationship – such as it turned out to be – had hindered her progress far more than it had helped her. There was little doubt that if she'd set her sights on a nice, safe job in the press office, she'd probably have been made up to inspector in record speed – but Nessie hadn't wanted her in Murder.

Iris closed her eyes, trying her best to shove memories of the father she thought was hers to the edge of her thoughts. It was actually preferable to think about Tony Ahearn and she liked him about as much as a wasp likes winter. The fact that he'd so obviously already set his sights at the DI's job didn't do a lot to change her mind. Detective inspector posts didn't come up that often. As bad and all as it was to be losing Coleman Grady to the lure of Cork's biggest Murder Team, Iris didn't want to contemplate working under Tony Ahearn for the foreseeable future. She needed to make the grade on this case, the alternative was unthinkable.

'You should apply for it,' Slattery had urged her a few weeks earlier when they were both pissed and Grady had told them he'd be heading off to Cork. Slattery had held his gaze steady. 'You'd be well fit for it, you know.'

'I'd be really popular. Old Nessie's daughter who couldn't see a mystery even when she was in the middle of it…' she said.

They both knew that she wanted to apply for the post. But in her head, she wasn't near ready to fill Coleman Grady's boots, no matter what cajoling Slattery did on her. Then again, neither was Tony Ahearn; he would be insufferable, she could just imagine him swaggering about, leering over the young female officers' desks. The more thought she gave to the job, the more she wasn't sure anyone ever really could fill the space if Grady left.

They drove almost a quarter of a mile north of Curlew Hall to a clearing in the woods that afforded parking for most of the volunteers and all of the Gardai vehicles. Tony Ahearn was walking purposefully around the clearing, sly eyes watching as Iris and Slattery made their way from the car. He was tall and perhaps, a decade earlier, had been good-looking, but now his dark hair was thinning and Iris had a feeling he might be dyeing it in some vain attempt to hang onto a youthfulness that had long since been driven away by cigarettes and fast living. His loud voice alternated between barking into a hand-held radio and guffawing inappropriately into the mobile he held close to his ear. Iris wondered if he was sharing dirty jokes with yet another girlfriend.

'His poor wife,' Slattery whispered to Iris, his eyes studiously ignoring Ahearn while he said it. 'She's the pity of it all.'

'She should leave him.' Iris knew she sounded hard, but no one could warn Rita Ahearn, she'd made her bed, and she seemed happy to lie in it. *Busy man,* Iris thought cynically and she wondered idly if he'd managed to get his shoes dirty in the active search yet.

Ahearn had deployed the team in four basic directions. An experienced garda led each team of searchers, the volunteers silently bringing up the rear, checking beneath undergrowth, perhaps hoping to find a sleeping Eleanor in their path. There were two dogs available locally and he sent one east and the other north. 'I just figured that at five o'clock in the morning she'd either head for the sun or head straight on from the door she'd exited,' he said self-importantly.

Cocky as ever, Iris thought. In fairness, there was nothing at the scene to indicate any particular route Eleanor might have taken.

'How's things?' Slattery asked Ahearn as they made their way back towards one of the parked Gardai vans. 'Any sign?'

'Well, it's early yet, and the volunteers are just getting into it… so…' He was competing with static from the radio. He turned it down, blocking out the constant updates from the various search teams, an in-joke already doing the rounds. Ahearn looked ahead, blue eyes finding it hard to focus too far into the distance. The thicket was as heavy here as in the height of summer, darkness snatching any view from you within yards. It made trying to find Eleanor Marshall here, if she did not want to be found, a complete nightmare.

'We're sure she came into the woods?' Iris asked.

'Forensics are looking at the prints bordering the edge of Curlew Hall. They're pretty sure she didn't travel through the gate headed towards the main road, so she must have headed back through the unlocked door that brings you directly into the woods. She certainly travelled this way at some point. It seems they bought her a couple of pairs of identical wellingtons recently; fresh prints are a perfect match, made after yesterday's rain. We could only track her as far as the old pillar.' Ahearn cast his eyes towards the woods behind Slattery. The pillar stood at the entrance to the woods proper, beyond this point the mud ended and a carpet of fallen leaves left little opportunity for muddy tracks.

'So why haven't we found her yet?' Iris asked, trying to keep the worry from her voice.

'The prints disappear into water, a three-foot drain going from east to west for about a quarter of a mile. After that, the forest floor is covered in leaves, they just spring back up as you walk on them. Once you come in about a couple of hundred yards, there's just layer upon layer of fallen leaves and branches too damp to break under foot and nigh on impossible to track.'

'Well, you have a big team, use them. They should be moving like blue-arsed flies, she shouldn't be that hard to find.' Slattery was turning to leave. The team were organised to search during daylight hours, beyond that they could do more damage than good. They assumed Eleanor would be back before dark. After all they'd heard about her epilepsy, surely it was more likely she'd be trying to make her way home now, wasn't it?

'Anything on the computer?' Ahearn said quietly as they were turning to leave.

'What's that?' Iris did her best to look down on the tall man before her.

'The victim's computer. Some of the lads heard the staff from the care home talking about it. It's missing, right?' Ahearn's voice was hollow. Iris couldn't blame him for trying to elbow his way onto the murder investigation, search parties were for uniforms, not detectives.

'Aye, it's missing. Why? What were they saying exactly?' Slattery moved nearer Ahearn, interested. Even Iris brightened slightly – overheard conversations, although not admissible, tend to be a hundred times more candid than official interviews.

'The gist, so far as I can gather, is that she went nowhere without that computer. Some of the lads on the search thought that she might be using it for record-keeping…'

'Record-keeping?' Iris's words were a flash of heat on a cold morning, and she huffed out heavily, watching the smoky air trailing away from her.

'Some of the lads' – Ahearn jerked his eyes dramatically towards the woods behind him –'some of them think she was keeping an eye on her colleagues, making notes of things she didn't quite approve of.'

'Bet that made her popular,' Slattery said flatly.

'Easy enough to check out.' Iris was freezing. Hot coffee was a million miles away. It felt as if they'd been standing here for hours, and she began to stamp her feet quietly to distract her from the shivers that were running through her too quickly.

'Not just that though, is it?' It looked like Ahearn had it all figured out.

'Motive?' Slattery cocked an eye towards Iris. 'You okay?'

'Sure, just cold.' Somewhere deep in her pockets her mobile phone vibrated – she ignored it. Text messages were rarely of life-or-death importance in Iris's experience.

'Well, I'd put more money on some of the staff up there doing her in than a kid who hasn't got the wherewithal to hold her own with kids her own age, wouldn't you?' Ahearn seemed oblivious to the low early-morning temperature.

'Maybe. It wouldn't explain everything though, would it? Like where the girl is now.' Slattery said reasonably.

They'd gone through a psychiatric report earlier in the incident room. Eleanor hadn't been pegged down as someone with violent tendencies; there was a diagnosis of depression, but that was hardly surprising considering where she'd ended up. To Iris, all she seemed to be was a lost kid, trying to find her way, but making a pig's ear of it.

'Well, no, but it's worth thinking about.' With that Ahearn's radio crackled and he was gone.

Iris couldn't get into the car fast enough. She fiddled with the heating knobs and realised it was the first time she'd felt cold in months. She pulled out Pardy's notes from Julia Stenson's conversation earlier.

'Julia Stenson says they would have counted and checked the medication press just before Eleanor turned in for the night. At that stage they administered Eleanor's evening tablets and everything was perfect when they signed off on the count.' Iris exhaled sharply.

'Aye, and by this morning we're missing half the contents of the meds cupboard.' Slattery was looking straight ahead, but his expression was taut. 'It had to be an inside job, Iris, someone who knows the run of that place – you saw the work an outsider would have to do to pull that off.' It was true, the medicine cabinet was double locked, with keys that were kept in a safe – even if you knew your way around, it would surely take some planning to succeed in getting what you'd need.

'So, you think Eleanor Marshall did it?'

'I hope not.' Slattery sighed. 'What about Nate Hegarty?'

'What about him?'

'Well, he's got the wherewithal, surely. Being security means he has the keys at least.'

'Motive?'

'Oh, I don't know, maybe Rachel saw something she shouldn't have… maybe it's noted on her laptop.'

'I need to meet this Hegarty bloke,' Iris said drily.

'Well, I'm sure he won't disappoint,' Slattery said as they made their way back towards Limerick.

'Anyway, I prefer the idea a lot better than the notion of Eleanor Marshall killing Rachel with a weapon she didn't have access to and then opening a numerical keypad she wasn't meant to know the combination to, to get out the door and keep quiet as a mouse while security didn't register so much as a dicky bird.'

'See what I mean.' A smile played around Slattery's lips. 'Tell the truth now,' he said as he elbowed her softly in the upper arm. 'The only rotten thing about it is that it came from Silky-Socks Ahearn. Apart from that it fits perfectly.'

'Mmm,' Iris responded, distracted as she fished deep in her pockets to find her phone, remembering the text message that had sounded earlier. 'Let's think about it…for a while.'

CHAPTER 6

Duneata House was as unwelcoming as it was striking. It rose like a bulwark from the brown craggy countryside around it. A grey monolith, it stood proud and stern alone on the empty vista. It was certainly imposing, if she had time to count off the number of windows and chimney pots, she knew she'd have run out of fingers before she made it even halfway through. The huge dark double doors, which should have been the smile of the house's face, seemed to stand in a permanent frown. The grounds were nice, she had to concede, plenty of work had gone into them to keep them pristine. Still, she couldn't imagine anything like a normal childhood in such a daunting place. There wasn't another house around for miles and the neat, narrow road, like a grassy spinal cord, leading to its tall entrance gates, was evidence that it was infrequently visited.

'This was the Judge's house,' Slattery said flatly. 'Back in the day, that's what it was known as – The Judge's House. Marshall bought it for a song, apparently, but he ploughed a fortune into it to bring it back to this.'

As they pulled up on the gravel drive, it loomed above them double-bayed and austere, the stone blacker, the windows darker and the land lusher than Iris would have expected. Two deep lines of tall chimneys trailed across the rooftop, but only two of those pots looked as if they were used regularly these days. It was a study in old-money charm and new-money opulence – Iris figured Marshall might have saved some of his cash and ended up with a more tasteful home. Slattery looked completely out of his comfort zone, as if he'd prefer to do a couple of rounds with Jaws rather than ring the doorbell.

'You're too old school for your own good sometimes,' Iris murmured as she trotted up the steps before him.

'It's not old school if it's listening to your gut and I've never liked the look of Kit Marshall – this place isn't making me any fonder of him, that's all.'

They waited for a moment for the door to open and when it did, Iris caught her breath; there was something unnerving about seeing someone you'd glimpsed so often in the papers over the years standing at their front door in an old-fashioned smoking jacket and slippers. Kit Marshall was as tall and reedy as she'd imagined him, but his face had a steeliness to it that couldn't be captured by a camera, or perhaps he'd managed to blot it out with good PR and fast answers fired at questions so there was no lingering when he didn't want it. He'd set himself up as a generous donor to worthy causes, probably to write off the enormous tax bill he'd have had to pay otherwise. The man before her now looked a lot less like Father Christmas than he did the wily businessman that he most certainly was.

'Ah, yes, I've been expecting you since early this morning,' he said, peering down his long nose disdainfully at their identity cards. 'Of course, the commissioner was onto me first thing. Those fools up at Curlew Hall lost Eleanor, he tells me.' He held the door open for them even if they had the distinct impression they were not really welcome. When he closed it behind them, Iris could have sworn she heard it echo.

The entrance hall was a lot larger and even more opulent than she'd have guessed from the outside, but it was not the double staircase, the original panelling or the low-slung chandelier – that wouldn't have looked out of place in an Emirate palace – that caught Iris's eye. Rather, it was the girl, a paler, blonder, green-eyed, younger copy of Eleanor who leaned over the top of the balustrade with a frightened expression on her face that made the biggest impression. The younger sister – Karena. Iris had seen her photograph in a newspaper piece about the family that she'd found on their journey out. It was hard to match this vision to the kid who Eleanor had spoken to every weekend as soon as she got her phone in her hands. It seemed as much as she could do was to fit in a long conversation with Karena before her phone was locked away again for another week.

'Right, well, I suppose you may as well come in here, it's got a fire and Susan will be along any minute.'

Kit Marshall positioned himself before the fire, overseeing the room with an unreadable expression, but certainly to Iris it didn't seem like worry or grief. He had already been briefed about his daughter's disappearance from Curlew Hall. The police commissioner himself had called, before there was any danger of it becoming the leading news story of the day. Marshall was as well connected as you got to any seat of power you'd like to name in Ireland. Now, he rubbed dry red eyes and kept his voice low and even, it occasionally rose at the end of his unfinished anguished sentences – he almost managed the right blend of worry, despair and mannish strength.

His wife, when she arrived, seemed to be a larger version of the familiar face that stood by her husband's side so often on their news feeds. She was still glossy, glitzy and at least a decade younger than her husband, but there was something more vital about her. It probably came with having all day to spend in the gym and the beautician's, still, you couldn't but admire her, she was in great shape – especially compared to her more uptight, overbearing husband. Perhaps they were the same age, but they looked like people from different eras. Susan Marshall had a peculiar glamour to her that would have marked her out of her own set. It was – Iris hated the term – *trashy*. As if she was trying too hard to let you know that they were wealthy. Perversely, Iris found herself liking Kit less the more she studied his comparatively vulgar wife.

'Susan, dear, maybe the detectives would like some tea. Can you call for some?' he suggested.

'No, we're fine for now. Thank you,' Slattery said slowly, but his eyes took too much in and there was no mistaking he set Marshall on edge. Perhaps Kit had met guards like Slattery before, or maybe he'd just met Slattery, it didn't matter – there was an unspoken mutual dislike hanging between them in the air.

'As you can imagine, it's come as something of a blow to us,' Kit began. 'My wife…well, she's just…'He looked about the room, as if the words could be conjured from the chintz on the sofa or the oil paintings on the wall. 'It's an awful tragedy, that poor young woman, impossible to get your head around it.'

'Yes, it's come as a terrible blow to her family too.'

'I mean, that place has top-class fees, you'd bloody think…' Kit stopped, seemed to gather himself. 'Well, it's just so…'

'Kit, come on now, it's just a shock,' Susan soothed him.

'It must be a terrible shock for you both.' Iris leaned towards Susan. 'There's a huge search party combing the woods now, so hopefully…' Her words drifted off. They didn't really know what they were dealing with; needle in haystack territory, but the Marshalls didn't need to know that. Susan nodded, mumbled something nobody quite made out and Kit coughed, to take the guards' attention away from her.

'Can you tell us about Eleanor, Mr Marshall?' Iris asked, trying to sound neutral, trying for all the world to pretend that there was anything vaguely normal in a daughter born to all of this ending up at a place like Curlew Hall.

'Oh, I wouldn't know where to start. She was a sweet child, until a few short years ago and then it seemed she changed and became very disturbed…'

'You mean she had mental-health issues?' Slattery cut in.

'Dear God, no. Nothing like that at all. I've always thought it was jealousy, you know, she's never been quite... well, I mean everything. She's the complete opposite of her sister, Karena – academically, sports ability, social graces.' Marshall looked about the room, waited a beat. 'I don't know, two children so close in every way, and yet, so completely damnably different. It's not as if we didn't try, but it seemed the more we put in, the worse it got.'

'Worse?' Iris prompted.

'Oh, yes, let me tell you, Inspector—' He stopped a moment, checking that he had the rank correct. 'It started with small things, running the bath until it overflowed, locking Susan out when they were here alone, you know, the sort of pranks that could drive a normal person mad on a daily basis, but then...'

'She attacked Karena,' Susan said flatly.

'Of course, she denied it, even had Karena lying for her – between them they blamed everyone they could think of – but in the end... well, you can't have a child like that and not take responsibility for them.'

'So, you sent her to Curlew Hall?' Iris managed to keep the judgement from her voice, even if it dominated her thoughts.

'Of course not, we sent her off to a psychologist first, then away to boarding school – that was a complete disaster. She was expelled – so much for that. In the summer she came back, she set fire to a cottage, just a few miles over from here.'

'Arson?'

'If only that was all. No, it turned out she'd had an argument with a local kid, locked him inside and set fire to the place. If it wasn't for Susan going to look for him... well... who knows? We were lucky she wasn't accused of attempted murder.' Now Iris could see why he'd aged so badly.

'But she wasn't?' Slattery asked.

'No. I spoke with the family, assured them it wouldn't happen again. They were very kind…' He looked towards the window; let his words peter off softly.

'Indeed,' Iris said eventually; they all knew what had been left unsaid, Kit Marshall had paid them off. She could fill in the blanks from there. Then with some input from a psychiatrist, maybe the GP and certainly some of his friends in the department of justice, he'd paid the fees to Curlew Hall and managed to slip in his daughter there. Amazing how any problem could be swept beneath the carpet if you had the money to buy a big enough brush.

'She was very *challenging*.' His voice had dipped further, his eyes as near puppy dog as any wolf can go. 'We couldn't watch her all the time. It came to the point where everything, everyone, made her more frustrated. I suppose we just weren't prepared or, that is, *equipped* to take care of her as she needed.' He had all the right words, drawn from a lifetime of diplomacy. A dab of his white linen handkerchief to redden his eyes and he might even fool someone. 'And then there was the epilepsy. We brought her to every consultant, but, really, she could have died at any time and that was when we knew she was safer in proper care. She was fourteen years old by the time she moved to Curlew Hall.' He looked across at his wife. It wasn't clear if he was inviting her to speak or warning her to keep quiet.

'She was only just fourteen when we had to let her go.' Susan's voice was Limerick city, even if it had been polished over with a posh veneer. 'It was the hardest thing, you can't imagine.' She met Iris's eyes, the sisterhood. Kit smiled tightly across at Susan as she continue speaking. 'I have to confess I found it very hard. They weren't keen on us visiting. I suppose it's all about getting her head straight.'

'So, you haven't actually seen her since?' Iris kept her voice clipped, neutral. Her eyes soaked in every tiny movement in Susan's face.

'No. It was for the best, or so we thought,' Kit said.

'I saw her.' Susan turned towards the dying fire. She got up from her seat and gathered four logs, throwing them across the glowing cinders. They sent a flurry of sparks up the blackened chimney. 'The last time, well, it was almost too awful for words.' She shuddered, drawing up her hands close to her chest, as though her palms cradled something precious.

'Tell us, Mrs Marshall. Anything that can give us an insight at this stage can only help our enquiries.' Slattery's voice was gentle, an unexpected balmy quality to it so it was as smooth as chocolate, soothing away your worries.

'It was in summer, about a week before her birthday. Remember, Kit?'

Kit shifted uncomfortably in his chair. 'I really don't see how going over these things will help anyone; raking up the past does no good.' His voice was granite and he cleared his throat, perhaps trying to shake the coldness from it.

'Please.' Iris said gently, and she leaned forward in the soft chair.

'I'd got her some clothes, just a few bits and pieces to keep her going. Karena helped me pick out some designer bits, and we'd made a special trip to Limerick just to get a matching outfit. I was so happy taking it into Curlew Hall. They said she'd had a good day before that, and I thought it would be okay for us to go for a little walk. It was May and the woods were in full bloom, I remember feeling such hope.' Susan looked out the window; perhaps returning to that far-off place for a moment. Sadness crept across her face. 'One of the staff – an older lady, Mrs Brady, she still works there – said she'd come with us, just for a short stroll. We headed towards the lake, if you can call it that, it's more like a large gully really.' Susan looked to the floor, her voice dipped, weighing heavily under the memory. 'Then out of nowhere, Eleanor just went wild.'

'How do you mean?' Iris asked.

'Well, when she lived here, her frustrations… you could see why she became upset. It was normally something very simple, like she wanted something she couldn't have or there was that terrible possessiveness of Karena, but this – this was different. We were walking along, myself and Mrs Brady, and we were chatting about how Eleanor might celebrate her birthday and then…' Susan lifted her head just for a moment; if her husband had been willing her to keep quiet, she wasn't listening. Her gaze fell in an instant towards her hands, which she began to knead over and back across the soft fabric of her jeans. 'I think it was the violence of it more than anything else that shocked us. The way she moved. She'd have hauled both of us into the water had she not lost her footing. There was no doubt in my mind it was deliberate and I'd never seen that before. Her rages had always been outbursts. I'm not saying she hadn't managed to hurt people, but you always knew, you could see – there was a reason, be it jealousy or whatever.'

'But that day?' Slattery whispered gruffly, his words were hardly audible above the hissing and crackling of a fat log in the fire that had caught aflame suddenly along its surface.

'I think that day she set out to push us into the lake. Maybe it was a prank. I'm not sure anymore. But, yes, I'm afraid that was when it became obvious that she was no longer the little girl she'd been at home.' She shuddered then, as if the memory had washed over her once more. 'Sorry.' She reached for a tissue, perhaps trying to cover up the tears that might force their way to her eyes.

'So they said you shouldn't visit her anymore?' Iris said gently.

'Yes.' Susan nodded. 'But they'd said it a million times before, only I couldn't just leave her there…'

'It wasn't an unusual request in the circumstances.' Kit bit down on his words, perhaps attempting to keep the defensiveness from his voice. 'Sending Eleanor to Curlew Hall is probably one of the hardest decisions we've had to make. We sent her for her own good, not ours.' Kit looked down at the fire; the flames were skipping high up the Victorian grate. 'The behaviour experts said our visits were unsettling her, putting two worlds before her when she could hardly deal with one. They said that for whatever chance we had of getting her back on track to work, she needed time to find herself first.'

'They'd been saying it for a while, saying it upset her too much, but yes, that was the day, that day in the woods, I knew they were probably right.' Susan's voice was barely an undertone.

Slattery nodded, silently, as though he somehow understood the loss. It was an unspoken rule; they had to keep these people on side. Iris had to keep reminding herself that Kit Marshall was not an enemy you wanted to make, especially when you were looking for his missing daughter.

'I can't imagine how hard it must have been for you.' Compassion thickened Iris's voice so her words were just a murmur lingering in the dead air.

'The police aren't interested in our sob story, Susan, they just want to do their job,' Kit cut in, his voice even, his eyes on the two detectives. 'Anyway, the people at the rehabilitation centre can probably tell you more about her now than we can.' He held out a hand to Susan who reached across obediently. 'Susan has a photograph somewhere around here. Maybe that would help?' He looked across at his wife and it seemed that some unspoken words passed between them, but Iris for the life of her couldn't imagine what they were.

'That would be great, Mrs Marshall,' Iris said. 'We can return it later in the day if you want.'

'You both understand that this is a murder case?' Slattery asked, and his eyes floated absently from Susan to Kit.

'Yes, it's very sad. Of course, we'll be sending our condolences to the family of the poor woman who died.' Kit Marshall's voice was smooth, intense and almost honourable.

'Are people looking for Eleanor now?' Susan asked shakily. 'They've told you about her epilepsy, you know she could...*die* in one of those seizures?' Her voice had risen, so there was no mistaking the panic that she was otherwise managing to keep under her well-polished reserve.

'Yes, Mrs Marshall, we've a huge team of Gardai out since first light and…'

'Can I join them?' Her words were a whisper of hope.

'Oh, Susan, I really don't think…' Kit Marshall stood abruptly, almost springing from his seat, when Iris cut across him.

'Of course, Mrs Marshall. We have a group of volunteers working with our own team of experienced Gardai searchers; some of the people who worked with her are giving us a hand too. The more people we have searching the better; come along in the morning.' She paused briefly before adding, 'But hopefully, we'll have found her by then.' Iris tried to sound reassuring and Susan nodded, a small tear scudded past her hand. Her 'thank you' was almost silent, caught up so deeply and almost wholly in the anguish of a mother's grief.

'Do you think that she might try to return here, to her home, to find you both?' Slattery asked.

'I can't see that… I mean, if she's decided to run away, surely home is the last place she'd turn up. What makes you think she might?' Kit said lightly, but there was a tinge of worry in his expression as he glanced across at his wife.

'Well, it's the only other place she knows beyond Curlew Hall.' Slattery sat watching their faces intently for a long silent moment. 'Either way, be aware that it's a possibility.'

'Are you telling us to be careful, Sergeant? Are you worried she might try and harm us?' Kit asked.

'You tell me – do you need to worry?' Slattery said.

Kit Marshall shivered and bent to stoke up the fire, sending a rasp of blue smoke into the room.

'Oh, for goodness' sake, have you not listened to a word I said?' Kit Marshall shouted now, the fear of losing face obviously having lost out to a very different kind of fear. 'She tried to hurt Karena… Do you not understand…?' He turned to his wife, as if sharing their stupidity with her. She was at his side in an instant, her hand on his shoulder, it seemed to calm him, his breathing slowed down and he wiped his brow as if he'd just done a hard day's work.

'Of course we don't need to worry,' Susan said sharply. 'If she comes back here, we'll let you know. That's all that there's to be done. I'm sure it's all just a big mix-up and when she turns up, we'll have it all ironed out very quickly.'

'Now.' Slattery smiled; a complex contortion of his features that held no joy, but had just enough warmth to alert them that he was moving on. 'We'll need to speak with Karena next.'

'Karena? I hardly think that you'll learn anything more from her, after all, she's only a child.' Kit Marshall folded his arms stubbornly.

'Even so.' Iris nodded towards the door and, with a sigh, Susan Marshall walked towards the hall and called the child in. It took only a few seconds for Karena to appear in the doorway, a frightened expression in her eyes.

'We just need a few words, pet,' Slattery said.

'Is she all right? Are you here about Eleanor? Have you found her yet?' Her voice was a tremble, just about holding back from falling into an emotional abyss that was far too complex and deep for any kid to navigate.

'We're searching the woods for her now. A huge team of people, all doing their best to find her,' Iris said gently. 'We just need to know if you can tell us anything.'

'Me?' Karena was perched on a sofa, as if ready to take flight at any moment. Everything about her was dainty, doll-like and expensive. Her ash-blonde hair fell in loose waves about her delicate features. China-blue eyes, whiter-than-white teeth and tanned limbs combined to make her the slightly lighter, brighter version of her beautiful sister. 'But I… I was here; I haven't seen Eleanor in over a year… I haven't a clue about any of this.' She gulped then, a huge tear making its way down her cheek.

'It's okay, we know that, it's just…' Slattery leaned forward.

'Look, you're the only one she talked to each week. Your phone call each weekend was the only contact she had with the outside world, so far as we can tell.'

'Oh,' Karena said and her expression dissolved into the tears and worry she'd been working so hard to keep at bay. 'We spoke every Saturday,' she said between sobs, glancing for a moment at her father. 'Not about anything really, just about how she was feeling, what she'd done all week. Sometimes, she'd tell me about some of the girls who lived across from her.'

'Did she ever mention Rachel McDermott?'

'She liked her. I think she liked her a lot. Rachel was kind and I think she was younger than some of the staff there, so they sort of clicked.' She smiled then, a convoluted movement of her pretty features as it fought against the tears. 'Yes, I think she was really fond of Rachel.'

'Is there anywhere she'd be likely to go?' Slattery asked. 'If she got out, did she ever mention anywhere she'd be likely to run away to?'

'No,' Karena said a little too quickly, her eyes searching the carpet for too long and Iris, for one, had the distinct impression that this was a conversation the sisters had had quite a number of times.

'It's important, Karena, really important. It could mean the difference between finding her alive and well and…' Iris let her words trail off, she didn't really need to explain about Eleanor's epilepsy or the fact that it was possible that whoever murdered Rachel McDermott could be out there, right now doing their best to find Eleanor.

'Don't you think I know that, Inspector?' the girl said and then she looked towards her mother with an unreadable expression that Iris had a feeling meant she was lying through her perfectly straightened teeth.

CHAPTER 7

The coroner's office had transferred Rachel McDermott's body to the county hospital and there, in the near-empty morgue, Harry Prendergast had started his day's work early. A mortuary assistant, he'd seen as much as any of them and probably far more than he ever wanted to see. Harry had been around as long as Slattery and these days he shuffled about slowly, eyeing the door, as if perhaps waiting for the day when he could walk out of there into retirement.

'Busy day.' He smiled happily from the opposite side of the desk and Iris wondered if she and Slattery looked anywhere near pleased to be here. They knew each other of old, and time was precious, so their small talk was brief. Iris looked at Harry's yellowing teeth and grey skin. He cleared his throat and placed his hands together, cracking eight fingers one after the other away from his torso. Whether he was gearing up for a day's work or for eating the mammoth beef roll that lounged in cling wrap before him, Iris couldn't say. 'Hungry work.' He smiled at her, and not for the first time she wondered if he could read her mind.

The gentle click of the door at Iris's back announced the arrival of Rafiq Ahmed, the pathologist and someone Iris had warmed to from the first moment they'd been introduced. Ahmed was around her age, early thirties, thin and symmetrically featured. He might have walked off a movie set, but for the fact that he was a little short to be considered a leading man. Always dapper, Ahmed was one of the few medical men Iris had ever met whose scrubs looked as if they had been designed by a couture house.

He was the antithesis of Prendergast who, after pulling out the rough notes that had been hastily put together to brief them and laying the five handwritten sheets of paper in a line on Ahmed's desk, unwrapped his sandwich.

'Miss McDermott was in overall good health for her age,' Ahmed began.

'What age was she?' Prendergast asked.

'Just twenty,' Slattery said. 'Bloody awful waste.'

'She obviously looked after herself, there's no sign of any damage to organs due to lifestyle choices.' He glanced across at Prendergast.

'What the good doctor is saying is that she neither smoked nor drank and she kept herself fairly fit. There's no sign of any drugs yet, but we have to get the pathology results back to confirm that.'

'Indeed.' Slattery cleared his throat. 'And yet, here we are.'

Rachel McDermott was dead and the only thing Iris wanted to hear was that she hadn't been killed by Eleanor Marshall. She and Slattery had argued it over and back on the journey from the station. He, in typical Slattery humour, refused to see beyond the fact that Eleanor had the opportunity and perhaps a motive. Iris tried her best to argue that at just about five feet, she would have to have phenomenal strength to wield a sledgehammer with the force that it took to inflict those injuries.

'Yes. Well, even Mr Incredible couldn't survive the kind of attack that our victim received. Multiple blows, many after she'd fallen and probably already lost consciousness, but…' Ahmed sent a ten-by-eight black-and-white photograph sliding across the desk. 'This seems to have been the lethal one.' He got up after they had a chance to examine it, leading the way into the autopsy suite where Rachel McDermott's body lay on an examination table. 'I completed the examination just half an hour before you arrived – I'm afraid I'm due to travel to Tipperary in the next hour…'

'Can you tell from the blows if our killer was shorter or taller than the victim?' Slattery put the question that Iris hadn't wanted to ask.

'You're wondering if it could have been the Marshall girl?' Ahmed smiled. 'Ah, if I could tell you that, then I suspect it would take all the fun out of things for you, Sergeant Slattery.'

'It's possible so?' Iris asked.

'Yes, it's possible. The first blow brought her down, she landed on her knees – from the blood spatter and prints – gripping onto the side of the sink. Then, with the remaining blows, she fell to the floor. The first blow wasn't to her head, it was here—' He pointed to the victim's back on the X-ray screen. 'At Rachel McDermott's height, anyone over four feet eleven could have served the blow easily. So, yes, it's possible that when you find the Marshall girl, you've found your killer,' Ahmed said, switching off the X-ray screen with a resigned flick. 'Now.' He looked at his watch. 'I need to be making tracks…'

'Oh, that house fire?'

'Yes. A couple and their grandchild, parents were away for the weekend and the fire officer is saying a candle may have been the cause of—'

'Oh, how awful,' Iris said and she exhaled deeply, the memory of death and fire too fresh in her mind not to send shivers through her. It was only weeks since Jack Locke had set fire to their home and himself and not much longer since she'd attended her first case with the Murder Team only to find that the victims were her own flesh and blood.

'I'm sorry…' Ahmed touched her arm.

'Don't worry, I'm fine.' It was a lie, but it was the one she was expected to say, and maybe if she said it often enough, it would become the truth.

'Right.' Prendergast pulled back the plastic cover to reveal Rachel McDermott's bruised remains. Now, while the blood, vomit and fluids had been washed away, the bruising from earlier had settled in mottled patches around her upper body and most prominently around her head. 'It's as you'd expect, the first blow probably put her down.' He pointed to a deep bruise blackening the skin at the area of her back that coincided roughly with Rachel's lung. It would have literally winded her. 'The rest were inflicted doubtless in frenzy, but there was some force here…' He paused for a moment. 'This was inflicted with the force of a madman.'

'Or woman?' Slattery asked.

'Yes, it could as easily have been inflicted by a woman.' Prendergast nodded and Ahmed agreed.

'Thank you for that helpful if perhaps graphic assessment.' Ahmed stood at the top of the examination table; he took a laser pointer from his jacket pocket. 'This wound, on her occipital bone, would have been enough to kill her within minutes. When we took a closer look, it struck directly into the centre of her brain – that would have rendered her unconscious almost immediately and instantly cut off oxygen to her brain, shutting down everything rapidly from her breath to her heartbeat.'

'Anything you can tell us that might give us more than she was assaulted by a nasty brute?' Slattery asked, peering closely at the victim's face, which was still, thanks to the patchwork of black, yellow and blue bruising, all but unrecognisable.

'We have a few occasions across the victim's body where the weapon has imparted a print. Prendergast has traced those, so they'll give you a copy of the weapon's appearance – we can say that it's certainly hammer-like in design and probably old. I checked with the lab. There's no trace of the kind of finish you'd expect to have left had it been a newly minted hammer head. You're looking for something that came from a tool shed, probably unused, as there are traces of rust here.' He ran the laser along the temple bone, but all that was visible now was bruising and a series of neat stitches that had been carefully inserted to try and keep the victim's face in as good a shape as possible for her family to view the following day. 'And that's about it.' Ahmed flicked off his little red beam and placed it in his pocket again before leading them back to the adjoining office. 'Of course, I'll have the complete report for you hopefully by tomorrow morning. I'll email it tonight when I get a chance to reread what I've just noted down today,' Ahmed said, gathering up his notes and placing them neatly in his man bag.

Harry peered into the half-empty mug before him and then looked hopefully across at Iris. Slattery's low cough reminded him to think better of it. The days of sending the woman to make the tea were well and truly at an end and it was no secret that Harry didn't think all change was necessarily good change. He swished the fast-cooling liquid around the cup before draining it dejectedly.

'So, no drugs, unless pathology comes back with something recent,' Iris said, although she hadn't expected to find anything in Rachel's bloodstream. 'How long will the reports from the technical bureau take?' she asked Slattery. Almost all the fingerprinting was completed now; hundreds of sets of prints, including some that they believed may be from Eleanor Marshall.

'Well, Kenny sent the fingerprints out earlier. They'll start analysing them today, so… I'd say within the next three days. All things considered it shouldn't take too long, the samples are fairly straightforward. It's just the large quantity that are going to cause delays.'

'Yes, yes…' Ahmed raised his head from the notes before him. 'Yes, beyond that, on her arms and abdomen there are a number of bruises, about a week old, you might want to check those out, but otherwise it's down to that trauma to her head.'

'Indeed,' Slattery said.

'Of course, the Marshall girl is still implicated at this rate. I haven't uncovered much to help you there. Are you any closer to finding her, do you think?' Ahmed rested his glasses across the notes.

'No, we've a huge search party in the woods but—'

'What about the marks?' Iris looked across at Ahmed, ignoring Harry. 'You said there were marks on her arms and stomach.'

'The marks could be from anything, but they look like they could be blows or bruising from some kind of fight.'

'Self-defence?'

'I can't say for definite, you know that, sergeant.' Ahmed smiled.

'I suppose that Marshall girl would have known how to use her fists,' Harry said flatly.

Iris cast a dark eye at Harry. 'Less of the past tense, if you don't mind.' She wanted to rage at him.

'All I'm saying is that Rachel McDermott doesn't look like the kind of girl who went in for boxing or street fighting. It's going to be easy enough to see if they were inflicted by Eleanor Marshall, places like Curlew Hall always keep a record of any kind of physical outbursts, especially if it's against staff – I'm sure they'll have had their fair share of insurance claims over the years.'

'Those marks, the bruising – they could have been there a while, don't just presume they happened yesterday.' Ahmed looked across at Prendergast now. 'They could be picked up from a fall – she was a fit young woman, who's to say she wasn't hill walking or mountain climbing on her days off.'

'Well, it's something for us to look into anyway.' Slattery glanced towards Iris meaningfully. *We can follow it up*. He didn't need to say it aloud. They planned to go back to the residential unit anyway; interviews were being set up with every staff member who had worked with Eleanor and Rachel. They could check it out then. The kids would be more difficult, they'd need parental permission and a social worker present; Iris wasn't having a statement pulled just because they hadn't done things by the book. She planned to do a lot of the questioning in the unit itself. Thankfully, Byrne had not yet begun to tie her up in budget meetings or the many other desk-bound duties that he'd foisted on Grady over the years. Most of the team had been allocated to searching the woods. The main objective now was to find Eleanor. Within the search team, hope was fading fast that they could find her alive, but they had to keep going, stay optimistic. Without hope there was nothing.

'It's a funny old world, isn't it?' Slattery was fingering the mug of cold coffee before him, delicately, the action out of sync with his voice and posture. Something in his words made both Iris and Ahmed lean closer to hear what he had to say next.

'What do you mean?' Harry leaned back in his seat, awaiting words of wisdom from a fellow philosopher on the sometimes abrupt ending of life.

'Well, you know who she is, don't you?' He looked at Harry.

'Rachel McDermott?'

'Yes, Rachel McDermott. You do know who she is, don't you?'

'Not the foggiest.'

'She's Imelda McDermott's girl, well, you know…'

'Imelda McDermott. There's a name I haven't heard for a while.'

'I bet you haven't thought about her in years.'

Iris looked between the two men, bewildered. 'Well, is this a secret? Was she an old girlfriend or something?'

Harry smiled. 'Not quite, but we did cross paths at one point, that was back in old Professor Waddington's day. I'd say Ahmed here was still in primary school last I heard of Imelda McDermott.' Harry looked at Iris, seeing beyond this case to a post mortem that had taken place many years ago. 'Healthiest man in Ireland,' he announced to no one in particular, or maybe just thinking aloud.

'Who is the healthiest man in Ireland?' Iris asked.

'Not is, *was*. Imelda's husband was the healthiest man in Ireland, bar the fact that he was dead of course.'

'I don't understand.' Iris set down her notebook before her.

'It's a long time ago, or at least if feels like it now anyway. A fine woman in her day, good-looking—'

'Ah come on, Harry – she had a face like a poker,' Slattery interrupted.

'Not to my memory. She was hardworking, but a tough woman. There was harshness in her that you don't generally see in mothers and certainly not in widows.' The smile was beginning to vanish and Harry closed his eyes, perhaps to get a better picture in his mind. 'William McDermott died from no apparent cause; he was only thirty-nine, with the healthy heart of a twenty-year-old. The usual suspects – heart attack, disease, trauma of any sort, none applied. The professor even tested for poisons, thinking maybe he decided to end things quickly himself – men of a certain age, and all that – but there was nothing, no apparent cause of death. It was a mystery to this day…sort of.'

'How do you mean?'

'Well, everyone dies of something. Some people are lucky enough to die of old age, with some it's an aneurysm, with others I think it can genuinely be a broken heart, but not with Mr McDermott.' His fingers stretched across the desk, and he paused a moment, seemingly wondering how to phrase his next sentence. 'I believe Mr McDermott, the healthiest man in Ireland, died of marital problems.'

'Hold on a minute, you're not saying you thought Imelda McDermott killed her husband?' Iris held her hand up, this had come completely out of the blue.

'It's what we believed at the time,' Prendergast said slowly.

'Why on earth didn't you mention this to me before we went to see her?' Iris turned on Slattery.

'I didn't want us both to have a clouded judgement.'

'So, I can't be fair-minded now?' Iris wanted to hit him over his fat head with the nearest thing to her, but she knew she couldn't let her temper boil over here; apart from all the professional reasons, she was not giving Slattery ammunition so he could wind her up at a future moment when he felt the need to amuse himself.

'I never said that,' Slattery replied softly. 'To be fair, Iris, there was no case to bring against her, nothing to prove.'

'Slattery's right. If Imelda McDermott killed her husband, there wasn't a shred of evidence, that's why we often joked he died of connubial complications.'

'Is it possible the daughter died of maternal complications?' Of course, that was madness. She could no more imagine Imelda McDermott taking a hammer to her daughter's head than she could imagine her murdering her husband all those years ago. But then again…

'I can't see her as a murderer, never did, not from the start, but it's a very unfortunate coincidence, don't you think?' Slattery hated coincidences almost as much as he hated pioneers.

CHAPTER 8

The forecast for the next few hours was not good. They had to find Eleanor, and soon, as dark clouds were rolling across the sky by lunchtime.

'We need to talk to Hegarty – he was there on the night, if not in that unit, he was certainly within the grounds and he has to know something more than I got out of him that first morning.'

Slattery had started the car before Iris had even managed to properly get into it. Iris sensed that Slattery's mind was racing ahead. The search team working under Sergeant Tony Ahearn in the woodland surrounding Curlew Hall had only a limited number of daylight hours, and the next few were crucial. The people at the care home estimated Eleanor could have had at least one grand mal seizure at this stage and that was assuming she was getting her medication properly. The truth was, that just because the meds were gone, it didn't mean that Eleanor had them, nor did it mean she would actually take them in time. *Grand mal*, the words raged through Iris's mind. From what little she remembered from learning French at school, she knew they meant big and bad. The staff at Curlew Hall said that's exactly what they were. Eleanor would lose consciousness and of course she could injure herself as she fell to the ground. There was a high possibility that she could die either by choking or from the seizure itself. They didn't hold out a lot of hope for her without those crucial pills, Iris could see it in their eyes. *Please find her soon.*

The Marshalls had rung every other hour at this point; June was fending off their calls, but really, it was a matter of turning over every branch and bush until they found her. It was as if she'd disappeared into thin air and that thought bothered Iris more than anything. After all, surely, someone would have spotted a girl on foot in the woods? Then she would toss over the idea of a ransom, but with the Marshalls checking up so regularly, she had to assume that there had been no contact from a potential kidnapper. They'd organised a press conference for later and Iris could only hope that involving the general public might be enough to track Eleanor down.

'Pardy?' Iris shouted into the phone, her patience a skinny wedge. 'I want you to pull any information Curlew Hall has on Eleanor Marshall – her personal file, psychology reports, behaviour reports, everything. I want to know all we can about her.'

She looked across at Slattery. This case had to be especially hard for him. Everyone knew about his murdered sister. He never talked about it, but it went with the territory of the Murder Squad, there were no secrets here. Una Slattery had been just nineteen when she was beaten to death in a little flat in the centre of Limerick. At the time Slattery was still at school – powerless, really. The family had neither money nor knowledge to track down the killer after the investigation had drawn a blank. Whatever had happened to his sister, Iris knew, as sure as she was sitting here, the spirit of that young woman infused this and any similar investigation with Slattery. *We've all got our demons,* he had once said, and she'd wondered just how far into her soul he had seen.

'Well,' she said flatly, 'so much for records… they don't seem to be able to locate her file… apparently, they're looking for it.'

'I wouldn't want to be the one telling Kit Marshall that.' Slattery shook his head ominously. 'I wonder how Ahearn is getting on.'

'Next call,' Iris said, scrolling down to find the sergeant's number. Tony Ahearn answered on the second ring, as if he'd been standing poised over the phone waiting for her call.

'Nothing. We're fanning out the search further, the chances of damaging the ground are lessening with the rain we've just had on and off out here, that'll do enough damage all on its own. Now, we're looking for anything: a catch of hair on a branch or a discarded bag, anything that might point us in the right direction…' His voice trailed off. They really had nothing, and depressing and all as that was, it was even more disheartening to think that they were looking for traces rather than the girl herself. 'Anyway, it's getting darker now, so we'll be calling a halt pretty soon,' he continued. 'They've set up a table here, with hot soup and rolls for the searchers…'

'Who organised all that?'

'Some of the people from Curlew Hall, I think,' Ahearn said absently.

'No, keep them searching, try not to break until the light has gone. Spread it out as far as possible. Bugger the overtime, I'll worry about that.' She jammed a thumb against the red button of her mobile and ended the call.

'Anything?' Slattery asked. He knew, of course, that there was no sign of Eleanor Marshall. He was asking only out of commitment to the vague hope.

'No.' Iris flicked into her emails. There at the top was a message from Byrne – well, she might as well get used to it. It went with the territory when you were in charge of an investigation, maybe more so when that investigation had an impact on someone as well connected as Kit Marshall. 'Byrne wants to meet,' she said eventually. She'd scanned through the email twice, drawing as much from its tone as the words. Marshall had made it clear he wanted to control how the media was involved and Byrne was passing on the message as neutrally as he could, but only because he was too wily to confer his opinions on written correspondence

'Budget?' It usually was. Still, they weren't spending anything that didn't need to be spent. These were difficult times, as Byrne liked to remind them with regular memos and lectures.

'No, not the notorious tighten-the-purse-strings sermon. I've a feeling it's something I'm going to like even less than that lecture.'

'Oh?'

'Kit Marshall.' It was all she needed to say. Marshall was friends with the commissioner, probably had the minister for defence on speed dial; they were all in the same big boys' club. She looked across at Slattery now, knowing only too well that he couldn't give a damn what Marshall or anyone else thought of him. 'I think he wants to make sure he finds Eleanor, but doesn't want her disappearance linked to the death of Rachel McDermott.'

'Well, that's fair enough, isn't it?'

'Yep, I suppose it is,' she said softly, but what she was thinking was: if Eleanor had already tried to hurt her sister and set fire to a house with someone inside, managing to avoid any major court case thanks to her daddy's money, did Kit Marshall think he could brush the death of Rachel McDermott under the carpet as easily?

'I know what you're thinking, Iris, but remember, all we need to do now is find her alive. We'll worry about charging her with murder after we question her and put a case together. If she killed Rachel McDermott, well, we have a job to do and that's all we have to worry about.' Then he smiled a little wryly. 'Well, that's all I have to worry about, now you're the officer in charge, you might have to think about how we're handling him.'

'You think Byrne asked me to lead this out because I'd do what I was told?' That rankled with her too: did he think she'd roll over for Marshall when it came down to it?

'I didn't say that, but let's face it, I wouldn't exactly be renowned for toeing the line just because Byrne told me to.'

'Christ.' Iris felt a trickle of sweat run down her back. Was that what they really thought of her? That she so badly wanted into the Murder Team and promotion that she'd do anything to get ahead? 'And if I don't, what's the worst they can do to us? Take us off the case? Move the investigation to another team?' She was thinking out loud, trying hard to remember Byrne's words – all he talked about was making sure that they followed procedure, nothing more.

'Why would they, Iris? Why would they?' He paused and she willed him not to say what they were both thinking. He did. 'She's probably dead anyway.'

'But we don't know that. They don't know that,' Iris said. They couldn't give up, not while there was still a chance.

'Look, the people who know her well, you can see it in their faces. You saw it for yourself, Iris, they believe they're searching for a body.'

'So? They could be wrong.'

'Let's hope so. Anyway, we both know that Kit Marshall doesn't want a daughter with a criminal conviction, we've seen that already.' A small smile played around Slattery's tired mouth. 'They won't take us off it, because look at us – you're damaged goods and I'm the legendary Corbally waste of space. In some ways, we're both dead men walking, aren't we?' His voice was low, not defeated, but smelling a struggle.

'If that's what they think, they're sadly mistaken.' Iris sounded more confident than she actually felt. Finding Eleanor Marshall was like searching for a mackerel called Mary in the Atlantic. They both knew that as each minute ticked by the chances of her safe return diminished enormously.

'Anyway, it's not all down to Kit Marshall,' he said before glancing at her. 'The girl has a mother too, doesn't she?'

'What about Susan though? She's a funny fish…' Instantly Iris regretted the words. Susan Marshall was in shock; she'd probably spent a lifetime missing the daughter that had been sent away ostensibly for her own good. But then, Iris knew, it was the way they spoke about their two daughters – Karena so perfect, Eleanor painted as the black sheep. 'She's a mother. Surely she wants more for her daughter than always being the almost ran?'

Susan Marshall had hardly said a word during their meeting at the grand house. Her empty eyes had searched the room for somewhere to land without staying too long in one spot. Iris had never met such a shadow of a person. It was as if she had always been only the wife of a wealthy man – there didn't seem to be any other dimension to her. But that was unfair, she was judging her on what she'd found online about the couple. Susan Marshall had come from one of the most deprived council estates in Limerick – the Cloisters. She'd managed, somehow, to dig her way out and had been lucky enough to fall into the path of Kit Marshall. Theirs seemed to be a stable and happy union, with plenty of evidence across the local papers of them at various fundraisers and charity galas. Long gone was the girl from the Cloisters, it seemed, in almost every way – her voice, her appearance and, of course, her social standing, all a million miles from where she'd started out. As they'd got up to leave, Susan had tugged her sleeve, her deep-green eyes piercing through Iris. 'You find her, find her for me.' She felt sorry for Susan Marshall for so much more than just her missing daughter.

'She probably always has but he's a—'

'Bully. He's a bully, but he's not going to bully us.' She looked across at Slattery, knowing that he couldn't be cowed by anyone if he thought there was a case to solve. 'Come on. We have nothing to lose.'

She smiled a thin smile at him. They had to find Eleanor Marshall, before it was too late. Too late for what though? With this case, with Eleanor Marshall, Iris sensed an enormous amount of vulnerability mixed with an admirable subversive streak. That was the unspoken message conveyed by the people who knew her. She was an unknown quantity. It was them and us. Staff versus Eleanor. That's what Iris was seeing. And people who saw things in black and white very often feared what they saw as different, and unfortunately it only added to Eleanor's already formidable reputation.

'You're right, fiddlers on them.' The creases that rutted across Slattery's forehead deepened, resolve shaping his face to make it look far older than his near sixty years.

'I'll follow up with Nate Hegarty,' she suggested, grounding them back into the here and now. 'Then I'll face the music with Byrne; see if we can't do a bit of a two-step.'

'We need to get this out there.' His voice was low. 'It doesn't matter how they spin it for now, as long as people know that she's missing and we want to find her.'

'Kit Marshall knows how important it is to make people aware. So, what's he playing at?' They should have it already, not waiting for it to be stage-managed by Marshall.

'That's a problem for us, isn't it?' Slattery affectionately rubbed the half-empty box of cigarettes that rested beside the handbrake. 'It's one of the questions we'll have to think about, along with what exactly Rachel McDermott was up to.'

'How do you mean?'

'Well, she didn't die because she'd done someone a good deed, now did she? And that bruising…'

'Suppose not, suppose not,' she replied, her mind scrambling through the woods, searching for the missing young woman. Slattery hadn't mentioned William McDermott – Rachel's father– since their meeting with Harry. Iris sensed that it was an avenue he didn't want to explore right now, but she knew it had to be done. 'Tell me about William McDermott.'

'Ah, Iris, he's dead and gone, old news.' Slattery sighed.

'You might as well tell me anyway.' She smiled at him.

'Look, I was hardly in the station a wet week when he died. I'd just transferred in from the border duties. I'm not the right one to ask.'

'Well I'm asking you anyway.'

He seemed to recognise the deep lines that furrowed into either side of Iris's mouth as a sign that she wouldn't let this go until she was satisfied. 'Okay, William McDermott died suddenly. He was a relatively young man and appeared to be in good health so naturally a post mortem was carried out.' Slattery took a cigarette from the packet and began to twirl it between his fingers. 'Anyway, the post mortem showed nothing, nothing at all. As Harry said, there was no cause of death, the man just died for no good reason.'

'And?'

'I was a uniform at the time; Bobby Nestor was my DCI so it was in his hands.' He replaced the cigarette in its box, his body language telling her that he was itching for a smoke. 'He made the enquiries at the time. I think he was suspicious because of Imelda McDermott's attitude as much as anything else.'

'Cold?'

'Yes, for want of a better word. She had every answer rehearsed and at the time, in financial terms at least, William McDermott was worth more dead than alive, Imelda had insured him to the hilt. When you looked at things on paper, she was the earner, he'd never done a hand's turn, from what we could make out.' He sighed then continued, 'All right, it looked like they were going to lose that house. He was a shirker and a gambler, his death meant that they kept the roof over their heads. Who knows what state the marriage was in anyway – back then you just stayed, kept quiet and put up with whatever was thrown at you.'

'Did Nestor really think she did it?'

Slattery indicated and began to move the Ford onto the main road, spending just a little too much attention with mirrors and gears. Iris knew he was considering his next words carefully.

'I think his instincts told him she was as guilty as sin, but Imelda McDermott was and is nobody's fool. You'd be wise to remember that.'

Was he warning her? She wasn't sure. 'Did they question her, at the time?'

'Of course, but there was nothing, she had herself well covered, there wasn't even a scrap of circumstantial evidence to point at her.'

'So, what did you think?'

'I think there was no proof and without it there was no case.'

If William McDermott were a nineteen-year-old girl like Una Slattery, would you feel the same? Iris wondered.

Nate Hegarty was minus one eyebrow; a large silver hoop penetrated the skin above the one remaining when Iris called to his flat. He appeared to be dressed in whatever clothes he'd woken up in. His sullen expression was only slightly more depressing than his slouched and pessimistic posture. Crooked teeth, brown fingers and a pinched face belied his youth. Iris would guess he was probably no more than twenty-five. He looked nearer fifty, like a man who'd put in thirty years of hard living. He hadn't turned up for work since the death of Rachel McDermott and appeared to be genuinely upset by the events of the last few hours. Iris wondered which would worry him more: the police on his doorstep or the passing of his colleague. In fairness, she knew that wasn't unusual. Most people, although completely innocent of any wrongdoing, tended to panic a little when faced with a questioning session by the police.

She watched him as his eyes furtively sought out the darkened corners of the room. Take-out cartons and empty lager cans littered the apartment. At his feet a sketch pad fell open on the floor, it seemed Nate was a doodler. He kicked it beneath his chair when he noticed her looking at it.

'Completely mental bitch' was how he described Eleanor, putting a dirty boyish hand up to his temple and screwing it around just to emphasise his point.

'The last time you saw Eleanor, what was her mood like? Did you notice if there was anything different about her?' Iris checked her notes. 'That was the night of Rachel's death?'

'That's right, I was on roster that night. I popped in, had a cup of tea, before I headed off to make sure the whole place was locked up securely.' He opened a packet of cigarettes and lit up what she guessed was his fortieth cigarette of the day, if the ashtray before him was anything to go by. 'There's a lot of boundary fencing there, it's supposed to be checked each night, that's my job, and when I've done that, I go and have another cup of tea, maybe something to eat in one of the other units.'

'Were you there when Eleanor was given her nightly medication?'

'I was nowhere near any tablets, if that's what ye're thinking. Rachel always asked me to double-check her counts, but I never touched a tablet in Curlew Hall.' He sulked now, dragging long and hard on his cigarette. They weren't going to leave, not until they'd got what they'd come for, so he dropped the scowl and carried on. 'Only care staff, ya see. Only smart ones, people who've been to college, they work in the units and give out the tablets. I've never even been near the store cupboard and I didn't want to be either.' He puffed out, almost self-importantly. 'Not after what went on a couple of months ago.' Iris had heard some tablets had gone missing weeks earlier. 'Funny, if ye'd asked me yesterday what was Rachel's drug of choice, Epilum wouldn't have been my first guess.' He smiled at his own weak joke.

'Oh yes?' Iris asked neutrally. Still, it bothered her that he knew the name of the epilepsy medication that was missing from the store cupboard.

'Come on, sergeant, I'm sure ye've heard the rumours? Rachel enjoyed an occasional joint, just to relax after a long shift.'

'They're not rumours so far as we know.' She was testing the ground; hopeful he'd give her more. This was like walking off a cliff edge, she had no idea where she was or where she might land. 'Was there anyone connected with Rachel's drug taking who might want to see her out of the picture, so to speak?'

'Jesus, what are you saying, that ye think she was killed for having an occasional spliff?'

'Yes.' She could smell it, Nate Hegarty knew something. He shrank in his oversized recliner, his already wizened face turning more scarecrow-like by the minute.

'Look, I don't know what Rachel was into, all I know is that she had the occasional joint, just like most people who aren't so uptight they don't know their own…' He stopped himself. His face became a blank and Iris knew that she'd get nothing else from him, not without having something to go on first.

'Who was her supplier?'

'Hey, if I knew that do ye think I'd be smokin' this shit on my day off?' Iris hoped he was joking, but then he was such a yokel it was hard to tell. No doubt, the drugs team would have more information on Rachel's dealings. If not, she'd be knocking on Nate Hegarty's door once more – sooner than he might like.

'Now, you told Sergeant Slattery in an earlier statement that you didn't see anything unusual on the night.'

'Well, if that's what I said…'

'You can cut the attitude right now, Nate,' she said sharply. 'It's like this: you're the one person who had access to every corner of that place and the only one working there who hasn't got even the whisper of an alibi. Everyone else was locked in and getting out would have meant setting off alarms.'

'So, it's hardly my fault if I was out doing my job, is it?' he said angrily. 'Anyway, that's just means, isn't it? I had no motive to kill Rach, we were mates, like I said, I'm gutted at what happened to her.'

'Yeah, well, maybe you'll have to be gutted down at the station,' Iris said, because as upset as Nate was at the death of Rachel, he was lying to her – she could see it easily. Whatever he'd been up to on the night of Rachel's death, it was not what he wanted them to believe.

'You're not arresting me?' he spluttered.

'No, but you can come along and help us with our enquiries.' Iris stood, tapping her shoe on the wooden floor, waiting for him either to catch up or talk up.

'Now, wait a minute, if you think you're going to fix me up for this—'

'You're lying to me, Nate, I know you are. So it's like this, either you start talking here or we move the conversation somewhere you'll feel a bit more talkative.'

'All right, all bloody right, I wasn't out at Curlew Hall all night. That's what you want to hear, isn't it?'

'I just want the truth, not a palatable version of it.'

'This will get me sacked, you know that?' He shook his head, perhaps he knew Iris might be thinking this wouldn't be such a bad thing at all. 'I did my rounds, had everyone locked up safe, but then, about eleven, I got a call from Tania.'

'Tania?'

'Girlfriend,' he muttered. 'Tania Quirke, you can ask her, I spent the night at her flat. Her kid was sick and she didn't want to be on her own, so she called me and I—'

'I'll need to check this out with her,' Iris said coldly, but now at least she had a sense that maybe he was telling something nearer the truth.

'Go ahead, check away, she'll tell you the same as I'm telling you now,' he said, and they both knew it; he'd had plenty of time to cook up an alibi. The thing he didn't know was that his car could be picked up on traffic cameras any number of times if he'd driven back into the city. She wrote down the address for Tania Quirke and the route he'd taken on the night.

'Had anyone threatened Rachel? Anyone who'd want to cause her harm?'

'I don't know. I'm not the cops – that's your job, isn't it?' He smirked at her. 'But I'll say this, when I heard what happened to Rachel, the only thing I could imagine was that someone had made a mistake – no one in their right mind would have wanted to kill Rach.' His eyes didn't falter and, for once, Iris knew that Nate Hegarty was telling the truth.

CHAPTER 9

Day 2

The woods were light again; in the distance, Eleanor could hear dogs, she never minded dogs, but she had a sense she should be moving away from them for her own safety. The world was closing in on her. She could feel it. It was a bolt of pressure at the base of her skull, wrapping around her head so all the thoughts and memories were jumbling up again. Eleanor continued to move through the damp green leaves, sometimes she stumbled on the soft ground.

They would be searching for her now, she was sure of that. She imagined them calling 'E-L-E-A-N-O-R!' calling out her name in their unfamiliar voices. When she slept, she dreamed she could hear them whispering and moving. The sounds were bending their way through the trees to let her know they were coming to get her. Each noise sent ripples of fear through her. She could hear them, hefty men in hi-vis vests, their heavy boots working their way slowly towards her. She knew, with the wisdom of dreaming, that she had to keep moving; she had a journey to make. Fate had handed her a chance, just one chance, and she was grabbing it with two frightened but determined hands.

Then, darkness had set in and she was back in a new nightmare.

Her own screams had woken her first. It was the same dream, a continuation, really. The wet stains on her back were from sheer terror. She couldn't have put a name to the panic that overtook her when Rachel's face visited her dreams. She felt the sweat seep from every pore of her body, her neck, her arms, even behind her knees and then she realised she'd wet herself too. She had seen too much – knew she was next. In the dream she felt those wet hands coming towards her and she struggled to get away. Worst of all, she realised that if Rachel was still here, she'd put her arms around Eleanor and tell her everything would be okay. Not today though.

The winter dark green of leaves and branches, still damp with the dew of morning and cut off from the day's sun, filled her senses. She thought she might burst with the sounds and smells. She'd closed her eyes and stumbled through. Then she flung her hands up in the air, caught up in the giddiness of freedom, her recently dormant senses bursting with the packed earthiness of the place. Curlew Hall had been just small rooms and timetables – this, this was living. Above, she could hear birds call out, at her feet the crack and snap of fallen twigs, and all around the cacophony of cascading leaves and moving creatures, all of them getting on with their tasks – not bothering her. There was no schedule now, no empty rooms and echo noises. No whispering staff, no agenda and no prying eyes or counselling sessions.

She knew the woods well. She walked here often, but this was different. Maybe it was that she hadn't taken the white tablets, her antidepressants – never liked them anyway, never liked the way they dulled her senses. Today she was actually seeing things and it felt good.

Later, she lay for a while with falling leaves tumbling gently around her. There were no alarm clocks here, no Rachel coming in to tell her it was time for her morning shower. No breakfast either, but there was plenty to eat, she wasn't worried about that. If she walked away from the early-morning sun, eventually, it would come to meet her. That was how it worked. She had places to be and the men in their bright jackets were probably working to her back so she could move as quickly as she wanted without fear of running into them.

She thought of home – her father's house. Was it still the same? Karena would still be there and that thought made Eleanor smile.

She walked for a while along the road; she guessed she was some distance from Curlew Hall. Her feet ached and her belly was empty. She was hungry, but she ate as she found and she took one precious tablet in the morning when the sun began to creep over the trees. It was less than they'd have given her in the home, but she was okay. Time was missing; she must have had a seizure, maybe more than one. She'd never been able to remember them nor had she ever known when they would strike.

She thought again of Rachel lying lifeless on the floor. Did she even know it was coming? Eleanor looked down at her hands. A vaguely familiar tingling sensation was rippling from her fingers. She fell to the ground before she had time to contemplate what the tingling meant.

Darkness descended and vomit pushed for escape from some-where low in her abdomen. Her body was taken over by firing sweat, pressure at the back of her neck, and then she was released. She looked beyond herself. Far down, far, far down, she watched as the rattle of the seizure overtook her body. She was a swallow. A summer bird, soaring loftily above her leafy bed, liberated in the frenetic rapture that took custody of her body. She wouldn't remember this freedom – probably just as well. Starting somewhere deep in her throat, the seizure worked its way throughout her body, until her limbs and torso rattled like a rag doll in the mouth of a very large and angry invisible dog. Her head lolled from side to side, trying to keep up with the incessant pace of her shoulders, deadening itself into vacuous numbness.

She'd forget all of this when she woke up. *If she woke up*, she thought as she watched a second seizure engulf her alien form, her body appearing smaller and spent. She closed her demented eyes and dreamed of home, as it once was, and then she was drifting away softly on the breeze…

CHAPTER 10

'But surely you can see, this isn't worth a thing to us,' Iris pleaded. Marshall had stage-managed the press conference so the media were running with a photograph of Eleanor that might have been taken four years earlier. It was an image of her that more closely resembled the virgin Mary than it did the spirited teenager they were getting a sense of. She could see why he'd done it. He didn't want a potential jury convicting her before they'd even managed to warm their seats in the courthouse. Iris wanted to shout that they wouldn't have to worry if she was guilty or innocent if Eleanor was dead. It may not have been Byrne's intention to have this conversation, but she wasn't leaving his office without raising it. She wanted another press conference and she wanted to be in control of it.

'The answer is still no. It's out of our hands,' he said firmly, and then he sighed; he agreed with her, but couldn't admit it. 'Look, Marshall has done the press conference, our only other shot at this is circulating something fresher when we have it. We really don't have a choice. The best you can do for the Marshall girl now is figure out what happened that night and make sure Tony Ahearn is doing his job out at Curlew Hall.'

'But you saw the image, she doesn't look like that now, she couldn't have been any more than twelve years old when it was taken…' It was screamingly obvious why Marshall had done it; did she really need to spell this out for Byrne?

'Look, I can see you're upset, you'd have liked to be there, get a chance to show that you're in charge and all that, I get it, but, she's his daughter, he has the right to go on TV and—'

'Dear God, it's not about that.' Iris exhaled; she couldn't lose her temper here. 'Don't you see? It's so not about getting our faces on TV – it's about Eleanor and putting out an image that people will recognise. We can't let them get away with this.'

'Away with what?' Byrne's voice had dipped into unfamiliar territory.

'Oh, come on, you can see it as well as any of us. He's trying to make her out to be some fragile little girl, so if we do make a case against her, it's going to take a bit less effort on his part to sweep this under the carpet like he's done every other time for her.'

'I must warn you, Iris, if that's a sentiment you repeat in public, it's highly libellous.' Byrne's tone had turned to ice.

'It's not libellous if it's the truth,' she said stubbornly.

'Look, I asked you to take on this case because I thought we would work well together…'

'I'm sorry, sir, but if working well together means covering up so a rich kid gets away with murder, then you picked the wrong sergeant,' she said, but she stood firm, because tempted as she might be to storm out the door, she knew it wouldn't get her what she wanted.

'Are you saying that Sergeant Slattery would?' He was playing games with her now.

'No, I'm not saying that. Ben Slattery is one of the most honourable detectives I've ever worked with. In spite of his faults, he would always do the right thing.' The words came like a default sentence, but when she said them, she knew they were true.

'Well, I admire your loyalty—' He stopped, because they both knew he was about to compare her to Jack Locke and comparisons to the man she'd believed was her father didn't apply anymore – it seemed at any level.

Iris was treading on thin ice, the last thing she needed was to make an enemy of Byrne; it already looked as if they were up against the whole establishment on this one, no need to bring him down on top of her too. 'I don't get it…'

'It's simple. If we proceed with something against her parents' wishes, we're going to get their backs up and we really don't want Kit Marshall playing against us. God knows what he'd pull out of that big purse of his. We can't forget she's a minor and he's her legal guardian.' He shook his head, put his hand up to stop her. 'Don't blame me, if anyone is to blame here, it's bloody GDPR and all the trip wires that go with it. If we so much as whisper her name in the press without her parents' consent, Marshall will tie us up in a legal battle that you can guarantee will spell the end of all our careers while somehow ensuring he comes out smelling of roses.' Byrne shook his head; at least it was good to see he wasn't taken in by Marshall either.

'And what if something happened to be leaked?'

'You can try, but if he finds out, I'm warning you, you could find yourself transferred to the Blasket Islands for the rest of your days.' He wasn't joking and she knew it.

'I could be in worse places,' she said flatly.

'Look, I know it's your first case and that's always a big pressure, but as long as you're following procedure, making sure you don't miss anything coming in from your team and trying to build up a picture to guide the investigation along – then you can do no more.' Byrne's face creased into a smile but his eyes were chary. 'That's the job, Iris. No one gives you superpowers just because you get a fancy new title.'

'I'm sorry?' Surely, she'd misheard him. 'There's a young woman missing, sir, I think that's all the reason we need to feel under pressure.' Damn it, this tightness in her chest, the drumming out of every second wasn't just about this case and how things might look to the powers that be. A year ago, that might have been the case, but things had changed. She had changed and now the old standards no longer held any bearing on her.

'I'm just saying, you're… well, you have a long career – perhaps a glittering career – ahead of you on the force, if you play your cards right. Whereas Slattery… well… you need to be careful that he isn't influencing you on this case, because we all know, he's going to have little time for the Marshalls of this world and his bleeding heart is likely to drive you both into career meltdown.' He raised his eyes to heaven as though they were discussing a naughty toddler. 'I'm just saying that decisions have been made, some very influential people are watching your progress, so don't step on any well-heeled toes, all right?'

'With respect, sir, Ben Slattery has probably solved more cases in his career than anyone else in this station and if his approach is a little unorthodox, I hardly think that it should take away from the fact that he's a good detective.'

'Yes, well, that's as maybe, but he's never going to be anything beyond sergeant and I thought your ambitions lay a little further up the line.' His glare hardened and almost immediately Iris regretted her outburst – after all, she wasn't sure Slattery would speak up for her if the situation was reversed.

'Sorry, sir, I'm probably just a bit wound up.'

'Well, if you're not fit for the job…' He turned his attention to the desk before him. 'There are plenty more out there who'll get on with it and bring in the same result as all this flapping will.'

'No, of course not.' Iris made her way back to the incident room with as much poise as she could muster. There was no undoing the certain knowledge that if she didn't keep Marshall sweet, and Byrne too, she could be out on her ear faster than she'd have thought possible. But, as she stood before the case board facing the images of Rachel McDermott and Eleanor Marshall, so many other arguments began to play out in her mind.

*

In the last few hours, locals out at Curlew Cross had begun calling to the station asking if extra police cover was available because Eleanor Marshall was on the loose. *Her reputation preceded her.* Her father might have kept her out of court, but this was small-town Ireland and everyone knew everyone else's business, no matter how much you paid to keep things quiet. The more Iris thought about it, she couldn't help but feel Eleanor was the victim of prejudice, the most dangerous kind of ignorance in the world. The kind that got you killed or drove people to kill. Still, as Byrne said – and Iris knew – she had a job to do, and if Eleanor killed Rachel McDermott or hurt anyone else, there would be no covering it up, she'd make sure of that. Then, all the big brass would do their best to pass the blame along the line. Marshall would be well out of the frame and the food chain could stop at her door. After all, she'd already seen Slattery was like Teflon and Byrne had never taken the blame for anything in his life.

God, all of this was making her head pound. She grabbed her jacket and headed for the small coffee shop nearby. She needed to stop thinking, just for as long as it would take her to walk there. On the way, she wasn't even sure if she'd brought enough change to pay for a small coffee, but it didn't matter, she felt her head clear with the breezy traffic fumes that knot-weeded their way about the city.

She ordered and paid for her coffee, took a seat staring out at the bus stop, waiting as the evening traffic passed by. Iris allowed her mind to empty for just a while until a loud thud against the window brought her back to reality. Outside, an old woman stood, fixing a scarf about her neck, probably; the shopping bags which lay spilling over against the window had startled her. It didn't matter, it was time to get back. As she passed the woman, she stopped, there was something familiar about her, not that she'd met her before, but she reminded Iris of someone. She took half a dozen steps when it came to her like bolt – Anna Crowe. There was something in her expression that reminded her of Anna. She turned back immediately, but the woman was just stepping onto a parked bus. For a moment, she stood in a no man's land, unsure if she should move forward or back, but then the door of the bus closed and it began to indicate before being sucked into the snaking traffic out of the city.

The short walk back to the station left her breathless; of course, she knew it wasn't the distance, but rather the shock of what she'd just seen. She'd never thought about it before, but perhaps there were other relatives out there – people she'd never met, Anna Crowe's people. Her people.

Iris reached into her bag and took out the case notes Bobby Nestor had carefully handwritten almost two decades earlier. In the end, they hadn't even been deemed important enough to commit to a database. She'd pulled them before she had met with Byrne. She hadn't mentioned the suspicious death of William McDermott all those years earlier – felt a little guilty about it, but it was only background reading so no harm done. Iris's phone rang just as she was about to settle into the file.

'Iris.' Pardy's voice was flat. 'I've hit a wall with Eleanor Marshall's file.'

'Oh?'

'According to their records most of her notes were archived. They haven't been looked at in years. In fact, they're pretty well permanently locked unless you get the parents' permission.'

'And?'

'Well, three weeks ago Rachel McDermott signed out the file, with the permission of Susan Marshall.'

'Have you talked to Mrs Marshall?'

'No need, we have her handwriting here and a blind man can see the signature on the file release is a forgery.'

'Do we know where the file is now?'

'No. I've checked at Curlew Hall. I'd say they're in for a cart load of bother now from the Marshalls. Slattery's going to call into Mrs McDermott, see if Rachel might have left it somewhere in the house.'

'Good work. Let me know how you get on.'

CHAPTER 11

Slattery hadn't worn a wedding ring in years. Actually, he'd lost it when he and Maureen went on honeymoon. He'd left it in the toilet of a little pub near the B&B where they started out on married life. At the time, Maureen had been beside herself; back then she was prone to superstition about the oddest things. How could he have known that skipping around ladders and blessing herself at every turn would one day turn into a commitment to the church which was grounded as much in guilt as it was devotion? She was convinced that losing that ring was an omen. Slattery figured the worst of it was he hadn't actually paid for the bloody thing. Now there would be six weeks of turning up at the jeweller's and handing over money that might be better spent on rent or beer with nothing to show for it. He'd only searched for it half-heartedly, after all, where Slattery came from, real men didn't wear jewellery – apart from the Bishop, but then since he wore robes that resembled an old woman's dress, he was hardly the most obvious male role model. Funny, when he looked back at it now, perhaps she'd been right; their marriage had almost run out of steam before the honeymoon was over.

In hindsight – well, thirty years later is bound to make you a little wiser – Slattery could admit that spending their honeymoon in a pub while his wife sat on a windy beach alone probably meant he had to shoulder most of the blame. That week, all those years ago, it was the only holiday they'd ever had as a couple, and if it hadn't entirely slipped from his mind, he'd certainly done his best to bury it beneath anything that could be deemed more pressing. And there seemed to have been plenty over the years that he could call more deserving of his time. Looking back, their marriage had been a fast rush of murder cases, countless late nights – spent mostly at the Ship Inn – and a long argument that had eventually settled into a simmering bitterness between them. Regrets? Sure, Slattery knew, sitting here watching Maureen nod off in the living room that should have been theirs, he regretted plenty. Still, there was no way of admitting he could have changed anything – he was far too stubborn for that. Maybe, his biggest regret was marrying her in the first place. It wasn't that he resented her now, the truth was, he felt an uncomfortable mixture of pity and guilt. She'd fired it at him once, the accusation that he'd thrown away her life with his own and he supposed that was true, but what he hadn't shouted back was she could have walked away. Of course, walking away, separation, divorce wasn't in her make-up. Even now, her wedding ring, thin and worn beneath the cheap engagement ring dug into her swollen fingers. There was no getting it off, not without cutting it, and Slattery had a feeling she'd lose a finger before she'd go out without her rings, miserable and flimsy as they were.

A slight harrumph signalled a drift towards wakefulness. It was almost nine thirty, the evening news at an end and Maureen had slept right through it; of course, the highlight for her had always been the weather forecast. A delivery of tomorrow's clothes-line pronouncements which Slattery's brain shut down for. He always figured he'd know what the days' weather was, soon enough when he got up in the morning.

'Uh, I must have just drifted off,' she said, straightening a little in her chair. 'Is the news over already?' she asked crossly, as if they might have had the decency to pause until she was ready to give it her full attention.

'Aye, fancy a cuppa?' he asked, knowing that tea at this hour kept her awake; she'd been saying it for years.

'No. It's time I was turning in,' she said pointedly. 'I'm sure you have better places to be too.' She flicked the remote control so it felt as if the only words likely to fill the air between them had been cut short abruptly.

'Right, well, I'll be going so,' he said getting up. He'd already checked doors and windows, unplugged anything that might be vaguely considered a fire hazard and tucked in drawers and chairs so there was little chance of her tripping. He couldn't think of anything else he could do, bar sitting in the garden all night to make sure she didn't fall out a window. So far, she hadn't taken to wandering about in her nightdress, but she had managed to get lost on her way to the supermarket. She'd ended up on the other side of town, forgot to get off at her stop on the bus and Angela had been beside herself, giving off yards to Slattery as if it was entirely his fault. He didn't tell her that they were only lucky she wasn't driving, but then they all knew– even if her car hadn't been smashed up in that tragic accident – thanks to the dementia, Maureen wouldn't ever be driving again.

'If you want anything…' He pulled his jacket on so it slipped over him at an angle. No matter if it had been made for him, clothes never seemed to quite sit properly – that was the thing about Slattery.

She smiled a half turn of her lips when she looked at him. He still seemed as if he'd just fallen out of the school gates, tie askew, shirt hanging out, and jacket only half pulled on. It was a mixture of disinterest and his unfortunate lumpy shape. He was never going to do a suit any favours, but if he took the time to straighten himself out before a mirror it would have made all the difference. Of course, like so many other things that had annoyed his wife over the years, they both knew that he couldn't give a flying kite about how he looked and cared less how other people thought he looked.

'Kit Marshall,' she said the name, it almost echoed away from them.

'That's right,' Slattery said, searching his pockets for car keys that were much too bulky to lose.

'He had an eye on me,' she said a little fondly, as if she had drifted from him to a time many years before.

'I knew that,' Slattery said, glancing at her. He didn't add that Marshall had his eye on every other girl in Limerick at some point. Always was a smooth fecker. Well, it hadn't got him any further than a marriage that looked as if it had more to do with his money than his sex appeal in the end. 'He still looks in good shape, not like…'

'Yes, I'd imagine he takes care of himself.' Maureen raised her hand to her hair self-consciously. 'But you have to live, don't you?'

'I suppose,' Slattery said, amused, because it never occurred to him that Maureen had ever given much of a thought to anything beyond cleaning the church and making the dinner.

'You know, I always saw through him,' she said thoughtfully.

'How do you mean?'

'Oh, just that. He wasn't half as sweet as he pretended. There was a dark side to Kit Marshall that I think a lot of the other girls didn't notice.' She shook her head now. 'I'm just saying it, because well, if you're depending on him to help you figure out anything about the McDermott girl, I'd take it with a pinch of salt. I think Kit Marshall would sell his granny for a bunch of hydrangeas so he could come up smelling of flowers, that's all.'

'There were never too many flies on you, Maureen.' Slattery smiled, because back in the day – and it was a long time ago now – Marshall had everyone he met fooled. He'd been a personable, eager young entrepreneur. It seemed to many as if he'd been lucky in his choices. Slattery always had a feeling that where he thrived, some unfortunate chump had been trodden on to get him to the next step on the ladder.

'He had a thing for another girl who worked at the bakery with me too. Lizzie, her name was. They went on a few dates and then she threw him over for some other boy.' Her eyes drifted, as if going back to a time, long, long ago. 'He sent her a dead rat in the post.'

'Marshall?'

'Well, she was sure it was him. It arrived into the bakery, delivered by some youngster on the street. Wrapped up in brown paper, it had a pink ribbon tied around it and a note that told her as much. After that, he never came into the bakery, I suppose he had what you'd call closure now,' Maureen said solemnly before handing Slattery his keys. 'Says something about him though, don't you think?'

Slattery headed out into the darkness willing Maureen to shut and bolt the door behind him, but instead she stood obstinately in its frame, knowing perhaps that he would prefer to believe she was locked up safe and sound. Perhaps he should count his blessings; too often he arrived here and she wouldn't let him cross the threshold – this had been a good evening. Maureen was like he remembered her, before they put a label on her that changed everyone's expectations of how things would work out in the end. He got into his car, turned over the engine and decided he would drive around the block a few times and then double-check the door himself, once she was inside it and deep in the middle of her prayers for the night.

The one thing he was fairly certain of, rat or no rat, Marshall was not their murderer. For one thing, he had spent the night at the other end of the country on a golfing trip that had finished up in the nineteenth hole around the time Rachel was being bludgeoned to death. That had been checked and for another, there was simply no motive. Marshall had nothing to gain from any of this. If anything, Eleanor Marshall roaming the countryside was making his life worse not better.

No, if he was putting money on anyone, he believed that she was killed not because of her connection with the Marshalls, but rather because of her link with Nate Hegarty. He was a bad egg and there was something he wasn't sharing with them. At this stage, Slattery thought he'd wager his week's wages on Hegarty: he had opportunity, means and now all they needed was a solid motive.

Although it was late, that nugget of annoyance was enough to send him back out to Curlew Hall. Suz Mullins was no different to her mother. Short and stumpy, old Gloria had spent her life draped over the gambling machines at the nearest chippie. Suz had the track of the Cloisters in everything about her, from her coarse Limerick accent to her mean mouth and darting eyes. Slattery didn't like her, but he knew if anyone could tell them how Curlew Hall ran, it would be Suz. He could see it: every movement registered with her, it came from a habit of looking out for the next opportunity. Suz had been served with bench warrants for shoplifting before she'd made her first holy. She'd learned from the best, her older sister stole like a pro. She was the square pin here, even if she wore the same expensive labels as the other girls. Theirs had been bought by parents who cared enough to pay through the nose to clean up their mess before it got too out of hand. Suz was here because there was nowhere else to take responsibility for her – the state had run out of options. She was too young for the women's prison and the only detention centre in the country was trying to empty out its residents, not make space for more.

'Drugs,' she volunteered before Slattery knew he wanted to ask. 'Off me face when I stole a car and rammed it into the back of the Lord Mayor's Mercedes.' She snorted when she laughed, remorse was obviously not weighing her down too heavily.

'You're clean now?' Slattery asked.

'Sure I wasn't even addicted. It was all just about having a laugh, but you couldn't tell the judge that. Me ma said I'd like this place, it's not bad either. Food is decent, all the channels on the telly and apart from all that counselling, it's a bit of a lark,' she said, looking then at Pardy as if she was trying to gauge her.

'Right, well, the way I figure it, Suz, you're the only one here who's going to have a choice about talking either way. Those other girls? All I'll have to do is ring up their rich daddies and they'll spill the beans quicker than it'll take to say their double-barrel names.'

'And I'm just going to roll over?'

'You have nothing to lose here.' Slattery reached into his inside pocket and slipped a fifty-euro note out far enough for her to catch a glimpse of.

'Sure, I have nothing to lose.' She smiled at him then; they were speaking the same language. 'What do you want to know?'

'Everything about the night Rachel died. Anything that you noticed out of the ordinary, anything you think we should know.'

'Right.' Suz sat back her chair, inhaling a long deep breath. When she went back over the night in question there was actually very little she could tell them, except that when she'd finished, Slattery had a feeling that even if Eleanor Marshall had her own private accommodation, Suz Mullins was the resident who'd have been better off separated from the rest of the bunch.

CHAPTER 12

Tim McDermott was not unlike his sister in some ways. Iris thought she knew every single inch of Rachel's face now; it stared at her accusingly from a ten-by-eight that hung in the centre of the incident-room board. Whereas Rachel was dark-haired, olive-skinned and green-eyed, Tim was fair, with a more generous mouth and his mother's eyes, a deep blue that would probably lighten as he aged. The big difference – he wore the red-eyed look of bereavement with stoic apathy. Both children thin, both of average height – he a little above, she a tad below – and they shared a certain set to them that Iris couldn't quite place, but it was somewhere along the jaw and it gave them a look of their mother.

'You left your card with Mam, and I knew you'd want to speak to me anyway, at some point.' He shrugged narrow shoulders. He was wearing a faded denim jacket over a white T-shirt and although he should be freezing, he looked as though he'd never felt the cold.

'Well, you're very good to come in. We'd have sent around a garda anyway, just to check you were both doing okay and…' Of course, Iris didn't need to say it, but the truth was, she'd already told Pardy to check in and see if Tim could give them any idea of people that would rather see Rachel out of the picture. She was also meant to check where he was the night she died, but Iris had a feeling now that Tim McDermott was no killer. Iris showed him into an empty office at the back of the main reception, he declined tea, which she told him was probably wise and he smiled easily, in spite of the edge of melancholy that lingered in his eyes.

'I imagine Mam wasn't much help when you called to tell her the news.'

'We wouldn't expect anything else. She'd just lost her daughter, it's unthinkable, and even if we see terrible things too often, it doesn't mean we don't understand,' Iris said, pulling a notebook across the desk and checking in a tray for a biro.

'Here,' he said, pushing one from his side across to her. 'Well, she told me you're looking for a list of Rach's friends?'

'Yes, anyone at all you can think of that she might have known or associated with, really; anyone that might be able to give us some idea of why someone would want to see her…'

'Killed?' Tim shook his head. 'It's okay, sergeant, I knew my sister better than anyone. She'd always had a nose for trouble.'

'How do you mean?'

'Well, she had a bleeding heart that always put her on the side of the underdog. Mam used to say it came from her being a carer, but I always thought she just sort of connected with people who were on the losing side of life, if you know what I mean.'

'They said she was really kind to Eleanor Marshall,' Iris murmured.

'Yeah, that'd be right. She'd see no badness in anyone – it was the way she was.'

'You don't think she'd have fallen out with anyone?'

'Don't get me wrong, she wasn't perfect. We'd rowed ourselves, only a few days ago. My mother won't have volunteered this, but I threatened to murder her with my own hands if she ever…'

'Oh?'

'Well, it all seems too stupid now. I'm sure you already know that Rach dabbled with drugs, smoking a joint was her way of chilling out. Rach never went to the pub, it wasn't her scene. The thing is, none of us are saints, but my mother – well, we're hardly kids she can brag about, but if she had to face her cronies at mass and they knew Rach was smoking weed… I think the shame would have killed her.'

'Of course, the toxicology will show up…' Iris said, thinking back to Nate Hegarty. 'She wouldn't have owed any money? There's no way whoever was supplying her might have…?'

'It's a bit bigger than that…' He shook his head. 'This was the real reason we fought, it frightened me, like I said, none of us are angels, but…'He reached into his pocket, took out a fat envelope and placed it on the table. 'This was left in a drawer in the kitchen.' He pushed it towards her, opening the end slightly so she could see it was packed with fifty-euro notes, probably a couple of thousand in all. 'After our fight, she said that was it. She promised to give this back to whoever it belonged to and well, I'm not completely naïve, I know that the sort of people who hand you this kind of money are hard to pull away from. After Mam told me, well, I had to get my head around Rach being gone and then I thought of this and I had a search about and there it was, sitting snug at the back of a locker in the spare room…'

'You think she was killed for this?'

'I'm not sure. I mean, I had hoped she'd give it back if it was owed to someone – Rach was just an occasional customer, never a seller or anything like that, as far as I knew, she just liked a smoke… but nobody hands you that kind of money for no reason, do they?'

'And, if she was involved in something – who else is likely to be part of it?'

'I wouldn't have a notion. She didn't have many friends outside of the people up at Curlew Hall, but I know she was close to Nate Hegarty for a while and trouble has never been too far behind him.' He shook his head and rolled his eyes to heaven. 'Regardless of what it's all about, I needed you to know that there was a far bigger chance of someone like… well, Nate Hegarty killing Rachel than the Marshall girl.'

'You've counted it?'

'Yep, about twenty thousand in all…' he said, then he stopped. 'Sorry, I probably shouldn't have touched it at all, should I?'

'You weren't to know. We'll need your fingerprints, not that I'd expect to get a whole lot, money is just about the biggest nightmare for forensics.'

'Sure, I'll do anything that will help, just…'

'What?' Iris looked at him now and found it odd, that strange mix of grown man with a lost and vulnerable quality that seemed to sit somewhere behind his eyes.

'Well, if you could keep quiet about the drugs… you know, my mother will die a thousand deaths of disgrace if anyone…' He shook his head. 'It's probably already common knowledge, Limerick is hardly a place to keep a secret.'

'You'd be surprised at that, Tim, you really would,' Iris said lightly, but she had a feeling maybe he already knew this to be true.

Iris rang Slattery after she wrote up her notes. Suddenly starving, she needed to get out of Corbally. She suggested lunch at a pub far away enough from the station where they wouldn't be disturbed. 'Two-ish,' they agreed and she didn't really care if he was late, it'd give her time to think, and maybe to breathe.

'So, Byrne gave you a flea in the ear?' Slattery chuckled as he sat down to a tiny cup of tea from the pot she'd ordered before he arrived. 'Better than a kick in the arse, I suppose.'

'Maybe, but it's not what I wanted.'

'Ara, sure, you knew going in there he wasn't going to agree to a second big media appeal when Kit Marshall had already had his five minutes of fame. His hands are tied as much as anyone's.

The only way we're going to make any headway with the media and getting a new appeal out there is if we come up with a new lead or an appeal on a different front,' he said, examining the teacup suspiciously. 'Here,' he barked at a young waitress who was wandering about looking to offload what looked like a barrel of soup and a hearty sandwich. 'Any chance you could find me a proper-sized mug in the kitchen somewhere?' He turned back towards Iris, ignoring the girl's startled expression as she scurried off on a new mission. 'Anyway, we can only do what we're doing and maybe we're doing better than we think,' he said picking up a menu from the table before him.

They ordered soup of the day, brown bread and another pot of tea. 'Thirsty work, this,' he said to the girl when she presented him with a travel mug that was big enough to fit the entire contents of the dainty teapot in it.

'Byrne said he wasn't *unsympathetic* to the plight of Eleanor Marshall, but from what I can see, he's more focussed on the annual fundraiser in aid of the local branch of Victim Support – now they've invited him to put in a speech.'

'Well, that'd be about right.'

'He's a big fan of yours too.' Iris smiled now.

'Oh, you'd be surprised how chummy we are,' Slattery said drily.

'You'd have to wonder, though, wouldn't you?' Iris said.

'What's that?'

'Well, they're her parents; surely they want her back safe and sound. The longer she's out there, the more chance she'll be dead and there won't be very much safe *or* sound about her. Marshall may be a good businessman, but he's no detective. I can't help but feel this needs to be said and said before it's too late.'

'Look, every investigation comes with something that holds you back these days, that's the way things are, I'm afraid.'

'I know that but still, there's no getting away from the fact that she's such a vulnerable girl.'

'I'm not sure that's how Marshall sees her. I was talking to an old mate of mine and, apparently, he's just put in to Special Branch looking for a Gardai presence around that fortress of his he calls a home. He already has two private security men patrolling the grounds twenty-four-seven and he just requested four officers from Special Branch, if you don't mind. From what I hear, the request has been refused so far, but if he pushed, the extra hours would have to come from existing budgets, so that would mean less bodies out on the search.'

'Does he think she's going to come after him?' Iris said, amused. The notion was ridiculous.

'Well, he was spooked enough to look for extra security, so that tells you he's afraid of something,' Slattery said.

When their lunch arrived, they began eating in silence. After a while, Iris spoke.

'At least the lake is clear,' she said absently, her mind considering the search out at Curlew Hall.

'How do you mean?'

'The lake. Julia Stenson said she had a thing about the water, went swimming there any chance she got.' An involuntary shiver ran through her at the thought. Julia had shivered too when she told them. *Urgh, full of eels, probably.*

'Bit cold for swimming though, don't you think?'

'Yeah, but remember she ran out of there in the black of night. She could lose her footing in the dark. God, it doesn't bear thinking about, does it?'

'Iris, they're doing their best. We're doing our best with what we've got, remember, we have to remain—'

'Focussed.' She cut him off. It wasn't easy, staying detached from the horrors that befell other people; you never really managed that. But Slattery was right; becoming upset just slowed you down. It stopped you seeing things, and that could literally be fatal. It was killing Slattery too, even if he wouldn't admit it in a fit. 'Okay, so where are we?' she asked as much to break the silence as to actually make any progress. They had nothing, not really; apart from gut instinct, a bundle of money, a missing file and a couple of fingerprints, but sometimes that was enough. Then again, if you could get a conviction on gut instincts…

'Good question,' he said and they returned to the gloomy silence.

'Come on, Slattery.' She exhaled. 'We know that for a girl who could do no wrong, it looks like there were a few people who had a grudge against her.'

'Hardly enough to kill her though.'

'Perhaps, but people have been killed for less,' Iris said softly. 'Those girls in the other bungalow, they said that Eleanor was exactly the sort to take revenge on Rachel for getting her transferred into that separate unit.'

'It wasn't Rachel's fault that those kids attacked Eleanor.'

'No, but that doesn't mean she didn't blame her in some way, you know what kids are like.'

'Yeah, and you're going to believe a couple of kids who can hardly tell the truth if their lives depended on it,' Slattery said. The only motive the kids had was perhaps jealousy of Eleanor, but it was hard to see what they had to be jealous of, once you took a good look up close. Each of them had fronted up to the fact that they'd given Eleanor a hard time, but it was plain to see that they were as fond of Rachel McDermott as they were of anyone in Curlew Hall. 'Anyway, they were locked up tight for the night, no way they could have got across that yard, even Nate Hegarty is adamant about that.'

'Well, he would be, wouldn't he?' Iris said. It was Nate's job to make sure that everyone was locked up securely, he wasn't going to go volunteering to anything different, not unless he had to. 'And what about Hegarty? If Rachel McDermott was taking notes, I can't think of anyone she'd be more likely to report for not doing his job well.'

'So, he'd kill her just to get out of a disciplinary meeting?' Slattery shook his head. 'Seriously, for the likes of Hegarty, that's chicken feed – no, if he had a motive, it's around that missing money.'

'You're right, of course, you're right.' Iris slumped down in her chair. 'Hegarty is the one person there who had the means,' she said softly. 'He could have let himself in and out of that unit seamlessly. But then, what about Eleanor?' Because she knew, that regardless of how much she wanted to ignore her as a suspect, Eleanor Marshall had motive and opportunity and there was no getting away from that.

'This isn't good for either of us.'

'Yeah, come on, let's go out and get on Tony Ahearn's nerves for a while.'

They pulled the car up at a stile; beyond it the ground had turned to mulch, thanks to the damp and increased traffic. Just a little way along, a trestle table stood, with huge flasks set out and the remnants of a lunch quickly eaten and then abandoned. In the distance, Iris could see the occasional flash of dayglo green where officers were searching through the undergrowth. They were making good progress, which at least was heartening.

Behind the official search, she spotted Susan Marshall's bent back, her thick platinum hair weaving and bobbing along. Her form was steadily juddering up and down, searching in places that could never hide Eleanor. There again, knowing that she wasn't there was probably better than always wondering.

'Hi.' It took an age to get to the woman and Iris felt out of breath by the time she'd ambled the short distance. 'How are you holding up?' Iris found herself cut short when she looked at the other woman's drained face.

Susan Marshall stood straight, replacing the blanket of ivy and moss that she'd just displaced in her quest. She quickly pulled down her sleeve but not in time to hide the scars that stretched well up her left arm.

'Ah, you know, as well as can be expected.' She pulled her wax jacket close around her body. It was the most expensive designer brand, no doubt, too good for walking in inclement Mayo weather. 'This is good…' She gestured a slim hand around the woods. 'Just being involved, it feels like something is happening, as though I'm helping her now.' The corners of her mouth twitched shakily upwards, there was little to smile about really. 'There's no news, it's just looking under every tree, but it's something, isn't it?'

'Oh yes, every pair of hands, it's all good.' Iris caught her breath. Pain seared up her back and she flinched involuntarily, almost losing her balance. It was strange, but since that night in Woodburn – when her whole world had been swallowed by the revelations that were still settling around her – she had aches and pains throughout her body, and only now did she realise that until this, she never had much more than an occasional stress headache.

'Are you okay?' Susan Marshall reached out a steadying hand.

'Fine, really, I'm fine – just stiff probably, too much sitting down and it doesn't suit me.'

'You need to look after yourself.' Susan Marshall lowered her voice.

'I couldn't rest if I wanted to… not knowing Eleanor is out here,' Iris said simply and honestly.

'I knew you felt that.' Susan's voice was little more than a whisper. Her hand reached out towards Iris. She gripped Iris's arm tight, her eyes locking, her face haunted. 'She didn't do it, you know, I'm quite sure she didn't.'

'I don't believe she did either, but we don't have a lot to go on.'

'I'm not a lot of help to you there, I know. But the people who worked with her, any of them, they knew her, surely they've told you. She…' Her eyes lurched, searching out answers in Iris's pitying face. 'No…They don't think…They can't… They loved her too… I know they did…' Susan Marshall recoiled, almost shrinking down into the luxurious jacket.

'They haven't said anything, Susan. They don't know what to think. Everyone is still in shock.' Iris looked around them, the search was moving forward without Susan now, giving them a little more privacy. 'Have you visited? Have you been to see Eleanor more recently than you said?'

'Not exactly, no.' Susan's face had the empty look of hopelessness. 'I couldn't just turn my back on her though, switch off and get on with things. It's not like that; it could never be like that.'

'You had some contact?'

'Rachel kept me up to date. When she accompanied Eleanor for walks, sometimes I'd watch from the car. She'd be so close, but a million miles away at the same time. Terrible really, I just wanted to shout out. Call her over and wrap my arms around her. What can you do? They probably do know best.'

'And your husband?'

'Kit? He didn't have a clue. He thought it was all just teenage rebellion. That it was a stage she was going through – that with enough money put into caring for her, she'd come good in the end. He couldn't cope with it all, with her, with what it meant for him.' A small tear rested before those striking green eyes and she rubbed hard at it with the back of her hand. 'I keep hoping this could be good. You know, that somehow things can work out for the best. You have to think like that though, don't you?'

'Why is he afraid that Eleanor might be coming to Duneata House, to your home?'

'He's not.' She took a hanky from her pocket, rubbed the end of her nose for a moment. 'He's just worried, I suppose, about

Karena. We've always thought Eleanor was jealous of her, but Karena won't hear a word against her sister. Still there's always that worry, after what happened last time.' She shook her head sadly. 'Kit really does love her, even if it's hard to see it sometimes with everything else. He didn't send her away because it would be easier for him; he thought it might help her.' The words seemed to drift between them, as if they might convince Susan as much as Iris.

'He's requested Gardai security.' Iris watched as Susan Marshall took this in. 'For your house, did you know?'

'Oh God. He thinks she killed Rachel, doesn't he?' Susan Marshall's eyes began to water and she let out a light hysterical laugh.

'It's possible.'

'Do you think so?' Susan's face was so earnest, it was hard not to tell her the truth.

'We hope not.'

Iris searched the other woman's haunted expression. She watched as she pulled up both sleeves of the jacket. Both arms, as far as Iris could see, were marked with what looked like scorch marks; scratches ran the length of both.

'This is why I had to let her go in the end. I always knew that there was a chance she'd do something terrible… but now… well, now it looks like we just sent her from the frying pan to the fire, doesn't it?'

CHAPTER 13

The incident room tingled with nervy excitement: something had happened, something big. Iris sat behind her desk, two messages, one from her mother from earlier. *Must have missed you, give me a call when you get this.* Iris picked it up and crumpled it into a ball, then dropped it in the wastepaper basket. The action was almost automatic now, but still she paused for a second, everything had changed. Her reflection in the window before her confirmed that. She was unrecognisable from the cocky detective she'd been only months earlier. Now, instead of walking with a spring, her feet moved with grim determination. Her pretty face had become gaunt and her eyes that had once smiled in spite of her mood were now troubled. Even the tarnished copper of her hair seemed to have faded to an ordinary brown. None of it mattered – Theodora Locke was the reason everything in her life had turned into a lie; she had taken Iris from the sister who loved her more than life itself and made a lie of everything she thought she was. Iris didn't want to become bitter, but it was too early not to blame Theodora for the mess that her life had become. Certainly, she was responsible for the death of Jack Locke and her sister Anna Crowe. Iris kicked the bin out of sight beneath her desk.

The second message was from Susan Marshall. *Good to talk today, hope it was helpful, take care.* Iris slumped into the uncomfortable chair at her old desk, waiting for the room to fill up after the search party returned. She'd never felt so tired, as if she'd spent the last twenty-four hours running into a concrete wall. Maybe coffee, she thought, but she was too tired to walk to the machine.

'Have you heard?' Pardy said. 'Tony Ahearn has been nudging some of the druggies around the town…'

'He's meant to be running the search party,' Iris said flatly and then wanted to bite off her truculent words.

'Some people can multitask,' Pardy said quickly. 'Anyway, it looks like Nate Hegarty is missing money. A couple of grand possibly, according to Ahearn's sources. Hegarty was putting the word out that when he found whoever took it… well, they wouldn't be sticking their hands in his pies again.'

'Hardly a surprise.' Iris had suspected at one stage that Ahearn and Pardy could be shagging each other; they were so well suited it almost made horrible sense. Now she wondered; no one could remain in awe of Ahearn that long and still play second fiddle to the wife and kids, surely? 'So that's the big news, is it?'

'Come on, Iris, it's a break, isn't it?' June placed a steaming frothy coffee before her, and she knew then she must look every bit as tired as she felt. Mind you, June didn't exactly look as if she was bursting with energy either. Then, June always looked a bit worn-out, not surprising really, a widow raising two teenage boys with a full-time job on the Murder Team. She was a good egg though, June. A fifty-something-year-old detective who still believed in happy endings – quietly, mind, because there was no point getting up Slattery's nose over things like that. June was smart enough to pick her battles. She wore a badger stripe of grey along the centre parting of her hair, drank fair-trade tea and loved sugar-free muffins. Her figure had descended into the shape of a bag of spuds, but she was as bright as a button with a sharpness to her that people underestimated at their own expense. 'I'd have thought you'd be delighted. Of all of us here, you seem to want Eleanor Marshall to be innocent the most.'

'That's not true.' She took the cup gratefully.

'It's no harm, Iris. After all, from what we've seen she's had a shit life so far, no one really wants to see her go down for this.'

'You're forgetting something.' Iris looked across at Jo Pardy as she blew steaming air across the hot beaker. 'We have to find her first and that's down to Tony Ahearn, right?'

'Okay, okay.' Byrne had arrived in the incident room with Ahearn at his heels. 'I want to thank everyone for coming in tonight. I appreciate it has been a very tough day for all of you – this won't take long.' Byrne loosened his tie and placed his uniform jacket carefully across the back of a nearby chair. 'Just very quickly for the officers working on the search first thing, Tony?'

Tony Ahearn stood up front: standard-issue navy outdoor jacket with the collar turned up, pristine compared to the rest of the dishevelled search party. Iris suspected that he managed the rescue effort for the day from a discreet distance, focussing more on building up brownie points with Byrne than actually finding Eleanor. Iris switched out of his droning voice. But she watched as he walked to the whiteboard and pointed out the ground covered over the day and the directions the search teams would take in the morning.

'Any questions?' he asked as he went to sit down.

'Am...' Iris raised a weary arm. 'Just, the search team have found absolutely nothing, right?'

'Right.' Tony Ahearn maintained eye contact; his face steely.

'Well, we're out there now, what twenty-four hours, or as good as, with two dozen searchers – surely we should have found something.'

'Not all of our team are professionals, sergeant, you know that.' Ahearn's tone was short.

'It's not that, I'm not implying that the team isn't working well, or that it's not being led out well...'

'That's good,' Tony Ahearn grunted cynically.

'Go on, Iris.' Byrne was leaning forward.

'Well, I suppose what I'm thinking is, we have a good team, being well run and we have a young woman – hardly the most experienced in survival techniques, yes? We should have found something, a hair, a catch of material, a scuff mark – something. Doesn't it strike anyone as odd that we haven't even come across a rib of hair?'

'Iris, you know what those woods are like, we knew it would be the devil's own job to find her there,' Ahearn cut in.

'Maybe she's not there,' Slattery said.

'Maybe,' June said softly. 'Or maybe someone helped her to get away from Curlew Hall the night before last…' The words were soft and dreamlike – of course it was wishful thinking. Most of the searchers thought she was dead. 'Maybe she's made her way onto a main road, maybe she's miles away at this stage…'

'Yeah, and maybe we'll find another hundred officers and pull apart the whole county.' Ahearn's words were blunt and his face mocking. He didn't have time, didn't have resources and he – like everyone else in this room – just wanted to go home after a long day.

'With respect, sir, I'm not talking about another hundred officers…' Iris's words were even, determined.

Byrne was leaning against the crumbling plaster of the very furthest wall from the action. 'No, but we all know what you are suggesting, another public appeal, and I'm not having this conversation tonight.'

Slattery smiled slyly at Iris. *Nice one*. But all she'd managed was to get up Ahearn's nose and she could do without him thinking she was trying to undermine him. Byrne cleared his throat, and began to call on various detectives to brief the assembled officers on how the case had progressed over the day.

Tim McDermott had dropped in an envelope full of well-thumbed fifty-euro notes. He'd blubbered like a baby that he felt responsible for his sister's death. He, at least, was convinced that Rachel had been dealing with some dodgy characters – his only reason for believing it being the cache of loot and his sister's history of enjoying an occasional joint. Some of the fingerprints were back, nothing to get excited about there either. PULSE – the fingerprinting database and search mechanism – automatically cross-referenced new prints with stored files.

There was nothing in Curlew Hall that raised any red flags with previous crime scenes. Tony Ahearn's input was what they called soft information, not much good to them, really, apart from pointing them in a general direction. Nate Hegarty had an alibi, of sorts, he'd been at work, he'd called into one of the other units. Later, after they'd pressed him further, he changed his story. He'd skived off, between his rounds, met up with his girlfriend. His girlfriend swore blind she was with him on the night in question. But, as they ran through the details again, he was looking more and more like their man. He had access, motive and, crucially, he would know how to handle Eleanor Marshall. Girlfriends, and especially ones like Nate Hegarty's – old before her years, tough enough to sell you out if she thought you crossed her, made the worst false defence of all. Iris wasn't worried about Hegarty's alibi. A small suggestion of him playing away would bring any lies crashing down around Nate Hegarty's ears faster than he could imagine.

'Iris.' Byrne was at her elbow. 'Thanks for that.' He nodded back towards the top of the room where officers were making their way home for the evening.

'Seriously?' She'd never understand Byrne. 'It didn't do a lot of good though, did it? You still said no.'

'You'd be surprised. It'll keep Ahearn on his toes for a day or two anyway and that's never a bad thing.'

Iris was tired, too tired for small talk. 'Why didn't you tell me about Hegarty and the money?'

'I only heard five minutes before the briefing. Ahearn brought it to me in the hall when I arrived… I didn't get a chance.'

'Even Jo Pardy knew about it…'

'Aye, well she would, wouldn't she?'

'They're still at it?'

'Looks like it. It's not going to play out well for Ahearn if he does go for promotion; no one likes a cheat.' Byrne was renowned for his sermons; they only stopped when some of the boyos circulated a Christmas email mentioning 'Pious Pete'. Iris looked towards the door now. The place was almost empty, desks abandoned, computers whirring on standby, a buzzing army, waiting for orders. Most of the younger officers would be down in the pub for a pint to round off the day. 'It's only one lead, Iris. You know how these things can pan out.'

'Yeah, but we don't have a lot of panning time now, do we?' She could feel her face had scrunched into a million lines, matching each dart of pain that cruised just for fun in her head.

'Go home. Get a good night's rest and don't show up here too early tomorrow, nothing's going to happen tonight and if you take yourself out to Curlew Hall tomorrow, you'll be in plenty of time arriving after nine.'

'Thanks, sir.' She dropped her voice then. 'You don't think she's…' Iris couldn't say the word.

'I hope not, but what you said is right, we should have some trace of her by now. Tomorrow? With a bit of luck, she'll have shown up tired and hungry, yes?'

'Yeah, tomorrow,' Iris agreed wearily.

CHAPTER 14

Slattery turned out of the cul de sac, his mind not on Maureen for once; he hadn't called to see her this evening, no need when he saw Angela's car parked outside. In some ways, his wife and daughter were a perfect match. They were built in equal parts to play the martyr and quietly bully each other. It made for a strangely tight equilibrium that fashioned itself into the kind of unalloyed loyalty that went beyond what Slattery recognised as any normal relationship. Perhaps he should have made an effort to spend a quarter of an hour in awkward, punctuated silence with them both, but it had been a long day and really, all he was fit for was the pub.

The sound of his phone on the dash vibrating was an irritation. It was Corbally station, work; no one else ever rang him. It was an odd thing, he lived for the job and yet tonight he'd pulled down the shutters on his day, he wanted nothing more to do with it. When had that started happening? He cursed, yanked the thing to him and swiped his fat finger across to answer it.

'Sergeant Slattery?'

'No, Mary bloody Poppins,' he answered gruffly.

'Oh, right.' It was one of the new youngsters, Slattery couldn't put a name to him, but he was all fresh-faced and eager-eyed and probably couldn't understand why Slattery had to pull himself around the station and never managed so much as a fleeting nod to job satisfaction.

'There's been a report of a body out in the woods around Curlew Cross,' the voice said neutrally and Slattery waited a beat. 'Acting

Inspector Locke said you were to go out there immediately, there's a connection with the McDermott case.'

'Right.' Slattery managed not to curse, but he put the phone down morosely. The fact that he was gasping for a pint meant very little to him suddenly. If he'd hoped for one thing, probably they'd all hoped for the same, it was that Eleanor Marshall could be alive and well. That somehow, going forward, her life could be improved. Finding her body in the woods was the one thing he'd hoped wouldn't happen. He indicated left, pulled out on the quiet road, ignoring the traffic light that was stubbornly sitting on red. Usually, he liked sitting waiting for the green. If he was lucky it gave him enough time to light a cigarette and grumble about having to hang about. Tonight, his complaining counted for nothing.

Curlew Cross at its busiest was little more than an intersection with a convenience store, a pub, a church and a school. The only tourists here were surfers brave enough to take on the Atlantic, which rushed in treacherous waves and hidden currents onto a pebble beach a five-minute journey towards the west. Rush hour was either mass or a funeral. Parking was along the main road, with two streetlights to get you from your car to your destination and keep you out of pot holes if you were lucky. If you weren't lucky, they could result in a soaking up to your ankles if the rain was heavy.

Curlew Hall and the woodlands that some gentleman farmer had planted a hundred or two years earlier ran off to the east. They fanned out from there, drawing all the way back to the Comeragh mountains, running from birch to pine, covering a stretch of land that even now you could see was more suitable for grouse than for potatoes. The landlord had done the people of this place a favour, even if it didn't seem like it at the time.

Slattery turned right for the woods. There was only one road in from here and Traffic corps had set up a marker alerting drivers on the road that there could be a Gardai presence about. It was enough to slow down most motorists. He pulled up his car next to Iris's. They were among the first to arrive, most of the techies would have to be called from their beds at this stage, but Iris was here and it looked like there was one Traffic team who'd probably been in the area and decided it made a change from night duty on the motorway. They had set up between them a couple of lanterns, cutting into the darkness and creating a narrow path to the victim. Slattery checked in his boot, he had two more lanterns and his Maglite – they couldn't hurt. Soon enough the crime-scene boys would arrive with huge lights and cover to keep the scene as virginal as possible. He hated this, dreading seeing Eleanor Marshall out here in God alone knows what kind of a state. Maybe it was better that the machinations of crime-scene procedure had not been put in place to dehumanise her just yet.

He cleared his throat, knowing he couldn't put it off forever, cursed and threw his half-smoked cigarette on the ground, stamping it out viciously under his shoe. The incline was not steep, but it was enough to knock the wind out of him all the same. Near the top, Iris stood with a tall thin man, decked out in running gear.

'Slattery.' Iris nodded to him, informally making introductions. 'This is Matt Deering, he found the body when he was running through here.' Even in this light, limited as it was, there was no mistaking the shock that filled the man's face.

'It's a bit of a jolt, I'm sure.' Slattery gazed towards the mound of leaves and twigs, covering an unnatural knoll just off the main path.

'It's a crude attempt to cover her over.' Iris put words onto some of Slattery's thoughts.

'Her?' he said then, turning to look at her and immediately noticing something unexpected in her expression. Shock?

'Yes. Her,' she confirmed darkly. Her expression told him they had lost, the investigation had timed out and they'd been too late to save Eleanor Marshall. 'You can get a little closer, take a look if you want,' she said, but they both knew he did not want to see her, even if he had to.

Slattery walked around a tight trail circling the body. The flattening of grass looked just about wide enough to have been created by a badger, which may not be good news for forensics. He pulled his Maglite from his pocket and angled the glare onto the form beneath him. From up here, there was no mistaking, this victim had been battered every bit as violently as Rachel McDermott, but the link here was not drugs or any other gang-related activity they'd been focussed on.

Karena Marshall's cold dead eyes met Slattery's, her once pretty face oddly angular thanks to an almighty blow to the side of her head. The sickening sight of open skin and bone protruding was too fresh to have attracted foxes or other scavengers who would have quickly set to work had Mathew Deering not almost fallen over the body. Slattery would guess, from the condition of the wound, Deering had found her very quickly after the poor kid had been murdered. She'd obviously been walking here, dressed in an expensive weatherproof jacket and expensive hiking boots, which poked out beneath the mound of leaves.

The question was why? What on earth was the girl doing here, in the middle of nowhere, when her mother had been so convinced that she was in danger from Eleanor? Slattery sighed; he bloody hated the idea that the Marshalls had been correct all along.

'Right,' Slattery managed when he made his way back down to Iris and the shocked jogger. 'What time did you find her?'

'Just when I called your lot, about half an hour ago. I was coming along here, my flashlight had grown weak—' He held up a headband with a small light that might not look out of place on an old man's bicycle. 'I began to slow down, I'm parked just over there.' He jabbed a thumb in the direction of Slattery's car. 'And then just as I came over the hillock, the light caught her eyes… the poor wee girl was just staring up at me and I…' Deering was shaking still, probably cold and definitely in shock. 'I must have tripped, because the next thing I knew, I was rolling towards her… and…'

'You're not hurt?' Iris asked, checking, but she'd already carried out a visual and there was no sign that he'd been given the same rough treatment as the victim.

'No, no, I'm fine, just…' He shivered. 'It's not what you expect to come across…' At that, Slattery saw a couple of squad cars arrive, their blue lights filling up the trees with unnatural vivid eeriness.

'Come on, let's get you warm at least,' Slattery said, guiding Deering towards the clearing beneath them and away from the crime scene. God knows it'd be hard enough for the poor man to sleep tonight without making it worse by hanging about here any longer than it was necessary to keep the foxes away. 'You didn't notice anything else, you know, running through the woods? Other people? Lights or voices? I'm presuming you run here regularly – there was nothing out of the ordinary?'

'No, not that I can think of. I tend to run here because I don't want to meet people. It's a way to de-stress after the day, just me and my thoughts. I'll have my iPod going sometimes, but not tonight.'

'Often people remember things, later, you know, when they're back in their normal routine, away from all of this.' Slattery ranged his hand around the clearing now, where various officers were gearing up to cordon off the scene and techies were emptying out of a van and suiting up for a long night ahead. 'If you think of anything at all – cars you might have noticed on the way, or even just sounds that didn't seem right—' He reached into his pocket. 'Give us a buzz, yeah?'

'Sure.' Deering took the card and began opening a pouch he had attached to his waist, but his hands shook too much to make any real headway.

'Here,' Slattery called to one of the uniforms, 'take care of Mr Deering, will you? He'll need a lift home and someone to take his car back.' He leaned into the opened boot of one of the squad cars, pulling out a foil blanket and placing it about the man's shoulders. 'These lads will take care of you now. They'll need to take contact details and we'll be back in touch for a full statement in the next day or so,' he said, leaving Deering next to a marked car that would take him safely home while Slattery made his way back up to Iris at the crime scene.

'Well, what do you think?' she asked him now they were alone.

'I don't know what to think. That poor kid.' Slattery shook his head. If he thought about it, this feeling that was welling up now – apart from shock at the utter waste of such a young life – was probably guilt. They should have done more, although, Slattery was damned if he knew what. 'Same as you, not what we expected... a bit...'

'I know. Shit.' She shook her head. It was terrible to feel as if they were somehow at fault, even if they couldn't put the words on it. 'It looks like Marshall was right all along,' she said quietly. 'If I'd only listened, instead of thinking I somehow knew better.' Iris had tears in her eyes now and he could see she was taking the worst kind of beating up, the kind you can only inflict on yourself.

'I was no better. It wouldn't have mattered what you'd thrown at me, I wouldn't have believed that the kid could be that bad to the bone.' He shook his head; it was the utter loss of innocence. Karena Marshall had been a good student, a caring sister, a naïve kid – she deserved better than this from a Murder Team charged with keeping the city a safe place.

'It's definitely Eleanor?' Iris sighed wearily.

'I think we have to accept that it is. Whoever killed Karena got her out here on purpose. It's too much of a coincidence that she's walking out here and Eleanor is missing in the same woods and then the kid turns up dead.'

'How in God's name did they find each other out here? I mean, there isn't even a phone signal, never mind anything much to mark it out as a spot much different to any other across the miles of woodlands.'

'Who knows? Maybe it's a place that meant something to both of them? Maybe Eleanor knew she'd come here anyway and waited for her… who knows? We'll have to check with the Marshalls.'

'Oh. God.' Iris drew in her breath. Visiting the Marshalls would be a nightmare. How on earth were they going to break this to them?

Slattery had no answer to that, he turned towards the narrow route, there was no putting it off anyway.

'Sergeant—' Deering was making his way over to them as they scrambled down the incline. 'I've just remembered something.' He looked to Slattery as if already he might be recovering slightly. 'You asked if I noticed anything different, saw or heard anything?'

'Yes.' Slattery loped towards him.

'I heard a scream…I didn't think about it at the time, just one of those noises, assumed it might be a bird or youngsters playing deep in the woods… over there.' He nodded deep into the forest off in the general direction of the Comeragh mountains.

'A scream?'

'Yes, after I stumbled over the…' He looked back at the child's remains. 'The more I think about it now; it was definitely a scream. Just the one, loud and long.' He shivered again, as if he could hear it in his head. 'A young girl, I'd say, and dear God…' The realisation of what that could mean. 'A frightened young girl. You don't think…?'

'No, Mr Deering, I don't think anything at all,' Slattery said through gritted teeth and turned to light up the cigarette that he'd needed since he'd looked into Karena Marshall's dead eyes.

CHAPTER 15

Eleanor felt as if she had walked for miles. The rain had stopped now. There was a bland punctuation of wet leaves and sodden earth. The voices were fading, as if their activity was gradually being absorbed by the trees. Now only the occasional whisper – and that sounded so familiar that she assumed it was coming from somewhere in the back of her memories.

She would sit for a while, try to assimilate what had happened; it was too much to take in. She dropped down to her hunkers, breathing as slowly as she could manage, knowing she had to try and stay calm. There were plenty of logs, cut and abandoned, waiting to be seasoned. She took possession of one, sitting astride it, and let her eyes travel up to the tops of lush, dark trees. At the back of her mind, she knew she should find somewhere to sleep for the night. A rush of exhaustion threatened to overtake her. In the distance, she could hear again the rustle of the undergrowth. Foxes, badgers and hedgehogs were all getting ready to waddle about in their nocturnal world. As the night drew in, the other inhabitants were getting more boisterous in their work and Eleanor pulled her flimsy sweatshirt around her.

The search party had left the woods now. She had heard them go, the dogs yelping, the forced laughter, backslapping, their voices strained. Probably wishing that their quarry had been found, but at the same time conscious that they'd meet another day. This strange non-time, suspending real life for another few hours, she should be alone in the woods now until first light.

The images of a thousand different days played through her mind, a medley of words and taunts and fairy tales, strung together so she couldn't make out anything clearly. She could see Rachel lying there, her head angled, bloody and desperate. And then Karena – she'd come across her in their secret place and she'd run, knew she had to get away. She'd left her there – what did that make her? She could hear Karena's voice, soft and reassuring. She was not meant to die, Eleanor was sure of that. And then she knew. It was her. It was meant to be her.

CHAPTER 16

Day 3

Duneata House was in darkness apart from a few lanterns lit to show a path towards the front door. Iris knew that not sleeping in twenty-four hours and the memory of Karena Marshall's battered body probably had as much to do with her shivering as the cold morning.

'You know the way you hate PMs?' She shot a look at Slattery, but she knew he felt the same. Of all the shitty things they had to do in their jobs, breaking news like this was probably the worst.

'Yeah, I hear you, but it's an hour for us, a lifetime for these poor buggers.' Slattery flicked his cigarette out onto the gravel drive. From where they stood on the steps, Iris saw one of the security guards lurking in the shadows, watching them. They'd already had to show their identity cards to his sleepy muscle-bound colleague on the gate.

'Amazing how Kit Marshall goes from self-important git to poor bugger in the space of a few hours,' Iris murmured as a light flicked on somewhere in the vast emptiness behind the heavy door. Susan Marshall pulled back the door gently.

'Yes?' She also looked like a woman who hadn't slept in too long. Although her hair was as groomed as if she'd just stepped out of the salon, her face was free of make-up, showing worry lines and dark circles about her eyes that added ten years to her. Worry? God they weren't going to make it any easier with this news.

'Mrs Marshall, can we come in?' Iris said softly, as if afraid to wake the birds in the trees.

'Of course, has something happened? Have you found Eleanor? Is she all right?' She was pulling her fingers through her hair now, her words trying to keep up with her thoughts and perhaps outpace her worst fears.

'Is Mr Marshall here?' Slattery said then, looking towards the stairs. 'It's best if we speak to you together.' Iris and Slattery both knew this was code for the very worst news. Perhaps Susan Marshall knew it too. Iris felt a pang of compassion for the woman – she had no idea just how bad the news was.

'Of course, I'll get him, just give us a minute, it's very late…' She looked at her expensive wristwatch. 'Or early.' She shook her head, mumbled something to herself as she made her way back upstairs.

It took Kit Marshall all of two minutes to arrive downstairs, looking as if he'd been roused from the deepest sleep, his hair a crow's nest of silver and gold, his lips dry, his monogrammed smoking jacket thrown unevenly about him and firmly tied over matching pyjamas and slippers.

'So,' he said when he reached the bottom step. 'You've found Eleanor?' His words carried no sentiment, as if he'd always expected someone to turn up in the early hours and tell him she was dead.

'No. Perhaps we can…' Iris gestured towards the room they'd sat in last time they'd been here.

'Of course, of course…' He looked at Susan, who had joined him now, a little brighter, as if she'd taken time to douse her face in cold water; suddenly she looked more alert than anyone in the room. *A mother surely knows*, Iris thought as she looked at Susan sitting straight-backed in a huge winged chair.

'I'm afraid it's Karena we've come to tell you about.'

'Karena?' Kit looked as if he'd missed a thread in the conversation. 'Should we call her down? Surely you don't want to speak to her at this hour?' The familiar disdain had once again returned to his voice.

'I'm afraid that won't be possible,' Slattery said and looked across at Iris.

'I'm sorry to tell you both that we were called out to an incident at Curlew Cross this evening. I'm afraid Karena was the victim of—'

'That's not right. She's been here all evening, there's been some mistake…' Susan started, but her words petered out as she took in the grave expressions of both detectives. 'No, she's been here. She had a headache… I checked on her myself at nine o'clock, she was sleeping…' She looked around the faces now, and in a tender soft voice whispered across at Kit, 'In her room… she was…' But the words ran out and it felt as if the air had been sucked from the room. Time stopped – suspended between all four of them – in that horrible moment before the worst is confirmed and nothing will ever be the same again.

'So where is she now? Can we go and see her, ask what she was doing out at Curlew Cross?' Kit asked, but maybe he already knew.

'I'm sorry, but Karena died in the incident. She's being taken to the regional hospital in a few hours, for now…' The words hung like meaningless static between them for what seemed like a long moment and then the most awful sound Iris thought she'd ever heard seemed to usurp the silence. She looked across at Kit Marshall, his body seemed to have crumpled into a fraction of that proud man she had believed him to be.

'Not Karena, please, no… not Karena…' he whispered and in an instant, Susan was beside him, her arms wrapped tightly about him. They sat for a long time, a huddle of grief vibrating with soft, disconsolate sobs, almost unrecognisable from the people Iris had met that very first day.

*

There were no words, Iris knew that. Anything she said now would be trite, meaningless at best, irritating and jarring. So, she and Slattery sat, at opposite ends of this over-cooked monstrosity of a room, silently waiting until at least some of the fog of loss had cleared. After about half an hour, there were the sounds of movement. Whatever staff were appointed to run this house and by extension the Marshalls' domestic arrangements, had woken up to a day that would be like no other they'd experienced in their employ. Sadly, Iris knew, it was the first of many days that would follow a pattern, woven with grief and loss and perhaps guilt. Iris understood that – feeling guilty, although you'd done nothing wrong. She felt it every time she thought of Idras Locke, the baby buried without so much as a marking over his grave. Perhaps, they were on different ends of the same spectrum, but as surely as she thought about the child she had replaced, she knew that the Marshalls would be as eaten up with guilt for believing their daughter was tucked up safe in bed, when in fact she'd been roaming about Curlew Cross and being beaten savagely to death. That was a terrible weight of guilt to carry.

Somehow, tea and coffee and buttered homemade brown bread were ferried into the room. Slattery had nodded, when the housekeeper had peered around the door. He'd shuffled her back into the hall and no doubt towards the kitchen so when her grief exploded into tears, she was at least out of earshot of the Marshalls. No doubt, he'd set her about doing what she normally would, or at least a shade of it, tea and coffee, bustling, keeping busy, it was, Iris knew from experience, the only answer they could give now.

Iris had stopped thinking sometime after 6 a.m.: the details of the investigation seemed to be in a traffic pile-up in her exhausted brain and she found herself drifting off in the car while Slattery smoked. She woke when they arrived back at the crime scene, abruptly – perhaps he'd said something – to see the perimeter fence and the technical team yellow-taping around anything that might be valuable in building up a picture. She and Slattery remained at the crime scene until just before the sun tried to poke through the silken morning sky.

It was still dark in Limerick, but daylight trailed their car on the return journey to Corbally. It seemed to Iris that there wasn't much point in going home.

She stood under the hot pumping shower in the female bathroom for twenty minutes, washing the tiredness from her bones, if not from her brain. She made her way to the locker room, feeling as if she was carrying pockets filled with rocks, her every footstep weighing heavily on the old-fashioned marble floors.

Clean at least, she sat for a moment in the incident room, thinking – not for the first time since she'd taken over this investigation – that she'd give anything to have Grady back here now, taking responsibility for all of it. Grady had steered her first case with the Murder Team: the fact that it had taken everything from her was probably half the reason she felt this undeniable connection to him. He was the kind of man she'd thought her father to be – as it turned out, she was wrong about Jack Locke, but she knew, deep in her bones, that Grady was the real deal. Slipping into his job, sitting at his desk, it had made her feel as if he was still looking out for her in some ways, but today, with the death of Karena Marshall, she felt his absence more starkly than ever. Perhaps if he was here, this case would already be solved, maybe they'd have Eleanor Marshall home safe and Karena Marshall may not have been murdered last night.

There was no doubt in her mind that they were looking for the same killer for both murders. She didn't want to believe that the murderer could be Eleanor Marshall, but really, she knew, everything was pointing at the girl now. Quite simply, she had convinced herself it couldn't be Eleanor; even in the face of all they'd known, she'd squandered precious time looking for a killer when perhaps she'd been in plain sight all along.

Iris wandered over to the case board, mentally fixing Karena Marshall's face to the investigation. Later, they'd have a photograph; for now, copies were being rushed off in a bid to make this personal to everyone on the team. It wouldn't be hard; you couldn't not see what a tragic waste this was. Rachel McDermott, Karena Marshall, both dead and still Eleanor Marshall was out there, evading them – the answer was staring her in the face; she had to admit it now.

'Right, thanks to all of you for coming in early,' Iris said to the packed incident room twenty minutes later. No one wanted to be here, but by the same token, no one wanted to miss out either. Byrne had not shown up; he was putting in an appearance at the Victim Support conference on the other side of the country. Iris was just glad to have Slattery and June present, with other familiar faces like Westmont and McGonagle yawning at the early start. Pardy and Ahearn had each bagged table corners near the back of the room, perched either end like sleepy figurines gazing at her on an over-mantel shelf.

Iris cleared her throat to the murmur that fell softly across the room. 'Well, as you can see, the tragic news is that we have another victim this morning. Slattery and I spent last night out at Curlew Cross, where an unsuspecting jogger came upon Karena Marshall – Eleanor's younger sister. She was beaten to death. It looks as if the MO is the same as Rachel McDermott – Ahmed will have to confirm it, but we're looking for something between the size of a hammer and a sledgehammer.'

'Same murderer?' Pardy asked.

'If we knew that for sure we could all go home now,' Slattery grunted, not making eye contact with either Iris or the red-faced Pardy.

'There are too many connections for it not to be somehow part of our case: the MO is the same and it looks like the murder weapon might match also,' Iris said generally. Nothing was concrete until it was in a report from Ahmed and the techies, but there was little doubt in Iris's mind.

'Jesus, the Marshalls must be devastated,' one of the uniforms put in from the back of the room. There was no answer to that and the comment lingered about the team for a long, drawn-out moment.

'We're going to have to sit down this evening and really take a good look at possible motives, but for today, we concentrate on finding out who was in those woods last night,' Iris said, looking down at June.

'Of course, I'm on it,' June said wearily. She looked as if she'd slept less than Iris. 'There are cameras set up by the local birdwatching club – they move them around a bit, seems they catch as many canoodling couples as they do rare birds, but they're sending over everything they have this morning. Then, there are a few cameras in Curlew Cross, one on the pub, facing into a yard, which picks up number plates coming into the village, and another at the church, but I'm not sure that picks up much more than weddings and funerals for their webcam.' She shook her head.

'In the church?' Slattery echoed.

'Apparently, they all have them these days – too many Irish people in America, afraid to chance coming home for a family funeral in case immigration won't let them back in again. They're all up on the internet these days if you know where to look,' June said, ignoring Slattery's loud harrumph.

'Right, so apart from that, I want a team in Curlew Cross this morning, checking motorists and anyone who lives near the woods. I want to know who travels in and out of there regularly and if they've noticed anything unusual lately.' Iris looked down at her notepad. 'Tony—' She looked up now and met Ahearn's eye. 'You'll still have your team for the search today with a half dozen uniforms that Byrne has gifted us, just count out Westmont and McGonagle.' She saw Westmont grin. 'The ongoing search is probably the most important part of this investigation, finding Eleanor is our priority. Good luck out there today,' she said, levelling her gaze at the officers who'd spent the last few days trawling about the woods. Long days and nothing to show for it, the most unsatisfying kind of police work any of them could do.

CHAPTER 17

Iris called both Slattery and Tony Ahearn into her office when the briefing was over. Slattery had been wise enough to close the door.

'I want to look at the search again,' she said flatly.

'We're doing our best, the bloody woods are endless and that girl knows them like the back of her hand,' Ahearn began.

'Well, mate.' Slattery leaned on the word, as if he'd prefer to use any other, but it was the only one available. 'It looks like your best isn't good enough.'

'What do you suggest, since you're so bloody perfect?' Ahearn spat the words towards Slattery, but they all knew the venom was directed at Iris.

'Stop it,' she said firmly. Ahearn wouldn't have spoken like that if it was Grady in the inspector's seat – that was plain. 'We're not here to quibble. The fact is that girl is still missing. And while you're searching out there, we have another dead girl and you're no nearer to finding either our suspect or a potential future victim.' Iris's words were cold.

'We're following procedure, but you know yourself, it's slow, it has to be thorough and like I say, take a look at the map, the woods are huge. The dog handler reckons she's nipping in and out of the streams that cut through the place – she's neutralising any scent, so there's no way of tracking her. She can walk for ten miles in six inches of water in just about any direction. How on earth are we supposed to track that?'

'Well, we know one thing for sure – where you're searching is the opposite end of the woods to where Karena Marshall's body was found,' Iris said flatly.

'I can see that, but you still can't say that Eleanor Marshall was anywhere near that body. You can't even confirm if she killed the McDermott girl.' His voice was going slowly up. 'And then, you have the cheek to—'

'Careful there, mate,' Slattery said evenly. 'Remember, she's not a sergeant now.'

'Damn it,' Ahearn said and he turned his back to Iris. 'What do you suggest, so, *Inspector*?'

'I'm suggesting that you split the team. Work with the techies who are out there this morning, get what you can from them and then report back to me on what is the best way forward with the search.'

'Yes, ma'am,' Ahearn said sarcastically.

'I don't need to tell you, Ahearn, that we will be looking at the budget expended on that search. It's six times what we're spending on the investigation and that's not including the manpower from Curlew Hall.'

'Tut, tut, Byrne won't be very pleased when he starts crunching the numbers for the monthly stats,' Slattery said slyly.

'Oh, go find yourself a barstool to fall off, Slattery.' Ahearn banged the office door, just a little too loudly, as he made his way back to the incident room to pick up his jacket before the day ahead.

After a snatched hour or two of sleep, Iris felt as if her head had cleared a little. No one in the team was going to feel good, but at least when she sipped a strong cup of coffee, it felt as if she might be reviving herself a little.

'Marshall has made enemies along the way,' she said. 'There must be plenty of people out there who don't like him.'

'Aside from the pair of you?' June snorted.

'You wouldn't warm to him either,' Slattery muttered. 'He's a cold snob. Even if you can't pick that up from the telly, it's as obvious as Westmont's dandruff that he hasn't got an ounce of warmth in him.'

'Not fans so,' June said and Slattery realised she was warning him to be careful. She was right, of course. It's easy to look for guilt and lose objectivity when you're blinded by dislike.

'Yes, well, either way, we're going to have to go out there and talk to him again,' Iris said darkly; he would not want to see them, even if it might help to find Karena's killer. 'But first I'm going to have to finish off the statements from Curlew Hall and if I'm done in time, I can meet you over at the pathology suite,' she said to Slattery.

'Again?' Slattery moaned, but then he caught the tiredness in Iris's movements as she made her way towards the door. 'Sure.'

'Ahmed rang to say he'll start at two, so it would be good to be there and gowned beforehand,' Iris said, making her way out the door.

Harry Prendergast was hunched over at the rear entrance of the pathology lab, dragging deeply on a cigarette as if it might be his last, when Slattery parked, or more accurately abandoned, his car halfway between a yellow box and a double line.

'Social call?' Prendergast nodded at him.

'That's right, Harry, nothing I like better than paying my respects when you're at work.' Slattery shook his head, dug into his inside pocket and shook them out a cigarette each. Prendergast lit the fresh from the old and continued smoking.

'Should be fairly straightforward, most of the work was done already by the scene-of-crime boys.' Harry was smiling. Then he added, 'They were good enough to scoop up as much of her head as they could from the forest floor.' He exhaled a long fat cloud of smoke, it rafted as much from his nostrils as his mouth.

'You ever think about these things?' Slattery held up his fag for a moment. 'What with all you see every other day?'

'With my missus? It'd be a peaceful release for me. Anyway, I see plenty of men a lot younger than us, stretched out here thanks to killing themselves with stress. If I've learned anything in this job, it's that I'm going to go having enjoyed life because either approach is going to get you one way or another.'

'Jeez, Harry, I don't know if that's philosophical or the most depressing thing you've ever said.'

'Ah, well, it's all part of the service.' He nodded up towards the doors that had no sign telling you what was inside the building. Rather, at the end of the narrow car park a small arrow pointed you towards the pathology labs if you squinted and looked closely enough to notice. Slattery knew this building lay purposely to the rear of the hospital to distract patients from the obvious truth that while no one wants to be in hospital, it is far preferable to being examined in this department.

'Righty-oh,' Prendergast said as he took one long final drag on his cigarette, 'back to the party so, I suppose. Ahmed should be ready to go now, it's all set up and waiting.' The preparation of the suite was Harry's job. He was responsible for cleaning down after the last autopsy and setting everything straight for the next. He would already have organised Karena Marshall's body onto an examination table and laid out the various implements and tools Ahmed would require to perform the autopsy.

They walked through the glass doors into the hallway that was little more than a square with a post box at the bottom of noisy tiled stairs and double doors leading into a lift large enough to take a gurney and two orderlies. It was lit only by natural light and smelled heavily of a deep lavender scent that was used to mask odours that never actually made it this far through the building.

'You know, I was thinking about the McDermotts after you left,' Harry said as he pushed his way into what could be described as a reception area, if they ever had need of one.

'Oh?' Slattery knew that if Iris was here now, her ears would prick up: he'd seen the file left open on her desk. It was natural, of course, for her to think there might be some historical connection, particularly after the song and dance Prendergast had made of it. In the last case they'd investigated, the motive had hinged on a case some thirty years earlier – a case which had thrown Iris's whole world into confusion, leaving her very identity turned inside out. 'That death has nothing to do with this, Harry, come on. William McDermott was a long time back and it's time to let it go.' They both knew that since his death, so much had happened in the field of medicine and pathology. Ahmed could probably come up with a reasonable answer now within five minutes of looking at his case file. 'We shouldn't have mentioned anything in front of Iris at all, to be honest,' he said, still kicking himself for anything that might make her raw wounds more painful.

'Oh, Jesus, of course, of course.' Prendergast was shaking his head. 'Christ, it's hard to remember everything. I forgot about her old man…'

He sighed. Harry never really liked old Nessie. It was a funny thing about Jack Locke, but he was one of those men who divided opinion completely. You either adored him or you loathed him and over the past few weeks, it was becoming apparent to Slattery at least, that there were far more people in the latter camp than he'd ever realised before. 'Anyway, it wasn't the husband that I was thinking about, it was her – Mrs McDermott.'

'Rachel's mother?'

'Yep. She's a regular churchgoer, like my missus, and they knock about a women's group together a bit too, it seems. Anyway, we were talking about her last night, you know, so sad, the daughter dead, and the husband dead and so on…' Prendergast shook his head as if these conversations with his good wife were a bit like those Slattery endured when Maureen talked on and on and he let her words wash over him mostly. 'Well, then she says, *huh, indeed, Imelda McDermott wasn't always so holy*, and of course, that's when she got my attention too.' Prendergast laughed seeing Slattery turn his gaze on him. 'It seems Rachel was a *very overdue* baby.' He was nodding.

'There's no way,' Slattery said, because he couldn't imagine Imelda McDermott having sex with her own husband, not to mind having an affair outside of wedlock.

'Well, unless she was an immaculate conception.' Prendergast shook his head laughing softly.

'So who?'

'What am I now? The Holy Spirit? I don't know, but I know one thing, she might have been her mother's daughter, but she was never William McDermott's child.'

'Come on, Harry, I know what old women are like, God knows I'm married to Maureen long enough to know the way they can rattle on for hours. Who did they think might be in the frame?'

'Like I always said, Mrs McDermott was a fine-looking woman. I'd say she could have had her pick of men at the time, but the thing is, when whoever did the deed didn't step up to the plate, well, it's plain to see, isn't it?

'Is it?'

'Course it is, sure, it had to be a married man, or one that didn't want to lose face if word got out that he'd been having it away with the freshest widow in town.' He stuffed his cigarettes into his pocket as they entered the pathology suite.

Harry Prendergast had a habit of leaving thoughts in the air, like rabbits that didn't belong in a hat, but still, Slattery wanted to jam it back in. This had no more bearing on Rachel McDermott's death than the premature death of her father, did it?

'Ah, there you are.' Rafiq Ahmed was waiting for them, gowned and gloved in the heavily disinfected theatre. 'Slattery.' He nodded towards a pile of hospital garments that were left out for the police attending the post mortem.

Slattery grunted. It felt like it could be a very long afternoon.

CHAPTER 18

Ten past eleven and they were almost through interviewing the rest of the staff who worked with Eleanor. There was nothing here. Iris was convinced of that. She pulled the short straw this morning; it was either Slattery or a uniform called Kenny. And Kenny had asked if he could come along, so she figured better the willing officer than Slattery who looked as if he would have to fight to keep his eyes open if he had to take another statement.

'Didn't notice anything at all, well, not that evening anyway, there's been something off about her for a while. But then, she goes through phases, you know.' They were speaking to Julia Stenson again.

'So, how long have you worked here?'

'Oh, almost two years, on and off, but you get to know Eleanor pretty quickly, especially since she'd been on her own...' She continued to examine the glut of hardened yellow between her thumb and forefinger. Iris tried to forget that she shook hands with Julia on arrival.

'She's all right, I mean, I expected her to be a spoilt rich kid and most people probably told you all the bad stuff. I mean, she's here for a reason, right? But, from what I could see, she was no worse than any other youngster trying to push their parents' buttons.' Julia looked up at them now, her eyes almost pleading; biting her lower lip, there was more to say.

'Go on, we need to know everything.'

'Some of the staff, well… we think some of the staff picked on her…' Julia's voice trailed off.

'Did Rachel McDermott pick on her?'

'Rachel? No, never, Rach wasn't like that, she was quiet, she hadn't a cruel bone in her. But Nate Hegarty, now he's a different kettle of fish altogether.'

'You think he picked on her?' Iris leaned forward on the desk; some small part of her didn't need to ask the question.

Julia opened her eyes wide and brought her shoulders in a shrug. 'I don't know for sure, it's just a feeling.' She sighed deeply. 'I should have said this sooner, but… to be honest, that morning, when I found her, I couldn't think, not really.'

'What's she like? Eleanor?' Iris was conscious of Kenny's pen poised and waiting, like a court stenographer. It was off-putting; if Iris could feel it, she didn't doubt that this young girl could feel it too.

'Well, she could be cheeky, but then that comes with the territory of being a teenager. She had a soft side too just like the rest of us, I suppose. She wasn't all tantrums and throwing things, you know? Sometimes, she'd like to snuggle up to you, watch a movie, while you brushed out her hair. When she was like that, she could melt your heart. I think that's why most of us kept on coming in here every day. God knows it's not for the money.' She threw prematurely world-weary eyes heavenward. 'Probably have more out of the dole if the truth were told.'

'Was she like this with everyone?'

'She gave everyone a whirl. If she liked you then you got to see her like that more often. If she didn't like you and there's a few she didn't like, believe me, well they'd need to watch out – she was like any other kid here, she could make a shift hell with just being angsty and argumentative.'

'What about Nate Hegarty then?'

'She hated him. Well, I don't know if it was hatred exactly. Sometimes, I wondered if she was afraid of him. Some of the girls thought he might have hit her or something at some stage. I wouldn't put anything past him; he's a nasty piece of work.'

'Did you see anything?'

'No.' Julia was silent; her eyes veered towards the left and sideways. Both officers knew that she was racking her memory, not depending on her imagination for whatever came next. 'None of us actually saw anything.' She looked Iris in the eyes. 'Look, I know it's probably too late for Eleanor now, but there is just something about him. This last while, I always kept a closer eye on him than on her when he came into the bungalow.' She was silent for a moment, her hand moved across her soft leggings, feeling for the comforting edges of her mobile phone.

Iris willed Kenny not to say anything. Let the girl fill the silence. They could have a break afterwards, call her in again, but please let her say what's going through her mind at this moment. Iris leaned forward again, mirroring the girl's movements of her hands, working her left hand around the edge of her jawline.

'Look, this is only what I thought and I might as well say it. I've thought it for a long time, but, I wondered…Well, I wondered if she wasn't holding something over him.'

The room was silent. Julia exhaled, now she'd told someone. The words floated for a second or two in the air between them, like soft bubbles, perfect, honest. They'd never fit back in their box again. Julia reclined in her chair and waited as her words drifted, their effect lightening and depressing the room at once. Somehow, the burden had lifted, a weight was winched from around the corners of Julia's eyes and mouth. There would be more questions. There would be many questions and not many answers, just a feeling that something was amiss.

Iris drew in her breath. She did not want Julia Stenson to clam up now, not now. It would be difficult to gather details of abuse; it was just too sad, unthinkably depressing and unspeakably wrong.

'What made you think that?'

'Nothing.' Julia fingered the cigarettes before her. 'Well, that's nothing and then sort of everything. It wasn't anything really concrete, it was more in the way she reacted when he was near.'

'Did any of the staff notice this too? Would Rachel have had any suspicions like this?' Iris leaned across the table, her hands lying flat, faced upwards before her.

'God, no.' Julia's eyes became wide at the very notion of it. 'No, I'd say if Rach thought there was something really off about him, she'd have reported it straight away.'

'Not gone to Nate? She wouldn't have asked him, tried to intervene herself?' It seemed to Iris that Rachel McDermott was the sort who'd want to save everyone, not just Eleanor, but the weight of Nate being sacked might be something that she'd find hard to carry.

'That's the thing – Rach and Nate? Maybe?' Julia looked now from Iris to Kenny. 'He adored Rach, it was like unreal when she came here first.'

'Were they involved, do you think?'

'Rach was way out of his league and for all his swagger he had to know that. Still, it was as if, at the beginning, he thought there might be something. These last few weeks, he just hung about, like he was waiting for something.' She stopped for a minute. 'She was special, Rach. She wasn't like a lot of the other people you normally meet here. Eleanor saw that straight off and I suppose we all did. I'm not sure that she'd have dobbed anyone up, she wasn't the sort to pass on a problem. Yeah,' she said, confirming it for herself. 'If she'd had any inkling that Nate was up to no good, I think she'd have had it out with him.' She mulled that over and then continued. 'But she didn't…'

'How can you be sure?'

'Well, he was still here, wasn't he? And anyway, right up to that night, he was still hanging about like a puppy waiting for his treat.'

*

It was well after four when they finished up for the day. They had time to write up their notes and then, once Kenny had clocked off for the evening, Iris got herself a strong mug of coffee and settled into a half-hour drive on a mission that she wasn't going to share with anyone else on the team. She wasn't really expecting to find a pin that might slot neatly into the case they were working on, but she knew she had to put her doubts and questions about William McDermott to bed.

Bobby Nestor's case notes were old-fashioned, as though they were written fifty years ago, his spidery hand ranging across yellowing pages, earnestly seeking solutions, futile in the end. At least it answered her questions. There was nothing there, beyond gut feeling and Iris felt her own instinct running with Nestor's. There was more to learn here, but Iris was not yet sure what that could be.

'Jack Locke's daughter, eh?' Bobby Nestor appraised her as if she was coming to give him a quote on a particularly important repair job to his home.

How on earth could she explain all that was wrong with connecting her to the man they'd all known as Nessie Locke? Bobby Nestor must be, she realised, the only man associated with Corbally who wasn't aware that she was no more Jack Locke's daughter than she was the tooth fairy's sister. 'Thanks so much for making the time to see me,' she said.

'Ara sure, it's the one thing I have no shortage of these days,' he said dolefully. 'Plenty of time on my hands now.' He glanced about the small patch of garden before his semi, as if he was daring a weed to show up, the flower beds had been pruned to within an inch of life. 'Come on, I'll make us a nice cup of tea.'

Iris sat in Bobby Nestor's kitchen waiting while he went about making tea for them both. It was a kitchen that had reared a family, but there was no doubt in Iris's mind that Bobby was alone now.

'Yeah, wife left me, just when I retired, she's off in Spain now, living it up, I suppose,' he said a little wistfully; obviously, he had not been included in the travel plans. 'Anyway, what's this about William McDermott's case?' He put the tea before her. 'Well, it wasn't even that, not really.'

'No. I read your case notes. It was well managed and all of that and they're very helpful. There was no case – I can see that, but I suppose, with the death of the daughter and the fact that we went out there and met Mrs McDermott, you know…'

He finished for her. 'Lightning doesn't strike twice?'

'Something like that.' She sipped the tea, it was hot and weak, but still reviving, just a bit.

'At the time, I'd have put money on Imelda McDermott having killed her husband. It wasn't just the fact that the coroner couldn't find a reason for him dying, it was a whole lot of other things too.'

'What kind of things?'

'Oh, I don't know, something of nothing and everything too, I suppose.' He sipped his tea thoughtfully. 'It's funny how life changes the way you look at things. If I was leading out that investigation now, I'd probably think very differently.'

'But you had reasons for suspecting her, I'm sure.'

'Yes, but I wonder now, looking back, if it wasn't my own small-mindedness that made me pursue it for as long as I did.' He sighed, a long and worn-out sound. 'Those were different times, Iris. I don't expect you to understand, but back then there wasn't the same amount of tolerance for things, if you know what I mean.'

'I'm not sure I do.' She smiled.

'That man wasn't very long in the ground before she had a baby on the way, people said… well, they said all sorts, but everyone knew it wasn't William McDermott's.'

'No?'

'No. She was a good-looking woman. I'd say, before she married McDermott, she could have had her pick of men about the place.

According to the neighbours at the time, there were plenty of them sniffing about her door, although, God knows, once McDermott was gone, she didn't need any of them. He left her well provided for – well, his life assurance did at least.'

'So, at the end of all that, you think?'

'I think it was an unlucky turn of events for poor old William, but quite a fortuitous one for his widow. I think, if it happened now – apart from the fact that the medical examiner would have all the answers for you either way – there wouldn't be the judgement. If I'm honest, at the time, I saw her taking up with another bloke so quickly as a reason to suspect her all the more.'

'As you say, different times,' Iris said softly.

'Indeed,' he replied, glancing about at the emptiness his own wife had left behind.

'What is it, is something up?' Her voice was bleary so it matched the rest of her body perfectly, she must have dozed off. It took her a moment to get her bearings in the half light. It was Grady's office, her office, for now at least, but it had that unfamiliar feel to it as places do when you see them from a different angle or through a lens when you're so familiar with them otherwise; it seemed oddly – for such a small space – too big for her.

'We've just had a call from a uniform out in Comeragh Pass,' said Slattery.

Iris jerked up in her chair, the sleep draining away from her body, her thoughts raced instantly to the woods. Was there news of Eleanor? Had they found her? *Let her be all right, please, let her be all right.*

'Have they found her?'

'Not exactly.' He coughed into his hand, but it was more to clear his throat than a sign that he was coming down with something. 'We got a call a few minutes ago. She may have been spotted on Comeragh Pass. An old guy rang up the station out there, very upset.'

'And?'

'When the local garda came on duty, first thing he did was check the messages. This old guy sounded well shaken, he'd left a phone number and said he'd been involved in an accident, wasn't sure if anyone was hurt or not.'

'So it was an RTA, yeah?'

'Not exactly. He was driving along one of those old forestry tracks. Apparently, he does a little fishing in the lake. A lot of those tracks are hardly wide enough to walk along, but he came around a bend and ran straight into a girl. We're lucky because the garda had just come off overtime out in the woods. The description fitted perfectly with Eleanor Marshall.'

'Did he question the guy?' She hoped he hadn't, didn't want the eyewitness account getting confused.

'No, don't worry, he's clean. Our colleague rang here straight away and we can go out now to talk to the fella.' It was a break – a small one – but a chink of hope that Eleanor was still moving, still alive.

'Okay, you want to come along?' she asked, shrugging into the jacket she'd hung at the back of her chair earlier. She was making a habit of not taking for granted that he was always on duty. If she had one wish for Slattery it was that he could build whatever bridges he needed to with his wife before it was too late. She had a feeling he went to her house most evenings after work, before he ducked into the Ship Inn. Of course, he still never missed a night at his local, even if he did seem to be arriving a little later these days than he might have in the past.

'Of course I'm coming along, what else would I be doing with myself?' he said, completely unaware of Iris's silent glance willing him to say he needed to be at home soon.

At least it looked like Eleanor was alive today, which was something to hang onto. Was she injured? What had happened? Where had she gone? Various scenarios played out in Iris's imagination. All the while, a silent chorus chugged through her brain. *Please, God, let her be all right.*

Something of the conversation with Julia Stenson hung in the back of her mind. The way she spoke about Eleanor, breaking through the myth with a picture of the girl that Iris hadn't managed to capture until it was almost too late. She wondered if Eleanor Marshall really was their suspect.

'Is everyone all right?'

'Yeah, they're fine, the driver was badly shaken, but he's fine. He wasn't sure what happened, probably still in shock.' Slattery opened the door to the incident room, picking up his jacket from across a desk as he moved past the case board.

'Do we know where he picked her up?' Iris moved towards a magnified Ordnance Survey Map one of the junior officers had pinned up at the start of the search. It had been marked with highlighters of various shades to show where the teams had covered and spots where it looked as though Eleanor may have passed, but until now there was nothing concrete. She ran her finger along the map, tracing the perimeter of Curlew Hall.

Slattery watched the trajectory for a moment and then closed his eyes as if visualising the geography of the place.

'Let me see, he dropped her off near enough to Butler's bridge, drove along, quite shocked… coming from Tullyboy and then he picked her up at Tobair Mhuire.' He looked again towards the map. His eyes followed Iris's hand as she traced the route from Curlew Hall to Tobair Mhuire. It was almost eight miles. 'Good God…' Slattery's voice was little more than an echo.

Iris grabbed a ruler and held it against the two points. Using a thick black felt tip, she joined the points and let the marker run for an additional couple of inches west. The ruler ended centimetres away from the Duneata House estate.

'She's moving as the crow flies for home.'

CHAPTER 19

Day 4

Jack Locke always said, *it's an ill wind that doesn't blow some good* and Iris woke with those words in her ears. She wasn't sure if it was more disturbing that suddenly she was aware of the space he took up in her thoughts, or the fact that up until now, she'd never really noticed how large his presence loomed within her. Either way, she did her best to shake off the enveloping gloom that recognising what had become of the family she thought she knew brought on these days. Instead, she picked up her steaming mug of coffee and heard Mrs Leddy's carriage clock chime in the hallway beyond her room, as if to remind her precious time was passing. Time to get moving.

It was almost seven thirty when she arrived into Corbally to find the incident room already half full of officers. She went to her office to escape the banter that was too much to cope with under the gaze of Rachel and Karena from the incident board. She heard a light tap on the door and she looked up to see Slattery's outline in the glass.

'Having a little break, are we?' He looked as wrecked as she felt.

'Come in.' It was a revelation to realise that she was actually glad to see him. Somehow, his age and his curmudgeonly charm – if you could call it that – was comforting. 'I'm just getting my thoughts together for the briefing.'

'Oh, right.' He glanced down at the empty refill pad before her. 'Going well, I see.'

'If you're not going to say anything constructive you can just toddle off back under your rock.'

'Well, what do you want me to say? It's grunt work, that's all we can do, go through the routine enquiries and then spend as much time as possible going back over everything we collect to see if we can find some small hole that doesn't have a cover.'

'I know, but time is against us.' She looked out the condensation-filled window at the uninspiring view of the car park. 'How on earth is Eleanor Marshall still out there giving us the slip, Slattery?'

'She's bright, maybe brighter than any of the people who knew her ever suspected,' he said simply.

'It's still a long time to be wandering about the place.' She exhaled loudly on a raft of desolation.

'It's a done deal as far as Ahearn is concerned – the fact that she's given him the slip, he's convinced that she's our man, so to speak.'

'Oh God, Slattery, I hate to admit it, but this time, he's probably right.' Iris groaned, hated herself for it.

'Look, without her here, it's just shooting in the dark.' Slattery nodded out towards the incident room. 'We know what every other person who was around the building that night has to say for themselves, she's the only one who hasn't been able to give us her version.' Of course, he was right. They were meant to be in the business of justice, after all, being innocent until proven guilty. 'All I know for certain is that we are doing the best we can, right? And now, you need to get yourself together, put on your happy face and convince them you believe we can solve it.'

'Oh, yeah?'

'Well, otherwise, Tony Ahearn is only waiting to leap into that seat you're looking so comfortable in.'

'You're right. There's one thing…'

'Okay?'

'Well, Eleanor being spotted, it might help us put the pressure on Marshall to get an up-to-date photo on the news...'

They both realised Marshall's reluctance, in the face of losing his younger daughter, may no longer be the obstacle it was before. On the other hand, he may just decide he wanted to play the same game going forward – bad enough to lose one daughter, he'd surely want to keep the second safe. Even if Eleanor was obviously not the favourite, he would not want the weight of public opinion to fall against her, particularly if one day this went to trial with Eleanor in the dock. Iris couldn't blame him if he continued to try to control the information given out about his one remaining daughter.

'We need to get up there today anyway, to talk about Karena with him.'

'You can try, it won't do any harm, I suppose.' Slattery smiled wryly. 'So long as you don't mind risking another rollicking from Byrne.'

'I think it would be well worth it, if Marshall agrees,' Iris said, feeling a little more optimistic that maybe a renewed public appeal might help them find her quickly. 'We've spent far too long faffing about the place trying to keep everyone sweet, and why? What's the worst they can do to us? Take us off the case?' She shook her head, not sure who she was angrier with, herself or Marshall or Byrne for not having the guts to do the right thing.

One of the uniformed guards that Marshall had employed for his personal security was ex Corbally. He opened the gates for them when they arrived at the end of the scraggy road leading to the estate.

'Trev.' Slattery nodded to the officer. 'You doing sentry work these days? We'll have to get you a beefeater for Christmas, I suppose now.'

'Very bloody funny. You wouldn't be laughing half as hard if you were out here in all weathers and looking after a pair that won't offer you so much as a cup of tea if your life depended on it.'

'Ah well, I did hear life in the private sector isn't all it's cracked up to be,' Slattery commiserated. 'Are they saying anything about… well, you know…?' He was looking for something useful – anything that Marshall wouldn't share with the guards, but might say to his paid staff.

'No, but he's ramped up security all around the house since that kid got murdered up at Curlew Hall. If it was me, I'd be paying people to get out and look for my daughter, but there's no telling what kind of stupidity too much money can buy, I suppose.'

'Are the sentry duties new?' Iris poked her head out.

'Yep, thinks he's JF bloody K now. No one's going to tell him he's really not that important, but I think he's convinced that someone's out to get him. Chance would be a fine thing, if you ask me,' he grumbled.

'Since Karena's death?'

'No, before that, he's been nervy as hell since the McDermott lass died.' He pulled back the gates and let them through with a nod, closing the gates out behind them as they made their way up the avenue.

Today, at least, the sun was shining on the house, and unlike their first visit, Iris noticed the intricate mouldings in the plaster-work around the doors and windows and a cheerful array of shrubs at various points, punctuating the edge of the long rolling lawn. When they entered the hall this time, the sun shining through an impressive fanlight over the front door threw jewel-like colours across the otherwise lifeless entrance hall.

'Mr Marshall,' Iris said pleasantly as they followed Kit into the now familiar room, 'thanks for seeing us so quickly. We're sorry to disturb you again, but you know, with Karena's death, there are things that we need to find out and time is everything in situations like this. First, though, how are you both doing?' she asked as she took a seat, this time looking out across the gardens.

'Yes, Sergeant, we're as fine as you'd expect,' Kit said curtly, and Iris knew there would be no easy way to create some sort of rapport with this man.

'We do understand it's not easy and this… well, the death of Karena, it's such a tragic blow.' To be fair, Iris knew what it was like to lose everything in a flash, but saying that wasn't going to help Kit Marshall.

'I'm not sure it's really sunk in for either of us yet, to be honest,' he said, standing before the fireplace which held the ashes and the remains of a blackened log from the previous day. 'She was our pride and joy, an exceptional child, really.'

'Yes,' Iris agreed, because even for the short time they'd spoken, she had a sense that Karena Marshall was one of those rare kids who had been blessed not just with brains and beauty, but with a gentleness that went to her bones. 'The thing is, Mr Marshall, there's still time to save your other daughter,' she said softly.

'Eleanor,' he murmured, as if she was the constant worry, the booby prize when he'd hoped for first place.

'Yes. Eleanor. You know that whatever has gone on between you in the past, this…' Iris opened her hands in a gesture that encompassed everything about this terrible time. 'This tragedy, well, it changes everything. When things like this happen, you don't just lose people, you can find people too. It's a reason to mend any bridges, and if you get a chance, it might be an opportunity to bring her home.'

She knew, however, that Eleanor might be spending the next twenty years locked up if she was responsible for what happened to Rachel and Karena.

'Of course,' he said, as if he'd forgotten Eleanor was somewhere out in the woods. 'Susan is out there now.' He waved a hand towards the window. 'She's helping with the search. She told me you've moved along closer to here, on the road that heads over to the Comeragh mountains.'

'That's right,' Iris confirmed. 'It's part of the reason we came out here today. We got a call last night; Eleanor was spotted on the road. A driver was heading in this general direction and so, at least, we can say she's still…' Iris couldn't say anymore, she didn't have it in her to cause the man any more worry or grief.

'Alive,' Slattery said flatly. 'She walked in front of his car and—'

'Oh dear God.' Kit ran his hand back through his hair, as if it might somehow take some of the pressure from his head.

'We think she's fine,' Slattery said. 'No thanks to—' But he stopped when Iris sharply caught his eye.

'That's right, no thanks to the fact that we've practically turned over the woods out at Curlew Hall. The thing is, we're getting closer, but without the public having a good image of what Eleanor looks like now… Well, it's not helping her. They need to know and it's likely we'd have her picked up in no time.'

'You want a new press conference?' he asked.

'Yes.'

'You want to give the impression that Eleanor is some kind of crazed murderer and that she's killed that McDermott girl? I can't do that, don't you see?'

'We understand that you're afraid of how it's put out there, that if Eleanor did…' She couldn't say commit murder, not here, not now. 'Well, if there are legal repercussions you wouldn't want a jury to be tainted by what the red tops may sensationalise.' Iris stopped, looked at the man before her. Kit Marshall had aged by about two decades in the past few days, but while he might almost be a broken man, his eyes retained that glint of steel about them, so she knew he was still no pushover. 'Look, I don't need to spell it out to you. She's just a kid. All right, so perhaps she's had a knack of finding herself in trouble, but she's got epilepsy and if there is a killer out there in the woods with her, we both know she doesn't have much of a chance if faced with what Karena and Rachel McDermott came up against.'

'I don't know. I need to think,' Marshall said, moving from his position at the fireplace and standing with his back to them while he surveyed the gardens through the large casement window.

'Can you tell us what Karena might have been doing out at Curlew Cross that night?' Slattery's words cut across the room after they'd sat for a while in the silence.

'Your guess is as good as mine on that one,' Marshall said drily.

'Could she have made contact with her sister?' Slattery asked.

'I really couldn't say. I know that they were very strict in Curlew Hall about mobile phones. Although we'd bought her one, it spent most of its time locked away. In places like that, phones are a privilege, it's not like she could be ringing at every available opportunity.'

Of course, they knew this. Eleanor's phone was still locked away in Curlew Hall when they'd checked and it had seemed the only person she'd been in regular contact with was Karena; they'd kept in touch whenever she was allowed the phone. Karena's phone bore out a similar result. It held just the normal stuff any teenage girl was likely to have, nothing that flagged she was in any kind of personal danger.

'Well, it seems a little too coincidental that she just happened to be out there and then,' Slattery started to say, but stopped as Iris shot him another warning look.

She didn't want to blow it with Marshall. She wanted him to agree to a second press meeting. Having him believe that Eleanor might be in danger was their best bet. The problem was, she wasn't entirely sure that Kit wouldn't prefer to have a second innocent murdered daughter than he would a live one serving time for murder. That thought made her shiver.

'It's not just a random attack in the woods so?' He was checking, perhaps he'd tried to convince himself that it wasn't connected.

'There's no question that it's connected to the death of Rachel McDermott and by extension to Eleanor's disappearance,' Iris said, making it clear that there would be a Marshall connection regardless of how he tried to wriggle out of it. 'But that just means that if there's a murderer out there in those woods, Eleanor is in as much danger as either Rachel or Karena was.' She stopped for a moment. 'Mr Marshall, there's no reason not to believe that she was the intended victim when Rachel McDermott was murdered.' It was a long shot, but the truth was, they didn't know and when you didn't know, surely anything was possible.

'I suppose it's too close to be a coincidence.' Marshall shrugged, as if it had been worth a try. 'Well then, of course, we should make another appeal.' Marshall leaned forward, his head sunk low on his shoulders, his normally straight frame crouched. 'Could this be someone trying to get at me? I've stepped on plenty of toes over the years, but generally, I can't see any of my business adversaries stooping to that level.'

'We'll need a possible list of people that might have reason to avenge you,' Iris said, but the truth was, June had already trawled through every business deal. Marshall's career was a trail of derelict buildings and tracks of unused land, bought for peanuts and made good. He had an eye for potential. Back when Limerick's riverbanks had been little more than scrap yards, he had bought up vast amounts of land and transformed them into an empire of high-end business and luxurious living accommodation.

'You've heightened your security here,' Slattery said lazily.

'I suppose I've thought about the fact that perhaps… I've had threats in the past,' he said looking away from them now.

'Oh?'

'It doesn't matter now, but it was all tied up with a property I purchased about ten years ago on the Northern Ireland border and there was a suggestion that some of the renegade paramilitaries might be hanging about with the intention of kidnapping Susan for a ransom…' His voice petered out and Iris wondered if there was so much as a grain of truth in the words.

'It's not Eleanor you're worried about so?' Slattery cut across them.

'Yes. No, well, there's every reason to… Look, I don't know. None of us know what she's capable of and she's always had… funny ideas about us.'

'Right.' Slattery managed a thin smile, which unfortunately looked far too morose to be engaging. 'As I've said, Eleanor was spotted last night, between eight and nine, walking along the main road. We're pretty sure now she's making her way towards Duneata House.' The words hung in the air, leaden weights, somehow suspended, holding with them dark expectation. 'She may be making her way home to you,' he said flatly.

'Well, that's….'

'Good? Yes, we think so. At least then we'll be able to catch up with her. I suppose the only thing is, she still has to get here safely.' Maybe lies are okay if they're only told to save a life.

'How many miles?' Kit whispered hoarsely. It was hard to hear him. He'd closed his eyes and slumped down into his shoulders, the worry evident on his voice. 'How many miles was she away from here when she had this *accident*?'

'Am…let me check, I'd say about ten, but she's been travelling, from what we can make out, in an almost straight line, directly towards Duneata House, so ten by road, but less on foot,' Iris said. Eleanor's last known location was some distance further away, but that was almost twelve hours ago now.

'When do you want to do this press conference?' Marshall said with a ring of defeat in his words.

'We should go with it as soon as possible,' Iris replied. 'There's just one more small thing. We're trying to track down Eleanor's case file from Curlew Hall, but I'm afraid it's not there.'

'We had it archived. It seemed like a sensible thing to do, what with everything one hears about these things getting into the wrong hands.' He shook his head. It was understandable; who would want their personal notes at risk of being made public by some eager staff on the make? 'It hasn't been removed because we'd have been informed.'

'Normally, sir, yes, but this is a murder inquiry and even FOI allows that the police may request files without consent in a murder inquiry.'

'So where is it?'

'All I can tell you is that it was taken out a couple of weeks ago, we think by Rachel McDermott.'

'But she couldn't do that, she would have needed permission.' Kit's voice held a quiver that Iris had a feeling presaged a sudden boiling temper. 'Did Susan give permission?'

'No, sir. We have reason to believe Rachel forged a permission signature.'

'Where is my daughter's file now?'

'We're looking for it. I'm afraid since Rachel McDermott took it out, it hasn't been seen since,' Slattery said, perhaps enjoying the prickly disquiet that had settled in the room.

Marshall walked towards the door, stood for a moment, his hand on the frame, holding it open for their exit. 'Is that all?' He obviously had more important things to do than shoot the breeze with Iris and Slattery.

'One thing, where had you been last evening?' Slattery turned slowly, enjoying the slight stretch in the silence.

'I was in Dublin. I was giving a lecture in Trinity College. If you're trying to insinuate something sordid, Sergeant, it was a record turnout, one hundred and fifty witnesses. I was there all day and I had only just arrived back an hour or so when you started hammering on my front door. Have you quite finished now?'

'Well, for now, sir, yes.'

And then, suddenly, Marshall was marching them to the door as if they were participating in a fire drill and it was vital that they leave the building.

CHAPTER 20

Slattery was too long a garda to disregard his gut and if it was a feeling about a case, Lord knows he'd have been onto it like a fruit fly in summertime. But in this instance, he had ignored that slight shadowy feeling that glided somewhere at his back. He had moved through the incident room as if he hadn't a care in the world when, clearly, this inkling at his shoulder was becoming a new familiar reminder. Maureen.

When his phone rang, he knew before he answered that it could not be good.

'Have you seen her today?' Angela never uttered the name 'Dad'. Really, Slattery wasn't sure what name she'd use if she had to call out to him in public. He knew it was because he'd never earned the title. He supposed, on good days, she probably thought of him as Slattery, but there hadn't been many of those over the years.

'I drove by this morning, but you know, she won't entertain me any time before lunch,' he said stoically.

'Well, she's not there. It looks like she hasn't been there since yesterday. Her dinner dishes are in the sink, there's half a beef stew stuck to the pot as if she just walked out the door on it.'

'I thought you were calling in to see her every night—'

'Don't you bloody dare!' She cut into his words savagely.

'No, I didn't mean that, I just assumed, and so… look, I wouldn't mind dropping by but you have to let me know…' The truth was, he drove by every evening after work. Sometimes he just parked across the road, watched the routine unfold with lights switched off, Maureen padding upstairs, lights turned on and eventual complete darkness. She didn't want him anywhere near her. Not yet. Not until she had to have someone watch over her.

'Oh, please.' Angela sighed. 'So, from that, we can assume, you haven't been near the place since God knows when, right?'

He knew – maybe not because she was his own flesh and blood, perhaps, more so because he'd been a cop for so long – her irritation was not just with him. This angry voice had as much to do with her current fear as it had that familiar deep-seated bitterness towards her father.

'Fine,' she said and she hung up the phone.

He rang her back immediately.

'I'm on my way over there now. Are you at the house?'

'Yes, but I'm going to have to start searching for her, after I've finished opening the windows to let out the smell of the burning saucepan and disintegrating stew.'

'Fine, I'll see you in a few minutes.' He mumbled something at June as he made his way out of the incident room, could feel her eyes on him and he didn't need to check that she knew he wasn't on the case for now.

The city was mercifully clear, with traffic moving along at a decent pace. Slattery hardly noticed the ominous sky and murky river, but he spotted a huge raven perched on Thomond Bridge and thought back to some old saying about rooks and death and long waits and… ah, it was just nonsense anyway. Still, he shivered at the menacing water below him. He'd been on too many river trawls as a young garda for November darkness to ever leave him entirely.

Maureen's house was freezing when he pushed open the front door. The heavy stink of burning dinner clung forcefully to the air, as though it would never quite give in to the morning cold.

Angela looked like death, her round face managing to be pinched and drawn with a worry she would never voice to Slattery.

'She's been missing since five yesterday evening,' she said, checking her watch. Suddenly it seemed to Slattery that his daughter was changing before his eyes, as if her mother's diagnosis of dementia had somehow spilled over into her own features.

'She won't be gone far.' He tried to sound solid and reassuring – there was no point in hoping for dependable, not with Angela. 'Is her coat missing? Her bag? Anything else?'

'Her coat's gone and at five o'clock in the evening, the best we can hope is that she was wearing an apron and her ordinary everyday clothes.' Angela was searching through the kitchen units. 'No sign of her handbag either, so we can assume…' Perhaps she knew enough to know that with dementia they couldn't really assume anything.

'Right, so that's a navy coat?' Slattery waited for a withering glance from his daughter to confirm. He pulled out his phone and called an old colleague who had stayed out of trouble long enough to remain in uniform but never have the chance to move into stripes or command. He passed on a description of Maureen: 'Grey hair, five four, overweight, but not obese, a homely housewife and mother with blue eyes, and a determined expression,' was how he tactfully described her; well, it was better than saying grim-faced. Maureen was just sixty, but she was an old-fashioned sixty, with tweed skirts and a fondness for head scarves, knotted into submission between her first and second chin. Of course, he couldn't use this description before Angela – she might too easily see herself in it.

'They'll circulate that; it'll be in every garda's ear in the city within the next five minutes.' It was funny, but a year ago, he wouldn't have wanted any connection between his job and Maureen – and here he was now, when she'd get no mileage out of it, hauling in any favours he might still have to find her.

'You said she wouldn't have gone far. I'm going to head towards the church,' Angela said, pulling her coat about her and heading for the door.

'Right,' Slattery said and looked around the kitchen one more time. 'You've checked outside, round the back, the shed and…?' His voice drifted off when he met her eyes. 'Of course, you have, sorry.' He followed her out the front door, stood for a while, looking up and down the street. Many of the old neighbours had left here now, moved off to slightly more affluent homes, perhaps; Maureen would have liked that too, once. Slattery was never going to be one of those men who wanted to somehow advance his social standing by moving to the right area. In fact, he held any kind of social movement – particularly any desire for an upward climb – with a mixture of disdain and derision.

'I'll ring you… if I find her,' Angela said, and it struck him that perhaps, until she said it, she hadn't planned on letting him know, assuming that it mightn't bother him either way; depressingly, it wasn't even meant to be a taunt.

'Sure,' he said, heading for his car. 'And I'll ring you.' He sat in the driver's seat, drummed his fingers on the steering wheel – the truth was, he had no idea where Maureen might be now. He knew nothing about her, not really. He was familiar only with who she had been over thirty years ago.

He turned over the key in the engine and drove out of the little cul de sac of houses and onto the main Dublin Road. There was one place that now occurred to him, but it was a good five-mile walk. It was unlikely even Maureen would have the pig-headedness to take that on in the darkness of Limerick countryside with her injuries only healing after the car crash that had sent their worlds spinning. Her car had been written off and, for now, there was no mention of her replacing it. Dementia isn't a condition that lends itself easily to driving and a possible manslaughter charge hanging over her was enough to put her off the idea for good. He thought of Maureen, as black as any night in that dark coat, it made him shiver to think there was even a possibility that she would make the journey on foot.

Soon, he was out on the motorway, but only for half a mile before turning off. He turned into a narrow road, which was mean and miserable, wet and potholed – and depressingly familiar to Slattery, even though it was too long since he'd travelled it. The car jolted uncomfortably along the uneven track and when he pulled in next to a high weathered wall he felt as if he knew every inch of this place from memory, because it seemed nothing had changed here in all the years. He walked towards heavy iron gates, crosses wrought into their centre and painted white against the rusted black.

It was an old-fashioned cemetery, graves laid out in two halves with a central path just wide enough to accommodate a hearse for new arrivals. At its end, a marble altar was surrounded by various saints and winged angels who were perhaps meant to inspire some kind of hope in mourners that their loved ones were being looked over.

Slattery saw her immediately. She was the only other person here; it felt as if they were the only people around for miles. He stood for a moment, watching her; she was standing stock still, staring down at that modest headstone. He walked quickly towards her, half afraid to wonder if she'd been standing in that same spot all night long. As he neared her, he could see she was shaking and he couldn't be sure if it was cold or shock or something much, much worse – but what?

'Maureen.' He tried to keep his voice calm and even. 'Are you ready now? I've brought the car round.' He reached out for her, hoped that if he didn't make a big deal out of things, she might just trot along with him and he could get her home and warm and maybe call out her doctor to give her a once over.

'There you are.' She smiled at him, a rigid frightened move-ment of her lips that didn't reach her eyes, which were filled with tears. 'I thought you got lost on me, it feels like I've been waiting forever…' She shook her head a little crossly. 'But sure isn't that the story of our lives?'

'Well, come along, I'm here now.' He placed his hand around her back and the movement felt somehow strange and right. He couldn't remember the last time he'd touched his wife, even a casual rubbing together of their skin. There were no opportunities – they didn't brush against each other on the stairs or lie next to each other at night.

'God, it's cold out here.' Her teeth were chattering.

'It is that,' Slattery said and he looked back at his sister's grave, catching just a glimpse of her name – Una – and the small line of words his father had insisted they add as if it were an epilogue to her life. *Gone too soon.* Other families had written things on their loved one's headstones like, *Always missed* or *Pray for the soul of.* It struck Slattery at the time that his father was right. It was too simple – *gone too soon* – because they would never really be able to let her go completely.

Wasn't that it with murders, though? Wasn't it why he'd joined the Gardai and why he'd so badly wanted into the Murder Team? It was the reason he'd married Maureen – Una's best friend, the first one to find her that terrible evening. In the beginning she'd talked about nothing else, but as the time went on, it seemed to drift away from them – without it, without Una – there wasn't really much more to tie them together. Apart from Angela. That sent a creeping tingle of guilt through him. He looked back once more at his sister's grave. Its modesty was almost a recrimination: telling him, he should have done better. Perhaps that's why Maureen had ended up here today. Maybe Una was letting him know that it might not be too late to make something of the commitments he'd made all those years ago.

Back at the car, Slattery pulled his collar closer to his neck, opened the passenger door for Maureen and waited until she'd tucked the damp material of her coat around her.

'There was something,' she murmured as he sat in the driver's seat next to her. He tried to ignore a bulky quilt of cloud advancing from the west. It looked as if the rain was not finished with them yet.

'Oh?' he said, now turning his thoughts back to Eleanor Marshall and the interviews they'd been carrying out over in Curlew Hall. He was good at letting her prattle on while he escaped into his thoughts and punctuated her one-sided conversation with meaningless words of acknowledgement; he'd had a lifetime of practice.

'It was a boy…' She looked out the window as he turned the car. Perhaps they both rested their eyes one more time on Una's gravestone in the distance. 'Yes, that was it, Una told me it was a secret, but she was going to meet a boy that day.'

Slattery froze, felt as if the very blood in his veins had turned to ice. The car conked out beneath him and he stared at Maureen, who seemed to be completely unaware of what she'd just said.

CHAPTER 21

Day 5

'You look like shit,' Slattery told her as she hung her jacket on the old coat stand that stood to crooked attention by the incident-room door.

'And you think you look any better?' Iris said.

'I've never traded on my looks,' he said, and she knew he was just trying to knock a retort from her.

'Well, it's a bit late for you to start trying now, I suppose,' she said sweetly.

'Apparently, Byrne's been prowling about already,' Slattery said lazily. None of them bothered Slattery too much. Iris wondered if it was because he had no ambition and nothing much to lose or if he'd always known that, somehow, he was smarter than any of them. He looked sometimes at Byrne as if he'd wipe the floor with him, if he could be bothered. She'd seen him wriggle out from certain dismissal, with an ease that said much about his survival instincts.

Iris walked to the case board and spent some time organizing her thoughts about the details there. Too soon, the incident room began to fill up with their colleagues, the buzz of technology gearing up for a busy day. Coats were flung across chairs and there was a stampede, with yesterday's mug and spoon in hand, to the corner where a kettle was on constant boil at this hour. There comes a point in an investigation when the early-morning latte and freshly dry-cleaned suit are forsaken in favour of instant coffee and whatever looked cleanest on the bedroom floor. *Any news?*

'What's that?' Byrne was standing behind her.

'Nothing, just making small talk,' Slattery said as if he was a man who couldn't manage a gloomy silence with the best of them.

'Getting ready for the morning briefing, and the press conference, eh?' Byrne said, but his voice was clipped as if there was something he wanted to say, but he was holding back. Then he lowered his head. 'You called to Marshall yesterday?' It was a question, but it didn't require an answer.

'Yes, sir. We have the press room booked and we'll have packs made up beforehand,' Iris said, standing up to look him in the eye.

'Well done, carry on.' He made his way out of the incident room with a slightly lighter step than usual. 'Just give me a shout an hour before the conference,' he said as he headed back to his well-appointed office.

They already knew about the body. Iris had heard it on the news; of course, they couldn't confirm anything either way, not yet. You could smell it, here in the press room – probably the best room in Corbally, the equivalent of the good parlour in many an old Irish house. Still, for all the piped-in air freshener, there was no mistaking the scent of the baying journalists. It seemed half the media in the country had turned out – no mean feat considering that they'd only had three hours' notice. Still, they were sitting or standing where seats had run out, cameras poised, microphones and phones ready to record every detail that Iris was prepared to give and hoping for a few that she wasn't.

The truth was, Iris knew, she'd only called this to get a more up-to-date photograph of Eleanor in front of people's noses. The earlier one – the one that Kit Marshall had issued – had been of a girl four years younger than the image snapped by Suz Mullins

in the week before Eleanor had disappeared. It was a lovely photograph – no doubt about it, Eleanor was certainly photogenic.
Suz had managed to catch her off guard, a moment suspended
between patting a stray dog who'd wandered into the unit and
looking towards the camera. Eleanor's skin was flawless, her eyes
clear and her hair silky – unlike a lot of the images of teenage
girls that the press would normally have to work with, she was
make-up free, no ugly smears of shade and shadow to make her
into anything she wasn't. It was an endearing image; one that Iris
hoped would resonate with the public.

Slattery cleared his throat as Iris, the Marshalls and Byrne
all trooped towards the podium. It was loud enough to cause a
ripple of interest that spread like a Mexican wave to silence in
the room.

'Thank you all for coming here today,' Iris began, knowing
only too well that if a story had been bigger on the east coast,
they wouldn't have managed to get a full front row. 'I'm Acting
Inspector Iris Locke and I'm leading out the Murder Team on the
investigation into the death of Rachel McDermott.' She halted
for a moment, before introducing the Marshalls and Byrne and
giving the one or two old-school reporters a chance to scribble
down the names. 'I think you're all aware that another body was
discovered out at Curlew Cross.'

'Can you give us a name yet?' an eager reporter shouted from
the back of the room.

'Yes. I'm able to confirm now that the victim was Mr and
Mrs Marshall's daughter.' She stopped; she knew it was too soon
for them to know. The next words caused a shudder of greedy
excitement. 'Their younger daughter – Karena. We are, of course,
officially extending our condolences to Mr and Mrs Marshall.
You'll all understand how difficult it is for them to be here today.'

'But…' a young, glamorous reporter, local, from the front row
tried to interrupt, but Iris put up her hands to finish. None of

the waiting press had expected this – they'd expected this body to be Eleanor's.

'Karena Marshall's body was found by a jogger in Curlew Woods. We are investigating her death, as the circumstances are suspicious.' She nodded towards McGonagle who had already created folders with a copy of a press release and that one striking photograph of Eleanor, and who was now handing them out around the room. 'Obviously, we're appealing to anyone who might know anything about the events surrounding this tragic death to come forward. In relation to this latest tragedy, we're looking for anyone in the Curlew Cross area to call us, if only to eliminate them from our enquiries.'

'And the other Marshall girl?' A voice came from the back of the room. 'Eleanor?'

'If you look in your press packs, you'll see an up-to-date photograph of Eleanor. She's still missing and at this stage, as you can imagine, her family are really concerned for her safety. Since Eleanor went missing, she has been spotted only once, on a back road in the far north of Curlew Woods. We're really looking for as much help as we can get to bring her home safely to her family at this point.'

'Is she dangerous?' the glamorous reporter from the front row asked.

'She's extremely vulnerable.' Kit Marshall cleared his throat before leaning forward. 'She has epilepsy and so she could be very ill. We're just afraid at this point that she might be in danger from the person who murdered her sister and that poor McDermott girl.'

'There's been a mention of her having been kidnapped?' a reporter with a thick Midlands accent asked from the centre of the room.

'We're looking at every avenue, but there has been no ransom note and nothing in Eleanor's disappearance to point to that so far.'

'Although,' Kit put in quickly, 'it does seem pretty obvious to us that she is the target of some violent plan.'

'Our investigation is moving forward,' Iris cut him off. 'As Mr Marshall has pointed out, Eleanor is a vulnerable young girl and the fact that she may not have medication to treat her epilepsy is a huge worry in terms of getting her back safely. We really need to get this newer image into the public eye, if it's possible today…'

Iris looked around the room; it was a sea of risen hands, each one wanting to ask their own question which was a version of the same thing. Was Eleanor Marshall their killer? Or was she a vulnerable young girl caught up in something that was more dangerous than anyone wanted to imagine? Iris had to admit; those were exactly the questions she was asking herself.

CHAPTER 22

Nate Hegarty rented a flat in the centre of town. There was a slight smell of damp, covered over by the smell of yesterday's cooking and today's cigarettes. On the walls there was a string of broken lyrics from songs that Iris couldn't quite place, written in ornate yet strikingly different styles of calligraphy – talented boy.

Nate went through the night's events again, reluctantly, but to be fair, it was probably his hundredth time. Iris had a feeling Slattery was right; they were missing something and so they couldn't quite move on with the investigation without talking to him one more time. Everything about that night, except the last hour, slid firmly into place to build up a picture of Rachel's routine. They'd already documented this but Iris wanted to hear it again from Nate. He had left the bungalow for the night, leaving Rachel to carry out a number of mundane domestic tasks. He hadn't heard anything unusual.

'Could Eleanor Marshall have taken those tablets?' The question was sour on her lips. She knew the answer she wanted to hear.

'I don't know. I've thought about it a lot – the thing is, if she didn't take them, then that only leaves whoever killed Rachel.' His eyes wandered down towards his grubby hands. 'And, why would they bother? It's not like that sort of thing is going to sell on the streets, now is it? How would they get into the medication cupboard in the first place? It's locked up like the central bank. The only one there that night, except me and Rach, to know how to get at them was Eleanor, but I don't see how...'

'And Rachel would never have left the keys in the lock while she checked the stock or maybe cleaned out the cupboards?'

'I don't know. I was there when she counted them, but then we were chatting, you know, maybe she turned her back on them for a minute, it's hard to remember at this stage. A week ago, I'd have said *no,* obviously, we thought the unit was safe for Eleanor, otherwise…' Nate clicked his tongue, thinking as much as speaking.

'Are you doing okay?' she asked.

'Ah yeah, I'm fine.' Frosty sunlight streamed unkindly from a nearby window across his face, highlighting uneven skin scarred by acne when he was younger.

'It's a big shock, you know, all of this,' Iris said softly.

'It is,' Nate agreed. 'It doesn't help that my supervisor isn't that impressed that I'd skived off on the night when… well, you know…'

'In some ways, it was the worst timing, eh?' Slattery said, but of course, it meant that Hegarty had an alibi and if he'd been at work, monitoring a perimeter fence or whatever he was meant to be doing, he'd be in the frame now every bit as much as Eleanor.

'Story of my life,' Nate said.

'Sorry about that, mate.' Slattery was managing to keep his friendly side going.

'We're looking to track down Eleanor's file…' said Iris.

'Her file, like the files in Curlew Hall?'

'Her case file. It was archived, but someone, Rachel probably, had requested it a few weeks ago.'

'And you're wondering if I might know where it is now?' His interest was piqued.

'That's the million-euro question, I'm afraid. We're trying to track it down.'

'Oh well, I'll keep a lookout, I suppose.' Nate cast his eyes towards the window, no file here at least. 'I can't do much more than that for you.'

'We've heard it's not the only thing to go missing these past few weeks,' Slattery said softly.

'Oh?' Nate stuck his chin out, perhaps awaiting a charge of theft next.

'Yes, apparently you've lost a sum of money – we've heard that you've been very eager to get it back.'

'Oh, that. Nah, I got that sorted, last week. I'm all set now,' he said relaxing again, as if whatever threat he'd expected had passed.

'So, would you like to tell us? It's just we heard half a story and it wouldn't be the good half, if you know what I mean,' Slattery said coldly.

'Ah, well, then you haven't heard the right story so.' Nate shook his head. 'It was nothing, just a mix-up. I sold my phone and some old computer games, made a couple of hundred on them, collected the money on my way to work. I thought someone had swiped it, but then, later, when I looked in my car, there it was, under some old rubbish in the back seat.'

'Who did you sell them to?'

'It's all above board, I was saving for a new games console, deposited the money in the bank and then got myself a state-of-the-art set-up.' He pointed across at a sleek system.

'Hmm.' Slattery was non-committal, but Iris knew that he too was inclined to believe Nate. Like he said, bad timing.

The incident room was almost empty when Iris returned to the station. She walked over to the Perspex-covered wall. Scanning the various photographs, maps of the woods and lists of relevant people questioned, her mind returned to Curlew Hall. She unclipped a photo of the woods, holding it between her hands. It was one hundred and forty shades of green, peeling off into the distance, with no end in sight. The police photographer had taken it along one of the tracks winding around the countryside.

Where is she? Please, just one clue…help us find her before it's too late.

She thought again of the girls' mother. Susan arrived out at the search early this morning. There were twenty-six officers assigned now to patrolling and searching the woods, a pity they'd spent so much time – thanks to Ahearn – searching in the wrong bloody direction.

She had been hauled over the coals by Byrne earlier in the morning for almost an hour. What progress had they made? How could they spend so much and have so little to show for it? His mood had been black; his face flushed when he had offloaded the news that the powers that be were not happy with the way the investigation was being handled. There would be a new team put in place and the investigation would be handed over to Dublin Castle.

After it, Iris was actually happy to see Slattery slumping in his chair, gazing out the window as if he hadn't a care in the world, which of course, couldn't be farther from the truth. He was a ball of angry emotion, bundled up into an *I-couldn't-care-less* sham. Iris didn't ask him about his wife anymore, she'd seen him bark viciously at June anytime the subject was brought up.

'Well?' he glared at Iris. 'An update…' His head inclined towards the rickety chair opposite and she knew she was being invited to offload her worries onto him. She flopped down dead beat into the chair before him, grabbing a refill pad and cheap half-chewed biro from an otherwise deserted desk as she passed.

'So, what have we got?' He was chewing gum, never a good sign.

'Well, we have the search team out at Comeragh Pass. They changed their route to head in the direction we worked out on the map. I checked with—' Iris began.

'Ox balls. You know what Byrne said to me earlier when I met him in the corridor?' Slattery was livid. 'They're thinking of giving the investigation over to Dublin Castle. As if that crowd of Jackeens would have the first clue.' He managed to divert his attention to the door where a uniform was about to come in with a cup of tea, but on Slattery's bark reversed meekly in his tracks. 'Anyway, the upshot if we don't get this thing shaped up—'

'I know,' Iris said flatly. 'I met with him this morning, an hour-long sermon,' she managed to say before he started to chew crossly again. 'I was going to break it to the team tonight.'

'I just don't understand, they can't mean to leave a girl out there somewhere, God knows where, not a girl like that, she hasn't got a…' He dropped his voice, as if some of the pent-up fury was releasing through an invisible valve.

'Come on, Slattery, you know what it means. They think she's dead already.'

'She's out there and she was alive and well twenty-four hours ago,' Slattery said obstinately. 'What do you make of *her*, of Susan Marshall?'

'Honestly?' Iris thought about it for a moment. 'She must be at her wit's end. Scared too, I'd say, for all of them.' Iris walked to the window, looking out across the rougher part of town. 'Why, what do you think?'

'I suppose she is frightened.' He was thoughtful, carefully selecting his next words. 'We know she's married to a bully.'

'He definitely beats her, those marks…' The marks covering Susan's arms were old, meted out over years, but that kind of violence doesn't just leave a marriage. It outlives love; usually it lasts longer than either spouse.

'Come on, you know as well as I do that the best bullies never have to actually raise a hand to anyone. So we know he throws her the occasional punch, but it's deeper than that, much more than just beating her.' Slattery blew out long and slow, can't save them all.

'Okay, so she's scared of him, of Kit Marshall,' Iris continued, noticing a number of smoking chimneys in the distance. People were lighting their fires to keep out the west of Ireland's draughts and damp. Iris shivered. 'Maybe she's scared of something else as well. It's not unreasonable to suggest she's worried about her daughter, afraid of what might become of her.'

'And of course, now there's grief too.' Slattery looked at her, weighing it up. He faltered; he didn't want to continue with this line of thought. 'What if she's scared that we *do* find her, what if…?'

'Go on?' She was hooked now, an uncomfortable, sickly knot rising deep in her stomach.

'Ah, I'm going off on a tangent, sure. With what they've been through these past few days, she probably doesn't know how to react.'

'Will you just say it?'

'Right, but it's so off the wall. What if they wanted to get rid of her? What if the emotion we can't figure out is guilt, what if…?'

'Yeah, you're right. What if we got some real evidence before we go adding yet another suspect to our list?'

'It was just a feeling.' He turned the seat around towards the desk. They stayed in silence for a few minutes. The stillness was calming, Iris was glad; it was hard to get anything done while Slattery bitched about Byrne. 'Okay, then you might as well let me know how this morning went.'

Iris quickly filled him in on Byrne's briefing.

'Byrne thinks Ahearn is onto something with the drugs angle. He wants us to pursue it,' she said. They still had no other explanation for that envelope of money Tim McDermott had dropped off with them.

'Fair enough, except we're sure that Nate's explanation pans out?'

'Yes, I'm happy with the story about the missing money, that's easily checked.'

'But?'

'I still think he's lying about what he was up to that night. I don't believe him and I don't believe Tania Quirke.'

'Yeah, well I'm with you there and that means he's the one person who has means and, maybe, he has motive too.' Slattery looked at her for a moment.

'So, he's still in the frame,' Iris said softly.

Slattery swung about in his seat. 'June, have we found any connection between Karena and Rachel McDermott other than the Marshalls?' It was as if he'd uncannily read Iris's mind.

'No, still looking though,' June said, hardly taking her eyes from the screen before her.

Iris's phone rang out somewhere in the busy incident room, the trilling sound caught her attention for a minute. She looked at the clock on the wall behind Slattery's desk – plenty of time yet. Iris was glad of the opportunity to catch her breath and go over the casebook in the quiet.

There was no point going home now, wherever that was – Mrs Leddy's boarding house hardly qualified as home. She clicked the blue screen before her. It had been two days since she'd checked her emails. She might have felt guilty if she wasn't so tired and achy. Twenty-nine new messages; she hated emails. She scrolled down through them quickly: the usual newsletters, follow-ups from other cases that had slipped onto the back burner for a few days. Then, a name – unfamiliar – in her inbox. She was about to transfer it to trash, had right-clicked when her hand froze. The date was just two hours ago, the subject was Eleanor Marshall, but it was the sender's name that fired a jangle through her spine. *From: Rachel McDermott.* Someone was using her email.

CHAPTER 23

Slattery invested almost three hours in getting pissed before any of his colleagues arrived at the Ship Inn to end their day with an unofficial debriefing session. He called for another pint, pessimistically aware that his efforts were not working. He couldn't shake Maureen's words from his thoughts. He'd left Iris in Corbally, poring over the case book and a mountain of other paperwork. Slattery was a nose man – he never went in for combing through files: give him a couple of bystanders and he'd sniff out a suspect faster than any beagle. Iris was welcome to the inspector's job – if only because of the amount of paperwork that came with it.

Well, actually, she was welcome to the bullshit kowtowing and politics that came with it even more heartily, none of those skills were in Slattery's arsenal and he'd never had any desire to acquire them. Slattery knew it and Byrne knew it. Grady certainly knew it and so he'd never even asked him to step into the slot that was sure to become vacant at some point since they didn't seem to be able to hang onto a superintendent for any longer than it took tea to cool on a winter's morning. It would work out well, having Iris as the cigire. The inspector's job was vital to the smooth working of the team.

Even if they had resented her when she first arrived, now there was a quiet respect for Iris. She'd cracked a case that ended up pulling her own world down around her, but she'd done it. She had the determination to see the unthinkable through to the end and Slattery – for one – had every intention of being behind her as long as she needed him. She was young, true, but that didn't mean she wasn't fit for the job. People liked her, she was straightforward, no games, no agenda other than the one she put on the table from day one. She was ambitious, but then again, wasn't everyone? Even Slattery at one time had a flame of ambition within him. Without it, he wouldn't have made Murder. There were plenty who started out with him still turning up in uniform, pencil pushers now mostly, doling out forms or sitting at a desk in some forgotten outpost. Slattery had been hungry enough to go after the Murder Team and even if he had no intention of rising through the ranks, he was ambitious enough not to want to leave and hanging on sometimes took as much effort as getting in.

'Penny for them.' June plonked herself on the bar stool next to him.

'Hardly worth even that.' He barely lifted his head to acknowledge her, staring instead trance-like into his drink.

'True, but still, be nice to know what's so interesting that's keeping you here instead of sending you home to Maureen.' She nodded at the barman who was already reaching half-heartedly for an orange juice.

'Don't bloody start, it's been a long day.'

'I'm sure it has.' She fiddled with change, handing over the exact price of her drink.

'Yeah, well, it's not like she'd want me there anyway. At this point, it's only on rare occasions she lets me in the door.' He scowled. 'Anyway, I'm sure some of the neighbours think I've been dead for years.' He shook his head. 'And neither my wife nor daughter have bothered to put that notion to bed.' It might have been laughable, if it wasn't for the fact that Slattery could see it would have suited Maureen so much better to be a widow than, as she termed it, a deserted wife.

'You can't blame them entirely, Ben. You know, you've hardly been a model husband or father.'

'I know, but here's the thing... how do I step into the role that needs to be filled at this late stage...Angela bloody hates me.'

'Ah, now, I'm sure that's not true, "hate's" a strong word.' She shook her head, they'd both seen what hate could do to a person.

'Okay, well she doesn't like me. Actually, I have a feeling that while she wants me to step up to the plate in some ways, the more I do, the more she resents me being there.'

'And Maureen?'

'So far, she's putting up with me. She knows that what lies ahead is inevitable, for now, mostly she's doing okay, but the doctors have said the day will come when she's going to need full-time care and you know Maureen, she may be a martyr but she's determined not to be a burden.' He was dreading it; the idea of Maureen, always such a tower of strength, becoming dependent and frightened. He'd seen dementia before; it haunted him, that look of fear it branded across people's eyes. Maureen had never been afraid of anything in her life, but he knew, with certainty, that once the disease took her over everything in her world would shift, so life would become a routine of missing words, lost direction and then, most cruelly, depleting fluency until the woman he'd known for so long would disappear within herself.

'Maybe, Slattery, you need her more than she needs you now.' June said what he'd already known, but would never be brave enough to admit.

'Oh, June, can't I just have my pint in peace?' He looked at her as she got up to leave, but they both knew she'd won. She'd said what had been burning between them – that warning that there wasn't much time left if he wanted to make up for ground lost. 'Bloody hell,' he said, draining his pint and leaving a couple of coins on the counter beside his empty glass. He barged past Tony Ahearn and a couple of youngsters that had only just made it into uniform in the last year or two.

'Excuse us,' Tony said sarcastically, and Slattery chose to ignore whatever snide remark he was likely to make behind his back as he barrelled down St Anthony Terrace.

There was a cold wind whipping up and driving in from the Atlantic, up the Shannon and right through to the quick of his bones. It forced him into a steady speed, although he had no definite destination in mind. The truth was the Ship Inn was becoming too crowded these days. A man couldn't think when his drinking time was interrupted by do-gooders like June. She meant no wrong and, God knows, she'd saved his bacon enough times over the years to have earned the right to say her piece once in a while – but still, it wasn't her words that gnawed at him now. It was something else, the notion behind them. There was no getting out of his responsibility to Maureen at this stage. It was not born out of the vows they'd taken all those years ago, neither was it out of love. Rather, Slattery knew, even if June didn't, its seeds had been sown before they'd ever married.

The roots of responsibility towards Maureen had been planted that evening over four decades earlier when he had been called to a neighbour's telephone and she'd vomited the terrible news that she'd just found Una – his sister. Older, glamorous, a little out of hand, but not so much that she wouldn't settle, Una Slattery never got the chance. Maureen found her dead on a shaggy brown mat before the electric two-bar heater in the flat they shared. Slattery had been three years younger than the two girls; he'd watched them enviously make new lives in the city, earn their own money and come and go as they pleased. There'd be no more pleasing herself for Una after that, he'd thought as Maureen's words had echoed across the telephone line. It turned out, there'd be no more pleasing any of them. After that, the guards had arrived at their front door, but Slattery had already told his father the terrible news. That simple phone call from Maureen to him had been the start of forging a relationship that had lasted, in its imperfection and disappointment, for over thirty years. And perhaps it was that unguarded comment made at the cemetery that had sent his thoughts into overdrive.

The fact was, he thought he knew everything about what had happened to Una – well, everything he needed to know if her murder could have been solved. Well now, that belief had been burst, as if Maureen had stuck a pin in the balloon of his understanding of that time. They say a drunken mind speaks a sober heart. Maureen, when he'd found her yesterday, had not been lucid, did the same thing stick? Had those words been shored up for decades between them and only spoken because her guard had been lifted recklessly by dementia? And what did it mean anyway – at this stage, so many years down the line, did it really make any difference in the end? He wasn't sure.

Even if there was more to learn, he knew that extracting it from Maureen would be a job in itself, she was like a stone when it came to telling him things. He had believed that he had done that to her, over the years, her only method of retaliation was to keep whatever small secrets she had to herself. Honestly, it hadn't bothered him, if anything he was glad of the respite from her constant chattering, but this was different. This was something she'd known from the very start and she hadn't told anyone, not even the detectives running the investigation at the time.

He stood in a doorway for a moment, reached into his jacket pocket and pulled out his pack of cigarettes, lit one quickly in spite of the growing bluster about him. He was in the mood for rain. He turned up towards the quays, enjoying the moist breeze on his face. It cleansed some of the grime from his thoughts. He crossed the road and stood for a while, finishing his smoke, then tipped the butt into the river, knowing that Iris would probably have a fit if she saw him do it.

It was funny that she should pop into his head now. He wondered if she'd given up on the files for the day, or if she'd spend another night poring over the case book before rushing home and freshening up the following morning. God, he could remember when he'd done that, it seemed a long time ago. Was it worth it? It had cost him his marriage, his family – any stamp of normality he might have hoped for. And then, it settled on him…

Maureen hadn't known. She'd never known. Perhaps the psych boys would call it post-traumatic stress, but she'd never have lied or omitted a detail like that from the police. She just couldn't have.

Those words that had haunted him since she'd uttered them earlier – it was the disease that was all – anything else was unthinkable. He looked down into the black water, cold and unforgiving. PTSD. The term blanketed across his thoughts for a moment, as if it reverberated with something much more recent. And then it clicked.

That first time they'd met with the Marshalls, something had hung in the air between the couple. Kit Marshall had believed his wife had cut all ties – or had he? All of a sudden, Slattery could see a small crack, a question they'd never asked and one that might just go some way to settling a few of the nerve endings that bristled with this case.

CHAPTER 24

Eleanor saw it, or rather heard it, first. He ran through the woods, over and back, over and back. He would have trampled over her the second time if she hadn't scampered up the leaning oak. She moved as quickly as she could, high up, over the track and watched, and then her eyes followed him keenly for as far as she could. She wasn't sure if he was real or if she hadn't quite woken from her sleep.

When she saw his face, she knew. It was a face wizened with survival; a muscular body ready to pounce on any prey weaker than he was. He was no different to Nate Hegarty – that same stench, that same iniquity and if he came across her she might not survive. She knew it now even more than she'd known it when she hid among the thick rhododendrons earlier. It was in his eyes.

When he moved away, she clambered down the tree, running feral through the woodlands, jumping over dead wood, ran and ran and then, when it was safe, she cowered, low to the ground. She backed away from the hollow. She saw all she needed to see, she'd stay out of his way. She crept as silently as she could, competing with the smaller animals who furrowed through the undergrowth for silent footsteps, undetectable amid the rustling sounds of the woods.

She dug deep in the pocket of her jog bottoms. The last tablet. She should take it now. She fished it into her grubby hand and slid it onto her tongue. She never liked taking tablets, but somehow, it wasn't quite so bad when you were in charge of them yourself.

If only she could make people understand that. Her heart had been pummelling against her rib cage for as long as she had been resting here; now her head was beginning to swim.

She imagined that she heard them, close by, the heavy feet on the forest floor; unmistakable. They were moving slowly, determinedly, catching her up. She thought she could hear the dogs, the calls. She pushed herself forward, her hands in fists below her, and the weight of her body increased by the wet that clung to every part of her. She stank of the days and nights she spent here. She didn't smell of talcum powder and disinfectant anymore.

She had to move fast. The river had put some space between her and the searchers, but could they be on either side by now? Her head felt clearer today, clearer than it had been in years, it was the lack of medication. She could think, she could see. Then she heard a familiar voice, somewhere closer than the other noises. 'E-L-E-A-N-O-R.' It called out her name and there was that quality, what was the word people used? Musical? Dangerous.

So, she ran away from the searchers. She ran from Curlew Hall. All the while she prayed that what she was running towards wasn't a hundred times worse than what had come before. She had to keep running. Run to the death, she knew now.

CHAPTER 25

Ahearn and two of the uniforms picked up Nate Hegarty just as he was returning with what was probably his main meal of the day from the local Chinese takeaway. *No need to thank me*, Ahearn had said smugly. In Iris's mind, there wasn't much worse than a couple of hours in a windowless room with Nate Hegarty belching onion and garlic breath across the table at her. They drew the short straw and ended up in the smallest of all the interview rooms. Busy night.

Iris had set about putting together a few choice shots of Rachel McDermott, all of them in death. The images were grim, the brutal attack knocking out the essence of all that would have made her familiar to Hegarty. If Hegarty was the killer and he didn't already have nightmares, this would surely knock the stuffing out of him. Nate Hegarty was going to know that this was no fishing trip the minute he looked at these images. Iris included one particularly grisly photo, a post-mortem shot, just for effect.

When Hegarty arrived, he looked even younger than Iris remembered. A tatty dirty T-shirt covered his scrawny neglected body, and tracksuit bottoms that looked a few sizes too big only made him seem more adolescent. She shivered when she looked at him, but oddly he seemed oblivious to the cold weather outside.

'Nate Hegarty, for the purpose of the tape' – Iris barely nodded up at the camera behind her back –'I'm cautioning you, that anything you say will be recorded and may be used in evidence. You have a right to…' She pit-patted the caution, had said it too often to hear the words anymore. A lengthy prayer learned years ago, meaningless now.

'I won't be saying anything until ye get a solicitor for me, right?' Hegarty, for his part, looked suitably jaded, he had believed they were finished with him last time. His stance held the truculence of a teenager. Deep down Iris cursed: they could be here a while.

'Of course, Nate. The duty one okay or would you prefer to go private?' Iris's voice was smooth as velvet. She'd rattle him later, when they needed to.

'I've nothin' to hide, duty one will be just fine, thanks.'

Iris nodded to Ahearn. 'I think we might catch John O'Boyle before he leaves, he was in interview room number one – with Tania.' She watched as Hegarty flinched. They hadn't actually picked up Tania Quirke, Hegarty's girlfriend. Obviously, he didn't know that and from his expression he didn't like it.

'So, what's all this about anyway?' he said sharply, his eyes darting from one to the other.

'Just a friendly chat about Rachel McDermott to see if you might be able to tell us what happened the night she died.'

'Friends don't caution each other,' Hegarty said gruffly.

'No, but better to be safe than sorry, yeah?' Tony Ahearn was doing affable and he was good at it, Iris noticed. She could see how he'd go down a treat with the powers that be.

'Anyway, Tania told you already, I was with her that night– never left the flat all night.'

'Hmm.' Iris waited while Nate shifted in his chair.

'Ye're not going to pin this on me, if that's what ye think.' His voice had risen just slightly. It was enough to let Iris know he was becoming uncomfortable. He was hiding something and whether it had anything to do with Rachel McDermott was what they had to find out.

'Word has it that you and Rachel fell out a while ago, something about money owed?' Ahearn smiled across at the boy.

'Well, word is wrong. Me and Rachel were mates, good mates. I'm gutted over what happened to her.'

'My contacts must be mistaken.' Tony leafed through the pages that Iris had assembled in the file, laying each of the photographs out across the table. First to last, in ascending order of grotesqueness, this was hardly the Rachel that Nate would have remembered. 'Terrible thing to happen, though.' He waved a hand across each of the photos, gliding over Rachel's face as though caressing it with his long, tapered fingers. He halted at the last snap, taken during the autopsy. Most of Rachel's face had peeled away, her brain meaty and bloody to the left of her opened skull, waiting to be weighed, and then tossed back inside. Offal; dead, no good anymore. Tortured silence swathed the room, making their breathing resound loudly off the walls. Iris hoped Hegarty would want to end it, say something just to end it.

Eventually Nate Hegarty blew out a long breath. 'I know what you're trying to do here. I'm not stupid. You don't have anything so you're trying to find a patsy to stick it on. Well, that's not me.'

'That's not how we operate,' Iris said coolly. 'Nate, it's all very transparent here, everything is recorded. We've explained we only want to find the truth.'

'I need a fag.'

'You can't smoke here.'

'Fine, I need to get out of here so…' He looked across at Iris; suddenly she was the bad guy, but she was okay with that. 'Am I under arrest or what?' His eyes darted nervously between Iris and Ahearn, and then behind them at the camera trained on his miserable face.

'Of course, you're not under arrest, Nate. Like we said, you're just helping us with our enquiries, right?'

'Yeah, right.'

'Do you know, I wouldn't half murder a fag either,' Tony Ahearn said conspiratorially, and they both headed off towards a narrow doorway that led into a yard filled with lost and found and the great abandoned.

Iris set off to look for John O'Boyle. The solicitor was a mild-mannered man, in his early sixties, completely at odds with the people he advocated for and yet respected and liked by all of them. Iris sent him in search of the two smokers.

'He's consulting with his brief,' Ahearn said, his voice heavy with sarcasm, when he arrived back in the incident room. 'Too good for scum like that, pity the days are gone when you could beat a decent confession out of rats like him.' His coarseness caught Iris by surprise; she wouldn't like to be working under this man. She decided the best approach was *least said and all that*, they could be waiting a while, so she went back to her desk.

The incident room was quiet, save for a few hangers on. The buzz that marked the beginning of an investigation had slowed to a low hum. Everyone was tired now. She opened her mailbox again, scrolled down through the messages. Her fingers shook as she opened the one from Rachel McDermott. The technical bureau were checking it out – gone now was the initial shock of seeing it sitting there. There was something eerie about seeing it sent from the girl in the glossy black-and-white photographs she'd just spread out in front of Nate Hegarty. She read it for what felt like the twentieth time. *The answer's in that file, it will lead you to finding Rachel's killer.*

'Locke?' Ahearn called from across the room. He was standing in the doorway. 'We're on. They've just gone back into the interview room.'

Nate Hegarty looked more relaxed as he reclined in his seat beside John O'Boyle. The smell of nicotine reeked across the room and Iris thought she might throw up if he came any closer; now she really was thankful he hadn't managed to eat that Chinese takeaway.

'My client is prepared to make a formal statement in connection with the night on which Rachel McDermott died,' said John.

'Okay.' Iris looked across at the sullen features opposite her.

'I need to know if ye've spoken to Tania first.'

'I'm afraid they don't have to tell you that, Nate.'

'No? I thought she said we were buddies.' He pointed a stumpy thumb in Iris's direction. 'I want to know where I am with Tania before I say anything official like.'

'We haven't talked to her yet, Nate.'

'Fine, I wasn't with her that night. I told her I was working, then when Rachel died, well, she thought I was doing… family work.'

'Go on, Nate.' Iris looked at him. He was pathetic, still only a boy, really.

'I've been having it off with a young wan from the estates.' His head jerked towards the camera at his back. 'She'll tell you I was with her that night, but Tania…'

'Wouldn't be very happy?' Tony Ahearn grinned, peas in a pod.

'She'd have me bloody guts. Great girl, but she has a shocking temper on her.'

'We'll have to check with this girl.'

Iris began to fold away the papers before her. The day was catching up with her. A bath would be just the ticket, a long hot soak. Unfortunately, Mrs Leddy's bathroom was hardly designed to invoke anything near a relaxing experience; anyway, chances were she'd just collapse into bed, too wound up to sleep, too tired to do anything else. Another short night of tossing and turning lay ahead.

'What was it you were saying about Rachel?' John O'Boyle cleared his throat.

'Oh, yeah.' Nate butted his head towards the photos. 'It was just, Rachel seemed to have come into money, lately. She'd started splashing cash about like it meant nothing to her. Gave me a loan to pay for repairs to my car and she wasn't in any great rush for it to be repaid.'

'And you think it might have some bearing on what happened to her?' Iris heard her own voice, soft as a whisper.

'I don't know, do I? It might have come from her communion money in the post office for all I know for certain.'

'Well, hazard a guess for us.' Iris sat forward now, but Nate seemed to shrink a little further into himself.

'All the same.' Tony Ahearn leaned closer to him; they might have been sharing a pint, splitting a bet on a sure win in the national. Insider knowledge. 'It might give us a better picture.' And he ran a finger over the folder of photos once more.

'Once, a while ago now, we were both very drunk, but it's the kind of thing that stays with you.' He closed his eyes. 'Rach hinted she had something on Kit Marshall. I had a feeling it was something big, but…'

'Yes?'

'Well, that's the thing, if it was anyone else but Rach – at the time I couldn't imagine her blackmailing the cat, to be honest. She just wasn't like that. But then, I never expected her to be murdered either so…' He exhaled. More soft information. It meant nothing, it could mean everything – finally they had a connection outside of Eleanor. 'That was it, just drinking talk. We were both too pissed to know what we were saying. I probably told her I screwed my granny.' He grinned across at Ahearn. 'I didn't, by the way.'

The room fell into silence. The atmosphere absorbed another side to Rachel McDermott, a side Nate Hegarty had been aware of, but he'd have kept it to himself, if his own neck wasn't on the line.

'Anyway, about two months ago, suddenly Rach has all this cash, and like it's come from nowhere, but…' Hegarty's lower lip stuck out like a seven-year-old let down by his little mate. 'She wouldn't say where the money came from and, to be honest, I never properly asked. Well, it wasn't the kind of thing I could ask, you know?'

'So?'

'Well, it's obvious now, isn't it?'

'Is it?'

'She was blackmailing Kit Marshall, wasn't she?' Nate Hegarty's words rang too true around the room.

CHAPTER 26

Iris drove aimlessly and ended up at Cuckoo Lane. She knew this little road very well and although it led to nowhere of consequence, on the map it cut directly through Eleanor's route.

She hadn't planned to come here, but as she pulled the car to a stop, Iris knew it was inevitable. To assuage her guilt over having a dry bed to sleep in? Perhaps. On the other hand, maybe, just maybe, some small part of her thought she might actually run into Eleanor. That was just stupid. What would she do then? Convince her to get into the car, drive her coolly to the Marshall house and reunite her with her broken mother?

Eleanor haunted her all day, but night-time was even worse and this evening she had to get the sense of Nate Hegarty's words clinging to her thoughts out of her head. He couldn't tell them anymore; he said he'd never seen Eleanor's file, they'd no reason not to take his word for it. Still, the day proved difficult to leave behind. She was motivated by a combination of nerves and anxiety, probably as much for the past as for Eleanor, if she was honest.

The woods were silent, save for the few birds that were turning in for the night and the evening shift reporting for nocturnal duty; letting her know that the night-time sentry positions were filling fast. The car door squeaked nosily on neglected hinges as she threw it open. The noise pierced the otherwise sleepy woods, waking a grey crow from his stupor so he cascaded noisily from high branches, swooping over the bonnet and barely missing Iris's head.

Then she heard it. Not like the other sounds, this wasn't a rustling or a scurrying. It wasn't a bird high up tucking her head beneath resting wings for the night. This was more like a stalking. Movement that was stealthy, not stumbling. Eleanor, she imagined, would be running, or moving fast, bumping into things, tripping up – she wouldn't move like a shadow. That was the only word that came to Iris's mind as she turned the one hundred and eighty degrees to make sure she wasn't about to be set upon. Suddenly, she knew she wasn't alone; she shouldn't be here. Not now, not like this. Her car was only feet away, but Iris couldn't run, she could hardly walk and when she did, she barely trundled. A silhouette moved, somewhere to her left, only barely visible from the side of her eye, but it was enough to set her frayed nerves on edge.

'Eleanor? Hello? Eleanor?' Part of her knew the words were futile. If it was Eleanor, she didn't want to be found. If she had, she'd have got in that car the other night. Travelled in comfort to whatever hospital or Gardai station the old man arrived at first. If it wasn't Eleanor, then who was it? Iris moved forward. 'Eleanor, I'm here to help, it's okay. Please come out. I'm a garda. I'll take care of you…'

As she said the words, she felt a mass wrench of inhalation around her. It was as if all of the oxygen was sucked out from the woods. Perhaps, this presence – whoever, or whatever it was – didn't want the police anywhere near.

Instinctively she began to retrace her steps, backing slowly away from whatever was watching her, keeping her eyes on the foliage before her where the noise had come from only seconds earlier. The only thought going through her mind now was the location of her handgun. It was just a standard issue; she'd placed it in an inside pocket of her ridiculously oversized bag, on the passenger seat. *Shit, shit, shit,* the words tumbled through her. Retrieving it would be a nightmare in the dark. She cursed silently as she turned a throbbing ankle on one of the many gnarled roots that zigzagged across the boggy path. Only yards to go. She'd left the keys in the ignition, *stupid, stupid, stupid.*

The thing rustled again, too big – whatever it was. Too big to be Eleanor. She held her breath, held her stance. People talked about a predator cat roaming the woods that dashed along the butt of the Comeragh mountains. A few had even reported it at the station, convinced they saw a panther roaming freely beneath the trees. One of the national papers had come down hoping to get a picture of a bear or some other newsworthy predator, a wild cat escaped from a private collection, or perhaps set free from a travelling circus and not reported for fear of prosecution. All kinds of stories had done the rounds at the time. Dead sheep, once-off sightings and unexplainable damage had all combined to whip up local frenzy only months ago. Then, just as suddenly as the stories had begun, they stopped. Absently now, Iris began to wonder if they would surface again for lambing season at the end of the year.

That movement was too heavy for a wild cat and too menacing not to scare Iris to her very core. She stumbled once more, backwards slightly, stifled a small shriek that had escaped from somewhere beyond her belly, from some part deep in her rattling nerves.

Then she saw it move, properly this time, across her line of vision. It was moving hard and fast, across her path. Did it want to be seen? Did it realise she spotted it? She gathered herself up straight, stacking head and shoulders to make her as tall as she could be. The tingling feeling in her spine had disappeared, replaced now by full-throttle rasping darts that shot upwards and forwards just seconds apart, not allowing her to ignore her fear now.

The thing stopped, five, maybe four metres away, and assessed her. It was dark and long, sleek and smooth, with eyes that peered at her as if her presence here was even more surprising than his. Iris held her breath. For a moment, she was aware of every breathing, heart-beating sound around her, every rivulet of rain, every squeaking green leaf, but no pain. The shots and darts that she thought would tear her apart had faded away, her body on tenterhooks, waiting. Waiting for what? For fight or flight? Neither an option at the moment. She stood her ground, afraid to take her eyes away for those long seconds. Afraid that even one move could result in her stumbling, breaking the connection and then—

She imagined he'd be beside her in a fraction of a second. Those strong legs tearing up the earth, his hungry face breathing into hers. She shivered at the thought. Then he stood, perfect even teeth shining out in the darkness, but still, she knew it must be her imagination. In that second, she tried not to recoil, to hold on tight. She thought she might hit the ground, felt rather than planned her leg moving backwards, hands reaching behind her to break her imminent fall – and then she felt the cold metal of the car.

She placed her hand flat across the bonnet; it was reassuring, familiar, steadying. She kept her eyes straight on the woods before her, feeling her way round the side of the car like a blind woman, cast astray with no bearings. The familiar lines of her car guided her sweating hands, her body trailing, worn-out and scared. Surprisingly, her hands were steady and that, she knew, was probably a miracle. The fear that had consumed her when she caught sight of that emotionless face had managed to make her entire body shake involuntarily.

The door opened quietly this time. She took her eyes from the spot for only a second, and didn't see him blend into the enveloping foliage beyond. Once inside the car, she locked the doors immediately, reached for her bag and retrieved the handgun she'd placed there earlier. Had she dreamed it all? Had it just been her imagination? Why had he shown himself, she wondered, and what was he doing out here? It felt for those long few seconds as though he was warning her, threatening her to stay off his patch. Was he searching for Eleanor? She didn't want to think about that, prayed they'd find her first. Something told her that anything vulnerable finding itself in his path might end up paying a terrible price, even a temporarily vulnerable detective, and she shivered with a cold she couldn't blame on the mild evening.

CHAPTER 27

Day 6

The knock at the door was strong and authoritative. Real men never rang bells and Slattery had decided a long time ago, he was not a bell ringer. Imelda McDermott's shoes echoed on the Victorian tiles and he watched as she paused stiffly before a faded mirror to check that her normally immaculate hair sat just so.

'Mrs McDermott, I was passing so I hope you don't mind.' He was not tall, but his presence filled the doorway, he kept his smile lazy but his eyes were keen.

'You're welcome anytime, Mr Slattery. Actually, I tried to ring you.' She stood back from the door, holding it open for him. He walked past her into the hall and stood while she closed the door, his hands folded. His expression was almost sanguine.

He bent his head towards her. 'Is everything all right? Have you thought of something that might be able to help us?' He was following her now through the dark hallway, pulling up short when she stopped at the foot of the stairs.

'Well, there is something, if you'd like to take a look up here.' She was leading the way up the stairs, the carpet well worn, but perfectly maintained, cushioning the sound of her thick heels. She stopped three quarters of the way up, pointing at a small patch on the wall. Eventually she broke the silence. 'Don't you see it?'

'I see the torn wallpaper, but Mrs McDermott, I'm not sure what I'm meant to be looking at.'

'You don't understand…' She turned away from him, jerking her head towards the first floor so he would follow her. She made her way into a room facing the back garden; it was Rachel's room, neat and tidy. The smell of light, floral perfume still permeated the air despite the open window. 'Someone has been here, someone has broken in, I'm quite sure of it.' As she said the words her hands moved to her mouth and she turned away from him.

'Is anything missing?' His voice was gentle now.

Imelda McDermott looked at him for a moment, perhaps wondering how to explain. 'Not that I can tell, but I think I know what they were looking for.' She paused, looked at him now. 'Last night, late last night, I found a file. It was upstairs in the attic. We never go up there, to be honest. I'd never have thought, only Tim wanted a black tie for the funeral and I had a little rummage about. I didn't want to bother you, not at that hour, but I would have rung you…'

'Have you still got it?' He leaned closer to her, drawing her out, his words were soft whispers: *be not afraid*.

'Of course. It's the girl's file, a big thick file, all her notes probably. I know what that will mean to her family, I slept with it under my own bed.' The guilt, that's what the church gave you in the end, not peace, not calm, not even spirituality, really. Slattery knew the look well, had seen Maureen eaten up by it over the years. Imelda had chosen to take on the guilt for her daughter's death; even if they found her murderer, it would never be enough to lift the burden from her mother.

'Did you look at the file? Notice anything about it, any marks where maybe Rachel had been specifically reading?'

She was thoughtful, moving away from the drawers. 'I've never looked through anything that wasn't mine, never mind reading through a file that said "confidential".' She sat on the perfectly made bed, winding the thin wedding ring round her finger repeatedly.

Slattery had pulled latex gloves over his hands before further inspection. There was no doubt that the window had been opened with some force. Scrapings of white gloss paint lay forlornly on the heavily patterned carpet beneath the sill. 'What about your son? He wouldn't have opened this window just to freshen the place up?' He nodded towards the direction of the door, which shielded them somewhat from the slow thump of bass music playing somewhere downstairs.

'Tim?' The tone was incredulous, as though the very idea was ridiculous. She laughed a hollow sound from deep in her throat. 'Tim would be less likely to notice if the house needed an airing than Rachel was.' She returned her attention to the band on her left hand. Suddenly, she looked very old.

'I'm sorry, but I'm going to have to get some people here to look around, it may take a little while.' His eyes were almost apologetic.

'Look, there's something else, something about Rachel, something I didn't know when you came here the other day.'

'Yes?' he prompted. He was bending towards her, waiting, his face wrinkled with years of other people's worries and the weight of doing right. If someone had broken into her house, then she had to consider that there might be more to Rachel's death than just the frenzied attack of a madwoman. 'Imelda, is there something you want to tell me?' He was jolting her back – back to Rachel's room, away from her thoughts, back to the unfamiliar territory that had become reality.

'Well, you probably already know, but I didn't realise, I'd never have imagined…' Tears at the back of her eyes were welling up and reddening the normally clear whites. 'Just yesterday, Tim told me, he was…'

'Imelda, whatever it is, it can't hurt Rachel anymore.'

Down the stairs the sound of the Swiss clock that had hung in the hall for longer than she had lived in this old house called out the hour. 'I think she was involved with drugs.' The words were out; no other way to say it. The first words were the hardest. After that, they plummeted in a free-fall sort of way, releasing with them some of the pent-up grief that had so far only found expression with the odd single tear, dropped and quickly wiped away. There was no place for tears in Imelda's world. As she always had, she squared her shoulders and got on with things. She told him everything that she'd heard: her daughter liked to use cannabis. Imelda's imagination did the rest. Her grief conflated this one unexpected truth with the money and then she had taken the huge leap into the impossible.

'Do you think she might have been selling drugs?' The tears were streaming down her cheeks now, the familiar memory of her lovely daughter lost in a maelstrom of grief and shame. 'Do you suppose that's where the money came from?' Her voice was sad, as close to defeat as she'd ever been.

'No.' Slattery's voice was calm. 'No, I don't for one moment think Rachel sold drugs. I think that like every other youngster in this town, she wanted to experiment. These days, well, it's like smoking a fag was when we were young – no different if you're smart enough to pull away from it in time.'

'Thank you,' she said softly. 'Thank you for putting my mind at rest, I couldn't have borne to think…'

'Who told you about the drugs?'

'Tim says it's common knowledge, that every kid in the place is doing them and Rachel was no worse than any of them.' She searched his face, willing him to tell her that at least that much was true.

'Mrs McDermott.' Slattery leaned closer and his face softened. 'Imelda, Tim is right, so please, try not to worry about that now.'

'Thanks be to God for that.' She exhaled.

'But.' His voice was strong, low. 'We still can't figure out how she came into that large sum of money you found.'

'Maybe she was saving up, putting the few pounds aside?' Imelda could convince herself of that at least for a while.

'There was a lot of money in that box, Imelda, not the kind of money you put aside when you're earning what Rachel was and trying to live too.'

'It doesn't mean she was doing anything wrong though. I mean, there could be a simple explanation.' Her voice rose, just a decibel, but enough to sound desperate.

'I'm sure there is,' Slattery said softly, looking around the room again.

'It was the window,' she finally managed. 'Rachel never opened the window. She was the neatest person you'd meet, but she hated spiders, she was convinced that they'd invade in colonies if she opened the window. We'd stopped having conversations about it. I'd given up "preaching" as she'd called it.'

Slattery walked over towards the window again. He drew in close, moved the catch around in a fashion that looked almost aimless. The lock was the original, fitted with the sash windows God knows when. Years of paint had sealed it over, but someone had recently scraped the clotted paint and loosened the pin, so it moved with ease. Now the chipped white gloss lay like guilty fairy dust on the floor beneath Slattery's feet.

'There's no sign it was broken, it could as easily have been cleaved free from the inside.' He turned his head towards the door, registering her blank expression. 'They may have used this as an exit rather than a way of gaining entry.' Something else tripped along behind his words. 'Rachel wouldn't have given a key to the house to anyone, I suppose?' he asked, his tone already telling her he knew the answer.

'Never. That would mean a front door key, she'd never have done that.'

'There were no… boys?' He stumbled over the word. The girl was twenty after all, but Slattery knew it'd be a brave young man who would dare to cross the threshold of Imelda McDermott's house.

'There were no boys, Inspector.' She smiled at him. 'And if there were, they weren't brought back here.' Her smile was sad now, but thoughtful all the same.

'I'll have to call it in,' he said as he moved away from the flaked paint. He looked once more around the room. 'We'll need to cross match the DNA samples from both you and Tim, to rule you out and see if anyone broke in who shouldn't be here.' His voice was strong, commanding. 'Mrs McDermott?' he called to her from beyond the door. 'We'll have a technical team here in the next few hours, it's important that the room is left locked, nothing is touched, okay?'

'Of course, Sergeant Slattery, it's only me and Tim here anyway.' She opened a door along the hall, reached in and took out Eleanor Marshall's file. She handed it to him before they headed for the stairs.

He was lingering on the stairs, their business not quite complete, she guessed what it was he wanted. 'Some tea, Inspector?' she tried at last.

'Am... no, not today.' And he turned. He halted a second and took in her face while he asked, 'Do you know if Rachel had any connection with Kit Marshall outside of Curlew Hall?'

'Oh, dear.' Imelda's expression clouded over. 'I was wondering when you were going to ask me about that. Perhaps we should have that cup of tea after all,' she said, making her way past him and heading for the kitchen and her trusty tea pot in an attempt to set the world to some sort of rights.

CHAPTER 28

There were three missed calls on her mobile, so it was only reasonable to expect them to ring her at the station. The call from the nursing home was, if not unexpected, then certainly – Iris could admit to herself – unwelcome. Her mother was very upset, asking for her, calling out to see where she was.

'She's not my mother,' Iris said flatly.

'I do understand that, but she doesn't and…' The matron's voice petered out. She sounded much too young to be a matron and Iris tried to visualise the kind of woman who could fill matronly shoes and still sound so very fragile. 'She's being assessed by psych tomorrow and she's begging every staff member on their rounds to call you and ask you to visit.'

'It's really not my place anymore.' Iris felt empty saying the words. It was impossible to reconcile the notion of Theodora Locke with this woman they were talking about. Indeed, it was impossible to reconcile the woman she'd visited only a short time ago with the woman she'd always believed to be her mother. That woman had been articulate, perfectly groomed and taken care of as if she was priceless china by a man whose natural default setting was to protect fiercely the people he called family. Theodora Locke had been many things when Iris was growing up and she wasn't blind to the fact that her mother had a weakness for alcohol and a propensity to self-absorption, but the one thing she'd never been was pathetic.

'Perhaps the last thing she needs is my presence there to muddy the waters of her psych evaluation…'

She allowed her words to drift off, knowing too well that she might fool this woman, but she wasn't deceiving herself. The truth was she didn't know how she felt about Theodora or Jack Locke. She had invested a lifetime of love into two people who weren't who she believed them to be at all and every time she thought about Anna Crowe and how things had ended up she felt hollowed out – as if every emotion she'd ever experienced had been emptied from her; she wasn't sure she'd ever feel anything that passed close to love again. She wanted to tell Theodora Locke that she hated her, but she knew it wouldn't make either of them feel any better and the fact was that you had to have some feelings left for hatred and Iris just didn't have anything left.

'Look, Iris.' The woman on the other end of the line was still waiting for some kind of answer, presumably. 'Visiting her isn't going to affect the outcome of any psychiatric tests and I'm not going to say it's going to make either of you feel any better, but I can tell you this much and you may take from it what you will. After what you've both been through, moving forward, be it together or apart is going to be hard enough, but you're never going to make any progress until you make some kind of peace in your own heart.'

'Does she think I'm going to forgive her?' Iris whispered.

'I don't think she's even thought that far ahead. I think she just needs to know that you're around. Even if it's to scream at her and tell her that what she did was terrible.' She paused. 'It's the guilt, you see. She's been carrying all that around with her for years…'

'You sound as if you've seen it all before,' Iris said cynically, because if there was one thing she was quite sure of, it was that this woman had never come across a situation like theirs.

'No, I'm not saying I have, but I've seen alcoholics and I've lived with one and I'm fairly certain I can spot a suitcase full of guilt a mile off.' She sighed. 'Anyway, I'm only passing on the message. At the end of the day, the decision is yours and you know that you'll be welcome to visit here at any time.' The matron's voice returned to a brusque business-like pace and Iris imagined her, checking her watch, straightening out her perfectly white uniform.

'Well, thank you, I'll think about it,' Iris said, putting down the phone and knowing that there was no way she was going anywhere near Theodora Locke.

The last visit had been enough to put her off for life. They hadn't fought. Maybe it would have been better if they had. Instead it seemed like they might slip into some new reality that buttoned over what they both knew to be the truth. Iris couldn't cope with that. Theodora had led her to a bright and airy bedroom on the first floor. The nursing home was one of the most prestigious in the country. Jack Locke had invested heavily in health insurance as much as he had worked hard to keep their dark family secrets buried, it seemed. Now, Theodora had the advantage of living out her guilt-riddled days in the lap of luxury, while she waited to hear her fate from the state prosecutor.

Iris felt that familiar shiver run through her; overnight she'd become a stranger to herself and all of those things she'd believed predetermined by virtue of her Locke blood were brought to nothing in the stroke of a second.

Iris had shut herself away in her office with the Eleanor Marshall file so Slattery decided that since he couldn't think of anywhere else to be, he may as well head off out to Curlew Hall. Perhaps out there, he might be able to silence the growing questions that riddled him about Maureen. It was funny, being married to someone he thought he knew inside out and yet, here he was, wondering at four simple words. *It was a secret.* Maureen had managed, throughout thirty years of marriage, amid squabbles and heartbreak, to keep a secret from him that he had a feeling might have held the key to questions he'd spent a lifetime trying to answer. Of course, the way things were now, with the dementia, there was a good chance that the sliver of light he'd caught would fade behind that wall of mixed-up memories that seemed to slide casually over his wife's consciousness, so he hardly knew what was remembered and what was imagined anymore. There was only one thing for it. He had to deal with the case in hand – otherwise he could drive himself insane thinking of Una and the notion that there might have been some thread within his grasp all those years ago if only Maureen had not been such a loyal friend to her. This was the thought that sent shivers into where his heart should have been – loyalty to her killer.

He tried to shake off those circling black thoughts, pulled the car tight against the perimeter wall of Curlew Hall. He had a niggling feeling that there was something more to learn out there and it seemed as good a place as any to begin double-checking over what they'd already picked up. Tony Ahearn was still leading out a huge search team and even if they didn't say it, they all knew the fact that the girl had not turned up did not bode well for her safety. The unit, as they had come to call it, had become something of a base for the staff who had worked with both Rachel and Eleanor to drop in and probably unofficially debrief. Slattery was relieved to see one of the older dears there, fussing about the kitchen, cleaning out cupboards that didn't need to be cleaned and basically marking in time probably in the hope that no news was good news.

'You must be under fierce pressure,' Mrs Brady said unhelpfully as she scalded a cup in preparation for yet another round of tea-making. In so many ways, she was the last person Slattery would have imagined working in a set-up like this. But then, maybe, the fact that she oozed maternal consideration – even if she wasn't the fastest on her feet – maybe it made her the perfect person to work here. Her voice was soft; her movements slow, as though arthritis were making a hostile takeover bid on joints that probably creaked if she used them too quickly.

'Ah, every case is like this, once there are victims and families, everyone just wants to get answers… it becomes personal,' he said evenly and that was the truth.

'I suppose, it's like any job, you get attached,' she said philosophically and then smiled. 'Of course, there are the other sorts of attachments here too, they don't always end so well.'

'How do you mean?' Slattery liked nothing better than a good old gossip, it tended to yield some nugget amid the hearsay.

'Well, Rachel and young Nate, they were stepping out for a while, if you call it that these days. It's not right to speak ill of the dead, but I think we were all a little relieved when it came to an end.'

'When was this?' Slattery said, sipping his tea.

'Oh, a couple of months ago. I'd say he fell for her hook, line and sinker, but Rachel wasn't the kind of girl that was going to settle down with the likes of Nate Hegarty.'

'So, it was serious between them?'

'It was for him. I'd say he was as near broken-hearted after as he could be… you know, it's harder coming in to work every day, running into someone and pretending that you're over them.'

'She seemed to have got over him though?' Slattery asked, thinking back to the conversations that had been recorded with Julia Stenson.

'Ah well, I think she began to see what everyone else here could see. It wasn't meant to be and I told her here, myself, there's someone for everyone. I think that whole thing made her even fonder of Eleanor. I swear she'd have laid down her life for that girl.'

CHAPTER 29

The incident room was buzzing; word was out about Hegarty's statement. He'd sworn that he now believed Rachel had been blackmailing Kit Marshall. The truth was, they could find no other explanation for the amount of cash they'd found since her death. He was adamant he knew nothing about the missing file. Iris had a feeling he was lying, even if there was no pushing the truth from him – they had the file in their possession now so it was up to them to find what they could in it. Iris felt the excitement, palpable in the air. For her part, she felt it was as unlikely as the notion of Rachel McDermott selling drugs, but the statement was in the file now, so there was little she could do about it. There was backslapping among the men, easy jokes, Tony Ahearn was like the cat that got the cream.

When they got the full story, it was scant at best but it was enough to allow Ahearn to crow among the uniforms and bask in the glory of having made a breakthrough when it seemed the case was at stalemate. For some of the younger officers it was their first time to work a murder, and your first murder is always personal. Eleanor Marshall was still out there, somewhere, as the night was drawing in. Iris couldn't contemplate that thing she saw in the woods, didn't want to think of it running into Eleanor, maybe watching her now. She had reported it to the local parks ranger and maybe he was just a little pissed at the idea that she called it in as night arrived and he was just about to clock off duty. She pulled a file that had been compiled by various officers at the front desk.

Mainly locals, but a couple of tourists too, had reported seeing something that could have been a big cat or maybe a small bear – neither was going to make her sleep any better. At the briefing, it was just another detail to add to their worries.

The technical team were still working on tracing that email from Rachel's account. She'd checked with them earlier, but looking at her watch now, knew that the second floor would be empty – they kept regular hours, when they could. Iris plopped down next to June in the incident room.

'Time you were going home,' she said gently. They all tended to forget that June was a single mother. Granted, her two sons were big enough to look after themselves, but still, a case like this had to be hard-going. Iris couldn't imagine living anything close to a normal home life with the hours a murder investigation took up when they were in the thick of it.

'I could say the same for you.' June smiled easily.

'I'm not exactly going to be missed over in the digs.' Iris shook her head. 'Where as you…'

'My mother lives with us,' June said quietly.

'I didn't know that.'

And it was true, she knew very little of June, apart from the fact that she liked her from the moment they'd met. She liked the fact that she got on with her work; she'd never been threatened by Iris, just welcomed her on board with a quiet understanding that there was always room for another pair of hands. She was the one person who gave Slattery a hard time for not doing the right thing and didn't give a damn whether he wanted to hear it or not. She knew too that June's husband had passed away a good decade earlier and her wedding rings still shone as if they got the same attention to detail as she gave every minute of her time at work in the Murder Team.

'One bit of good news though,' June said. 'Finding that file, bet you're dying to dive into it as soon as you get a bit of peace and quiet.'

'It'll be interesting to see exactly what's in it, especially after that email,' Iris admitted, and then they both looked over at Tony Ahearn holding court at the far end of the incident room. 'What is it?'

'Ah, that shower, you'd swear he was Hercule Poirot.' June shook her head. 'He's done that much crowing about Hegarty I'm ready to go over there and tell him it'd be more in his line if he managed to do his own job properly.' She shook her head again. 'Bet that email to you got right up his nose.'

'Probably.' Iris smiled; getting up Ahearn's nose was just a nice little by-product. Even if the sender was just playing games, it was a lead, possibly to whoever had taken Rachel's computer and certainly to information that they hadn't managed to gather through the interview process.

It took another hour before the incident room emptied out. It seemed everyone was reluctant to leave and when they did, they were all planning on heading down to the Ship Inn to carry on the gloating conversation – although, in Iris's opinion they'd made only a tiny step on the way to getting all the answers they needed. She rang Slattery to let him know his quiet pint could be interrupted, she had a feeling the reason he hadn't turned up tonight was because he needed thinking time.

'As it happens, I'm not in the pub,' he said glumly, 'but I was going there next and you're right, the last thing I need is to be looking at Tony Ahearn for the night.' He sighed on the other end of the phone. 'Fancy a pint?' he said then and Iris had a feeling that he had things on his mind.

'Sure, but not in the Ship Inn,' she said, switching off lights as she made her way out of the incident room. She could come back for the file later.

'There's a small pub called Delaney's down the road from King John's Castle. I'll be there in about five minutes. I'll have a glass of Guinness on for you if you're not there by closing time,' he said hanging up.

Something in Slattery's tone gave her a sense that he had news. She made her way back to her office and grabbed her jacket. Delaney's would be low key, probably even further under the radar than the Ship Inn.

Delaney's was a short narrow bar, with six stools at the counter, an open fire in the hearth and a row of uncomfortable seats along the wall with a narrow bench before them that wasn't much wider than a bookshelf to hold your drink. A couple of ugly low chairs ranged along the other side, but it seemed that the regulars, all four of them, preferred the company of the barman.

When Slattery had chosen their table, he'd picked one as far away as it was possible to be in a room where cat-swinging was off the agenda. He sat next to the fireplace, a comfortable outsider that they all seemed to know well enough to leave him alone. If they raised their eyebrows at Iris's arrival, they managed to close their mouths and turn their backs on them both before it was noticed. Fortunately, Munster had knocked the stuffing out of a visiting French team earlier in the evening and the rugby match was being replayed on a small TV perched on the end of the bar. Regardless of the fact that they knew the result, it seemed lives depended on following every pass, try and scrum to the bitter, glorious end.

'So, busy day drinking tea with Mrs McDermott?' she said, slipping easily into the long bench opposite Slattery.

'Well, it was interesting,' he said, pushing over a creamy glass of Guinness for her to sample. She was not a porter drinker, but Slattery insisted on buying her one whenever they were in a bar he considered could put up a decent sample.

'You're trying to get me hooked on this stuff.' She grimaced as she tasted it. She actually liked the creamy top, but everything about the black Guinness, from its smell to its taste, reminded her of Jack Locke. 'And I'm telling you now, it won't work.'

'Never say never,' he said, leaning forward.

They must have looked an odd pair, Iris thought, if anyone was bothered noticing them. Slattery hardened by life and fattened by too much time in the pub, while she had become a shadow of the woman she'd been only months before, reluctant to fill out the same big space that once seemed to be her right.

'It seems that there is a connection between Rachel and Karena and it may go all the way back to Marshall,' said Slattery.

'Go on.' Iris found herself taking another sip, although she'd had no intention of touching the drink before her again.

'Well, you know there's some confusion concerning the gap between Rachel's date of birth and her father's death?'

'Yes, I knew that,' Iris said softly, it was no big deal anymore… not like it might have been twenty or thirty years earlier.

'Rachel was "overdue" by about three months. I suppose, back then, people just brushed it under the carpet. She was given her mother's name, which was Imelda's deceased husband's name and they all got on with things.'

'She's not…' Iris shook her head. She couldn't imagine old Mrs McDermott having it off with Kit Marshall.

'No, he's not, but obviously she knew that William McDermott wasn't her father from a young age and then at some point Kit Marshall called to the house. Imelda had won some sort of raffle at work, a Christmas hamper sponsored by Marshall – apparently, there was a photo in the paper. Knowing Marshall, it'd be milked for all it was worth. He made quite the impression on young Rachel, giving her a couple of bob on his way out the door and from then on, Rachel was convinced that Marshall was her father.'

'Wishful thinking?' Iris shuddered, because she'd never met a man she'd like less as a father. 'Didn't her mother ever sit her down and say, *listen*…?'

'I'm sure she did, but I think by the time she realised, it was too late. Rachel had already built up this whole fantasy and Imelda thinks it was all tied into the reason she was so very fond of Eleanor Marshall. She thought—'

'She thought they were sisters?' Iris shook her head sadly.

'Can we use words like *illegitimate* anymore?' Slattery shook his head, as far as he was concerned it was a world gone PC mad. 'Anyway, when she started working in Curlew Hall, her mother didn't initially see the connection, but then one evening she mentioned something about Kit Marshall and she realised…'

'Rachel had contacted them?'

'Well, she believes she contacted Marshall, who of course would have denied responsibility, but she has no proof one way or another.' Slattery traced the condensation down the side of his pint glass, it was almost empty but he was too pensive to register that he'd need another one soon. 'Imelda said she came home one evening on a complete high, as if she'd just won the lottery.' Slattery sighed.

'The money in the envelope?'

'Not exactly. She told Imelda that she finally had what he needed. Proof that – you're not going to believe this—'

'Come on Slattery, spit it out,' Iris said.

'She had managed to get proof that Kit Marshall was her father.'

'And is he?'

'Of course he's bloody not. Her father was a man who had lived four houses down. He had half a dozen kids and a wife who worked herself to the bone. When Imelda was pregnant, he scarpered, leaving his own family and Imelda in the lurch. As far as Imelda knows, he never made any contact with any of them since.'

Slattery nodded to the barman, *just a pint*. Iris still had most of her glass still to go. She'd have loved coffee, but knew it was unlikely they'd have anything bar tea bags and a kettle.

'Different times, Iris, those were different times.' He shook his head.

'So how could she have proof that Kit Marshall was her father?'

'That's the question, isn't it? But when she found that file in their spare room, Imelda said she just had a funny feeling that it – or something in it – must be connected to these notions Rachel was having.'

'It's a big leap from there to blackmail, isn't it?'

'I know it's only a very tenuous connection, but there's no way that the Marshalls are going to pay out money to someone just because they're making a wild claim which is easily refutable with a simple DNA test. I can't see how it fits, apart from the fact that it does give us a connection of sorts.'

'It's a pretty big coincidence all right.' Iris sighed, sitting back for a moment against the uncomfortable bench.

The barman had left Slattery's pint to settle on the bar and she was struck, not for the first time, that it was something of a ritual, pouring what Slattery considered a decent pint. He turned, following her eyes.

'In some ways, it's like she's the third of his daughters to be caught up in this, even if she's not.' She let her words drift off between them.

'Would you have wanted one?' he said, his gaze falling back down to the hardly touched glass before her. 'I'm sure they have crisps and soft drinks here.' He shook his head, just his luck to get stuck with a lightweight drinker.

'No, I'm fine,' she said, although she could feel her stomach rumbling and couldn't remember the last time she'd eaten.

'Iris, you're many things, but at this moment in time, you're not fine,' Slattery said softly, 'but we'll get you there yet.'

Something in his eyes made her feel as if there was the smallest chance he might be right.

CHAPTER 30

Day 7

Iris rubbed her tired eyes. She should go for a walk, move around, she knew that. She was almost drifting off now – the second time reading the case book wasn't throwing up anything she didn't already know. The clock told her it was three twenty in the afternoon, but she'd pulled down the blinds earlier in an attempt to stop her mind drifting out across the city. Now, it might as well be the middle of the night. It was all the same at this point. At night, in Mrs Leddy's uncomfortable bed, she'd just toss and turn, and during the day it felt as if she was pushing herself through a concrete wall just to hit some kind of normal pace. She needed sleep, proper sleep – she knew now it was never going to happen until she found Eleanor Marshall. Maybe, she knew too, here in her sleep-deprived state, that she needed a home, somewhere to call her own, that wasn't tainted by the past and didn't feel like a halfway house. She needed to move on in some way. This never-never land she'd been existing in – a kind of holding pen between past and present – she would have to find some way of breaking out of it. She would, she promised herself then, just as soon as this case was finished. She'd go and look for a new flat, maybe a small cottage, near the water. Somewhere with an open fire and the sound of the waves in the distance; she'd have to rent, of course, idyllic hideaways don't come cheap.

She shook her head – the reality of the incident room outside pulling her from her daydream. Iris swung her squeaking chair about and pulled the blinds up once more, revealing a cloud-covered Limerick. This window looked directly down on the car park below, but ahead, she could see the slates of a thousand roofs stretching out towards the skyline. The car park was fenced in on all sides, between Corbally and the administrative branch buildings for the Mid-West region. She'd completed a work experience there many years ago as a student; it seemed like a lifetime ago now. She couldn't imagine actually working there, insulated from the fabric of what it really meant to be a garda.

She turned back again to the file, flipped it closed. She would check Rachel's bank accounts. They were lucky, the bank had been very forthcoming, working with the McDermott family. Iris could log into Rachel's accounts and see every single transaction on both her debit and credit card. Iris had changed her passwords; the original hadn't matched the string of numbers they'd found taped to the back of the picture in her bedroom. Now, the pass code was her case-file number, prior to this, Rachel had used her phone number. Those numbers on the picture still gnawed at Iris, but at least they'd managed to track down every other payment Rachel had made from her wages over the last six months. One of the uniforms was still working through records prior to that, but she couldn't imagine there being much there to see. Rachel had been a cash girl. She'd withdrawn two to three hundred euro every time her wages hit her account, presumably, she paid for all her running expenses in cash. The only real payments from the account were bills like her car loan, her Netflix and a couple of subscriptions to animal welfare sites that she donated to.

Iris trawled through the older transactions, skipping over mundane occasional debit-card spends for things she assumed to be fuel and just before last Christmas a large payment to a local clothes shop – probably enough for a suit or a jacket– and then there was PayPal.

She searched through the case book once more. There had been no mention of a PayPal account among the myriad other details. Of course, most people use PayPal on their laptops, she reasoned, so it wasn't necessarily an account they'd have come across immediately. Iris sat for a moment, wondering about this – there was nothing sinister in it, but it needed to be checked out. It was just one payment, insignificant over the course of the investigation, just thirty-five euro, but there was no room in this case for dark corners or unanswered questions. She picked up the phone immediately and rang a detective she'd worked with a few years earlier who had gone into the fraud squad and was always happy to help out if she needed it.

'Ciara, I need to track down a PayPal account, can we do that?'

'Sure. How are you keeping? I heard about… well, you know.' Ciara sounded tense; Iris was getting used to it now. People didn't know quite what to say to her after the death of Jack Locke and then when details of the lies around her whole identity had emerged.

'Don't worry, I'm fine, just getting on with things.'

'I wanted to call, but…'

'It's okay, I know, people don't know what to say…I get it, really. I've been trying to get things straight in my own head. I can't imagine anyone else being able to find the right words.'

'Well, at least I can do this for you,' Ciara said brightly, 'shout what you know of the account holder's details.'

'It's a case I'm working on at the moment,' Iris said and then gave Ciara Rachel's bank account details and her email address.

'This is going to be easy – you have almost everything, leave it with me, I'll be back to you within the hour.'

Iris rang off and, not for the first time, wondered what her life might have become if she'd done as Jack Locke had always wanted for her and joined a nice white-collar unit instead of choosing to get her hands dirty in the Murder Team. She managed to nod off with these thoughts careering around her sleep-deprived brain, only to be woken minutes later by the shrill of her mobile.

'Right, back again. Now, they're lovely in PayPal – I've got a contact there and he'll just give you anything with the tap of a couple of keys.' The fact that Ciara had buckets of charm probably didn't hurt, Iris thought. 'He's sent me on a statement of everything that's come out of that account, but it's not much. It looks like your girl used it to buy a piece of vintage jewellery on eBay and then there's two more payments, both of them to a crowd who rent lockers. They're based in Limerick and it looks like she's had it for about a year. Any good to you?'

'Yes, I think it might be, can you send on the statement with...'

'Already in your inbox,' Ciara said brightly. 'Now, when you're up to it, we'll have to meet up, promise?'

'Next time I'm in Dublin, that's a promise,' Iris said, hanging up the phone.

When she looked at her emails, there was a list of half a dozen transactions sent directly from Ciara. She tracked down a number for 'Lockerby' easily and rang to see what she could find out. Suddenly the day ahead seemed to brighten just a little.

Slattery was soaked when he came back from wherever he'd been hiding for most of the day. Iris hoped that his disappearing act had something to do with helping Maureen, but she wasn't in the mood for having her head eaten off by asking, so instead she told him he could come with her if he felt like it. He didn't need to be asked twice.

Limerick University is one of those strange combinations of dynamic campus in an almost rural location. It's located on the River Shannon, far enough away from the city to be picturesque, close enough to be bustling. Iris cut through the drive, turning off into a parking area just short of the Glucksman Library. Almost every building on the campus is relatively 'new'. Iris felt it was something to be thankful for, she'd never found the realms of academia particularly welcoming and the smell of old buildings now would remind her too much of days spent trawling through museums and country houses with her father.

A young articulate porter dressed in khakis and fleece happily escorted them to the lockers. The company who leased the lockers had obviously told him they were on their way. He led them eagerly, talking about the building and the fact that he'd always assumed the lockers were only held by students. Perhaps he expected a grisly find when Rachel's locker was opened, but Slattery had barked at him to leave them alone when they arrived in the bright but empty corridor filled on one side with the row of red doors crammed together, as much a statement of modernity as of security. Sure enough, each of the lockers was secured with a numbered padlock. Number ninety-four was halfway along, on the bottom row. Iris quickly took out her phone, and bent down to the locker.

'I'm not sure we're meant to be doing that now,' Slattery said, but there was a catch of playfulness in his flat voice.

'What's that?'

'Storing evidence photographs on our personal phones. Haven't you been banging on about GDPR louder than any of us?' He shook his head, mock ruefully. 'Tut, tut.'

'Well, let's keep it as our little secret, yeah?' Iris said. Of course, she could have taken the photo of the numbers on her police phone, perhaps she'd get used to using it before Grady returned to take it over again. She dialled out the code on the lock with her examination-gloved fingers, waiting a beat for the tiniest click at the end. Slattery too was down on his knees now, waiting to see what this would yield. Iris slid the lock off and drew open the door. Almost empty, apart from a shopping bag containing about a hundred euro worth of hash, a cheap mobile and a single sheet of paper that looked as if it had been ripped from a file. Iris dived on the paper first, while Slattery had to make do with choosing between the bag and the phone.

'It's a social-work report,' she said, scanning the page. 'It goes back over twenty years, look, Slattery,' she said, holding out the page for him to read the words.

'Well, we have our motive for blackmail now, I suppose,' he said softly.

CHAPTER 31

'It's only made calls to two numbers,' June said, 'and the good news?' They had charged up the phone when they got back to the incident room. The tech boys had all gone home for the evening, apparently, some of them had lives.

Slattery flopped down in the chair opposite June. 'What we wouldn't give for a bit of good news at this stage.'

'We have both numbers on file, both of them linked to…'

'Marshall?'

'Spot on. We even have logs of when the calls were made and how long they lasted. There were no texts, no further usage. There's no browser, as you can see, it's cheap as chips and not as cheerful. It's a burner phone, she was only using it for one reason.' June shook her head.

'So, she thinks she's Marshall's daughter and she was trying to get what? Recognition or money out of them for her silence?' Iris asked.

She was reading between the lines, all they had was a report written up years earlier by a social worker who'd sat down with a very distraught Susan Marshall. At the time, Susan had talked about counselling for Eleanor because her family was in crisis and the child was coping badly. This was teased out two lines later, with the additional information that Kit had fathered a child through an affair some years earlier and the papers were on the brink of running the story if something couldn't be done about it.

Of course, when they'd checked, the dates would pass for working out with Rachel's birth.

'Can't be that simple, there's something not feeling right about this,' Slattery said, and he had the good grace to put up his hands, aware he was being a killjoy. 'Well, for one thing, why would they pay out?'

'Because maybe they just wanted to keep it quiet?' June said and shook her head.

'Yes, or maybe she blackmailed them with something else? Who knows, but this is what she was holding onto like gold – so we'll have to assume, for now, that it was what she was blackmailing them with.'

Iris looked at the clock. It was almost six. She picked up the page again, it was still sealed in plastic, although they'd made a copy of it. She understood what Slattery meant. Everything about the report felt wrong. The paper was too fresh – yes, there were marks and creases but it looked as if it had been aged on purpose, a coffee-cup stain and scratched-out ink – it almost looked stage-managed. It was handwritten, on an A4 sheet, pulled from a yellow refill pad. Was this how social workers had reported case visits back then?

'Maybe we should ask if we can take a look at something with a similar date by the same social worker,' Slattery said, reading her mind again.

'Yep, good idea,' Iris said and she rang the information officer who'd turned over every stone she could to find Eleanor's file last time round.

'Sure, we can let you see something, but what did you say the social worker's name was again?'

'Dermot Drummond,' Iris said, squinting to see the scrawled handwriting and date at the end of the page.

'That's what I thought you said.' The woman on the other end of the line even sounded as if she was shaking her head. 'You see,

I don't ever remember a Dermot Drummond turning up here, to be honest. I've been here for almost thirty years and the name doesn't ring a bell at all.'

'Can you check it for definite for me, with your HR department?' Iris asked.

'Sure, hang on.' She put Iris on hold for a moment, and even Slattery seemed to be willing the woman to come back and say yes, actually she'd forgotten all about old Dermot Drummond. 'I'm sorry,' the voice came back on the line again. 'They've just put him into the system and he's never worked for Curlew Hall.'

'Okay, well that's good to know,' Iris said.

'Do you still want to come and look at social-work files that were written up back then? It's just I'll have to organise permission and…'

'No, don't worry, I think we're good.' Iris put the phone down.

'You do know where we have to go now?' Slattery said, grabbing his coat.

Iris was too tired to guess. 'No, but I'm sure you'll tell me on the way.'

It seemed to Iris that John Street was even more derelict this evening than it had been the last time she was here. Slattery pulled up on the double yellows, snarled at a traffic warden, flashing his badge – 'Don't even think about it, matey' – and Iris knew you'd have to be either mad or stupid to put a ticket on the windscreen of his car.

'Here goes.' Iris rang the bell, wondering again if it even still worked. Upstairs a narrow sliver of light peered out from behind heavy curtains and Slattery waved a hand, obviously spotting Nate Hegarty checking who was looking to get in.

'It's only us,' he called up to the window above and they waited until they heard uncertain steps pad to the door and pull it open for them.

'Have you found her?' he asked, standing back to let them in out of the dark evening.

'No, I'm afraid not, but we've found something else you might be able to help us with,' Iris said, leading the way up to the dingy flat and the aroma of recently fried eggs and onions, which pinched at her nostrils. She remembered a time when standing here would have meant a trip to the drycleaner's for whatever jacket she happened to be wearing. Slattery launched himself at the old couch, which groaned disapprovingly against his cumbersome plonk. He was clearly oblivious to the fact that Nate Hegarty was just about to sit and have his dinner. Nate walked to the window and sat in the chair opposite him.

'Please, go ahead and eat, we can talk while you have your meal,' Iris said, willing Slattery not to ask for a cup of tea.

'Okay,' Nate said, and he folded himself back into the chair he'd obviously just left to let them in.

'You dated Rachel McDermott.' Slattery made it a statement, rather than a question.

'Well, I wouldn't say dated exactly…' A strand of hair fell across Nate's face, but he left it there, concentrating hard on his eggs. 'More like we had a bit of a thing, for a short while.'

'It's what other people are saying,' Iris said softly.

'We were… together, for a while, but…' They let his sentence hang in the air. 'I suppose it turned out we weren't as well suited as I thought at the beginning.' He laid down his fork, his appetite suddenly gone. 'When I first arrived at Curlew Hall, she was kind and I thought she liked me. I suppose I liked the idea of having someone like her, she just seemed so…' He looked up at Iris now, his eyes were transformed by vulnerability. 'So different to anyone I'd ever been with before. Settled? Normal? I don't know, but I just thought, for a while that maybe…'

'I get it,' Iris said softly, and she did. Nate Hegarty had looked at Rachel and Imelda and Tim and seen all that he'd never had.

Stability – that was probably it. Iris knew what it was to be outside now. She didn't want to think what it might have been like to be outside all her life. 'But things changed?'

'Yeah. It was great at first, but it didn't take long until it became obvious I would never be good enough, not for Rach's family, at least.' Nate smiled sadly. 'Whatever we had between us, whatever *it* was, it didn't mean enough to her to face up to old Ma McDermott.' He lowered his voice and when he spoke next Iris wasn't sure if his words were tinged with pain or embarrassment. 'I wanted her to keep things going between us.' He made a small sound, perhaps it was meant to be a self-deprecating laugh, but it didn't quite make it. 'I asked her, almost begged her, but she wouldn't listen. It turned out I meant nothing to her.' He bowed his head, finding the plate before him suddenly interesting. He wiped the tears from his eyes with a rough swipe, steadied his breath and eventually met their gaze. 'At the end of the day, it fizzled out into a fling, but...' His voice shook as he prepared to say the next words. 'I didn't kill her. You can't think that I did?'

'No,' Slattery said flatly, because the truth was, even though Nate Hegarty was the one person who had means and, it turned out now, maybe the motive; they'd never taken him seriously as their murderer for both crimes. 'That's not why we're here. We're more interested in Eleanor Marshall's file.'

'Oh.' It was a flat word, but it seemed to hold within it a caseload of answers. 'You know, so?'

'Tell us, from the start. And this time, Nate, you need to tell us everything. Obstructing an investigation carries serious penalties, we can charge you with that even now,' Slattery said.

'Oh God.' He began to cry, huge, ugly wracking sobs that rattled through his miserable frame, but he needed to know that everything had to come out now. 'When Rachel and I were... y'know, we talked a lot about Eleanor. I thought she wanted to help her, I wouldn't have got it for her if I realised.'

'You forged Susan's handwriting?' Iris realised. Of course, calligraphy was evident in the various sketches dotted about the flat. Nate had a flair for it. 'You helped her release Eleanor's file and then…'

'She asked me do it, in the end… I thought maybe it would make things right between us.'

'It doesn't matter, but you need to tell us everything now, even about Dermot Drummond,' Iris said quietly and watched as Nate flinched at the name.

'How did you know? Oh God,' he managed through his sobs. 'Rach told me, one night, when it was just the two of us in Curlew Hall, she told me that she believed Kit Marshall was her father. I didn't think much of it at the time. When you come from where I grew up, having a mother would be enough, wanting any more just seems like greed. I knew who Marshall was: bloody richest man in Limerick, everyone knows who he is. He was on telly at the opening of some big business one night when Rachel said it to me. I didn't pay much mind to it, but it was always there for Rachel, bubbling away, how she was going to put things right with her father, her sisters.'

He shook his head, remembering.

'It bothered her, that there were things about Eleanor she didn't know, while old Hilda Brady considered herself an expert. I suppose Rach always wanted to be the best, you know, number one with Eleanor? You should have seen her with Mrs Marshall when she called: syrupy sweet.' He looked now from one to the other, his eyes brimming with tears, a silent plea not to judge him before his next words. 'Anyway, I got it for her, filled in the forms and rang the girl in the record department, pretending I was Kit Marshall and I was getting my assistant to pick it up. It turned out to be easy as pie to get it released in the end. I brought the file back here, read through it first and then I had the idea about playing a trick on Rach. I thought it would be a laugh, a bit of revenge for her having dumped me.'

'We're not judging you, Nate, that's not why we're here,' Iris said softly, but she caught Slattery's silent warning flashing across his eyes.

'Still, I know it was wrong, but it wasn't meant to cause any harm to anyone apart from getting a swipe at Rach. I just thought she'd go marching out to the Marshalls' house and make a complete tit of herself before all those people who meant so much to her.' He shook his head now, bitterly regretting what he'd done.

'So, *you* wrote the case note that she believed confirmed she was Marshall's daughter?' Slattery asked, but he was just confirming what they knew now.

'I did. I was afraid to tell you before, I thought... I don't know what I thought, but I hoped that it was such a stupid thing, it couldn't have any bearing on anything.'

'Tell us now – Rachel made contact with the Marshalls?'

'Not with Marshall, he was away, I think he's always away really, but from what she said, she managed to get a meeting with Mrs Marshall. It was around a month ago?' He was trying to remember. 'Then, after that, she seemed to be flush all the time and she walked about the place as if... well, as if she owned everything and everybody in Curlew Hall.'

'So, you believed that the Marshalls had paid up?' Iris asked.

'Well, it was the only thing that fitted at the time, but they couldn't have, could they, because I made it up. Rach was no more Kit Marshall's daughter than I'm St Patrick's nephew.' In his eyes he was grappling with the predicament he'd invented.

'True enough,' Slattery agreed. 'Was there anything else in that file that might have given her an opportunity for blackmail?'

'No, not that I could think of, like I said, I wrote that note, but it was pure fiction – nothing to it and I have to confess, I only wrote it out of spite, but Rach fell for it hook, line and sinker and then it seemed to be too late to tell her the truth of it.' Nate's lower lip trembled. 'I have wondered if it was... You know, the reason she was killed, especially after Karena Marshall…I couldn't bear it, I really couldn't.' Nate finally descended into the kind of silence they'd both hoped he might manage to avoid.

'Will you be all right?' Iris asked as they got up to leave a little later.

'Yeah, I'll be fine, better than Rach now, anyway.' His lip trembled treacherously again. 'I'm probably going to get the sack anyway from Curlew Hall, this is just another reason for them to get rid of me.'

'Well, if you think of anything, anything at all, you need to pick up the phone immediately. It could mean the difference between Eleanor Marshall's life and death,' Slattery said darkly.

Iris wanted to kick him in the shins for being so hard on the kid.

'Sure,' he said, walking them down the stairs so he could lock the front door behind them.

Just as they were getting into the car, he called out to them again. Bounding down the street towards them, he tugged on Iris's arm. 'Hang on, there's something else,' he shouted and dragged Iris back to the flat again. Iris looked back at Slattery who was standing open-mouthed beside the badly parked car.

CHAPTER 32

It was a strange thing; once Slattery sped out of Limerick, the sky seemed to lighten, as if there might yet be another hour left in the day. All the same, there was no mistaking the heavy clouds rolling in from the Atlantic.

'Storm's coming,' Slattery said darkly.

'Shouldn't we bring it straight to the technical team?' Iris glanced uncomfortably at the laptop sitting in the back seat. In the end, she had a feeling that Nate Hegarty had been relieved to hand it over. Iris knew that for as long as he had it in his flat, it probably felt as if Rachel was still there lingering accusingly. There were other things too, Nate said, apart from Rachel's emails, she'd been planning on spending a sizeable amount on a new car, far more than the stash Tim had handed into the station.

'Rachel must have been putting the squeeze on them good and tight.' Slattery broke into her thoughts. 'That's enough of a reason to pay them both a visit.' He shook his head and Iris had a feeling that this trip was more about Slattery's gut instinct than it was about anything they might find on that computer.

'It looks like it's an awful night ahead,' Iris murmured, 'weather-wise.' She was thinking of Eleanor.

'We're getting closer to her. I can almost feel it in my—'

'Don't.' Iris put her hand to her forehead. The last thing she needed to hear was where Slattery had feelings.

'Him or her?'

'How do you mean?

'If you were a betting gal, who would you put your money on?' he said idly, staring out into the countryside, as they travelled further away from Limerick and closer to Duneata House.

'Well, I'm not,' she said sharply, because this wasn't a game and if she was honest, she didn't want to think of either parent maybe paying up to keep Rachel quiet.

They drove on in silence, Slattery sighing every so often, as if another problem had settled on him and he was carrying on bravely beneath the weight of all the responsibility. The gates to Duneata House were firmly locked, when Iris pulled the car up before them. Darkness had finally fallen across the sky, the moon and stars trapped behind dense carpets of clouds. Iris had a feeling it would be one of those long and black nights, but out here there were no church bells to punctuate the hours, only the rush and crackle of nocturnal creatures setting about their business beneath the blanket of darkness. Just then, a security guard appeared behind the gates, he waved at Slattery, obviously recognising him.

'Cold night for it,' Slattery said lazily.

Iris thanked her lucky stars she was no longer in uniform on night beats.

'Aye and it's going to get colder from the looks of it,' the man said grumpily.

'Overtime?'

'Why else?' He pulled back the gates and waved them through. The drive up to the main house was even bumpier than she remembered as they sped along. She wanted to get this over with, not because it was her main focus, which was strange, because normally, on a murder investigation it is the victim that keeps you going, but rather because of Eleanor. She had a horrible feeling that the longer their murderer evaded them, the more danger the girl was in.

Here, at the Marshall house, they were only a short distance from the search party. Through the trees, she could see lights shining, probing, small and inconsistent, futile amid the lushness of velvet night. She wondered if she looked as weary as Slattery did, she certainly felt it. She also felt as if she'd been wearing the black trousers she'd put on first thing for a week. Her shoes were too low-heeled to keep them off the wet ground and now a damp patch had risen from the trouser legs trailing the sodden earth and it wasn't helping her comfort levels. The cold and wet chewed at her calves and devoured any good humour that might survive beyond the tiredness and achy feeling that stretched through her.

Duneata House was in darkness, save for a porch light and a sliver of bright betraying life at the rear of the house. Slattery rapped loudly on the door.

'There *is* a bell.'

'Aye,' he said, 'but there's more satisfaction this way.' He beat the door again with his fist. Inside, Iris watched as the unmistakable shape of Kit Marshall made his way towards them. He peered through the glass side panel before opening the door slowly.

'Yes?' he said, reluctantly moving back to let them in when Slattery pushed the door and marched past him. 'Has something happened? Have you found my daughter?'

'No, not yet, but we have some more questions for you.' Slattery stood square, as if he was baiting the taller man. Iris looked at them both, they were similar age, but you could see the differences in their lifestyles. Slattery's shape and lazy gait spoke of his time on a bar stool. Maybe the thinness of his mouth conveyed some of the depravity he'd seen, but it was in his eyes. Those calculating hooded eyes that told you he was no fool, regardless of what Kit Marshall might believe. Marshall stood tall and thin, his ash-blond hair had all but turned to grey, reading glasses perched upon his forehead. He was every bit the country gent, an austere intellectual, Iris caught her breath – a murderer?

'Mr Marshall.' Iris managed to gather her composure. 'Could we ask you a few questions?'

'Will it help find my daughter and put this terrible business behind us so we can mourn Karena properly once and for all?'

'It might,' Slattery said, his eyes travelling about the dark hallway.

'Right so,' Marshall said and he led them back towards the soft light streaming from the library. The room was warmer than Iris had expected for some reason and it occurred to her that perhaps the frostiness she'd felt here before wasn't all about temperature.

'We've managed to get our hands on your daughter's file and a piece of evidence has been thrown up that's… well, we know about the blackmail,' Iris said. She had walked along to the furthest side of the room, was standing next to one of the twin windows. In the distance, the searchers' flashlights were sprite-like within the eerie darkness.

'Blackmail?' Marshall echoed. He stood next to a small table beside the fireplace, picked up his glass of whiskey and sipped some of the drink thoughtfully. 'I think you've got yourselves confused, I'm not being blackmailed.' He smiled, said it so smoothly, that if Iris hadn't just left Nate Hegarty, she might have believed him. He laughed first, but then something like realisation stripped the laughter from the room and he dropped heavily into a chair. 'Dear God… but…'

'The threat was a hoax. It was based on a lie,' Slattery said flatly, assuming that Marshall would be more concerned with whatever dirt the blackmailer had gathered on him. 'But then, you'd have known that already, wouldn't you?' Slattery looked at Iris, suddenly, everything was falling into place.

'Where's Mrs Marshall now?' Iris's voice came as if it had travelled from a great distance away. When she caught Slattery's eye, they both knew they'd had it wrong – well, *she'd* had it wrong. On the journey out here, he'd asked if she'd wager on Kit or Susan – she'd have lost, she realised now. 'Where is she?' Iris was shouting now, but she knew the answer, they all did. The lights in the distance had begun to die down – Iris hadn't noticed them reduce from half a dozen to three, to two and now there was just the one. 'Does she stay out there alone? Has she been trying to find her all this time because…' Iris didn't need to finish the sentence.

'Look, there has to be a mix-up, you've got it wrong. Susan wouldn't…' Marshall was staring too at that single flash lamp moving stealthily in and out of the trees in the distance. 'You don't realise, Susan couldn't, she's weak and damaged, she'd never do something like this. All these years, I've had to protect her from herself.' And he waved towards his forearms and Iris knew then, that the marks on Susan's arms were not inflicted by her husband, but rather by herself.

'Rachel McDermott was convinced you were her father,' Iris said.

'But that's nonsense.' Kit seemed to sink lower into his chair.

'Really? Well, maybe Susan didn't think so and an illegitimate child surfacing after all these years, spreading it about the papers that you'd sent one child to Curlew Hall and turned your back on the other? It wouldn't do your reputation a lot of good, would it?' Slattery shot across at him.

'So, you're saying, you think Susan killed the McDermott girl because she threatened to go public?'

'Someone paid her a couple of thousand to keep her quiet,' Iris cut in.

'And then she went there? That night, to Curlew Hall, hit this… blackmailer over the head and then killed Karena?' He was shaking now so much that the whiskey began to spill over the side of his glass. He placed the drink as gently as he could on the occasional table next to him. 'Not Karena?'

'I'm sorry,' Iris said softly and she meant it, because suddenly she could see Marshall for what he was – a vulnerable older man. Since the start of this investigation, he'd lost a daughter, perhaps he'd pushed the other away, but it didn't mean he couldn't regret it and now, facing a trial, all his money wouldn't keep this out of the papers.

'No, no, you have it wrong, don't you see?' Marshall was shaking; his whole body had begun to tremble with something Iris wasn't sure qualified as shock or delayed guilt. 'Susan would never hurt Karena, she loved her as much as I do… you can't think she's out there to hurt, Eleanor, you just can't!' he said before wracking sobs overtook his body.

'Let's go, we'll deal with him later,' Iris said and she was almost at the front door before Slattery had made it to the hallway. 'Come on, we can't let her find Eleanor first… we know she's close at hand, she has to be, we need to get her before Susan does.'

CHAPTER 33

When they pulled in to the clearing – where until only a short time earlier the search team had parked – it was empty apart from Susan Marshall's Range Rover. They stood on the verge of the woods, surrounded by an unnerving silence and enveloping blackness. Iris did her best to keep her eye on the weakening glow of the only flashlight left in the trees.

'At least the rain's stopped.' It had, if only for a brief respite. Slattery had told her coming over that there would be a thunderstorm in the next hour; they needed to get Eleanor out of here before that struck – no one wanted to be in the middle of the woods for the damage that lightning could cause.

'Look,' Slattery said and she saw where he was pointing: the tiniest pinprick of light.

'Christ, she's headed for the mountain?'

'Currant for cakes,' Slattery said as if there was nothing he'd like better than scaling the side of the Comeragh mountains in a force-ten gale with thunder and lightning thrown in to liven things up.

'And reasons for everything?' Iris finished for him. When Slattery said it, he pronounced *reasons*, *raisins* and always smiled at his own humour. 'What's she thinking?'

'Bloody mental cow,' Slattery said under his breath, 'but she must have a reason, perhaps she's seen something, she has to be following her, otherwise, there's no way…'

'Christ.' It was enough to mobilise Iris. If Susan Marshall was following Eleanor up the side of that mountain in this weather and if they were right about her having already killed two people in cold blood, then finding and killing Eleanor would surely be child's play.

They set off along the track. Slattery had called for back-up on the bumpy road across from the Marshall place. It'd take them half an hour at least to get out here. Now, as they moved along a muddy path, Iris listened as the rain began to spatter overhead, first a light fingering of the leaves and spindly branches at the tallest point of the trees, then, gradually, building up to a full downpour. Soon, the rain was cascading from the canopy overhead, at the sides and beneath their feet in unseen ditches. Water gushed, hard and frantic, as if it couldn't get away from what was ahead fast enough. It was a combination of the sound of it and the fear that bubbled up in her, that made Iris's heart beat fiercely in her chest. They couldn't let her die. They couldn't let all of this be for nothing.

After a while they came to a wide drain, separating the mountain from the woods. Iris could see the soft root-strewn ground give way on the other side to stone and uneven rock. A slim stile provided a bridge from one side to the other and, somehow, Iris felt that once they crossed over, they were leaving behind not only the cover of the leafy canopy from the rain, pouring fast and furious now, but also the protection of the trees from something much darker.

'It doesn't make sense, any of it. Why would Susan Marshall pay out money for an illegitimate child that didn't exist?'

'Because she doesn't know. She's afraid of anything coming between her and that lifestyle she's got going,' Slattery puffed.

'So, she just paid up without even asking?' Iris said breathily.

'Perhaps she just went out to Curlew Hall to buy more thinking time?'

'With a hammer?'

'As far as she was concerned, probably Rachel had them over a—' Slattery cursed. He'd made a good attempt at getting across the stile, but banged his leg on the way down, falling awkwardly on the jagged stones below.

'Are you all right?' Iris bent down, flashed her phone at where he lay on the ground to inspect the damage. There was almost no need. From the crack when he'd fallen, she could have told him he'd broken something.

'This is the last bloody time I bring you on a bloody romantic walk,' he panted, but there were tears in his eyes and she knew the pain must be excruciating. Iris switched on her flashlight to examine the wound. He'd managed to land awkwardly – a good chance he'd broken his ankle at the very least, never mind the rest of his leg or the bones in his foot. There was no point saying that to Slattery, it wouldn't do him any good.

'Oh God, I'm sorry, look, you can't move…' She started to search about frantically, there was no cover here and an ominous roll of thunder scudded about in the sky overhead. 'You'll have to wait until the emergency services get here.' At least Slattery had called them already. They'd have an ambulance on standby, the only problem was, it was meant to have been for Eleanor.

'You're not going in there on your own,' Slattery said as sternly as he could manage, but they both knew he couldn't stop her and maybe, they also knew, he wouldn't have anyway. A girl's life was in danger; no one joined the Murder Squad to sit on the fence.

'And I suppose you're going to come with me, are you?' she said, keeping her voice even.

'Iris, the woman is mentally unstable. She's killed two people.'

'All the more reason to go in there and give Eleanor a fighting chance. Now, stay here.' She smiled, he couldn't move even if he wanted to. 'You have your gun, if that thing…' She let the words fade, not wanting to make it any more real than it might appear in her nightmares. 'Well, you know, we can account easily enough for a bullet in a' – she straightened herself up – 'in self-defence.'

Then she looked towards the mountain. It was in complete darkness, perhaps her own torch had alerted Susan that she was being followed.

'Well, be bloody careful, no flipping heroics, right?' he shouted after her.

'Not on your life, I'll be back before...' She smiled then, looked at him, lying there prone, was that concern in his eyes? 'Promise, I'll be back before closing time.'

'Bitch.' He called after her, but she had a feeling he'd have smiled if it wasn't for the agony of his ankle.

In some ways, walking on the rock was easier. At least here, the ground was solid. There were no roots crossing unexpectedly, tripping you up and throwing your movement out of rhythm. The only downside was the rain, making everything slippery, and Iris wasn't sure if she was imagining it or if it glittered on the ground beneath her feet as she ran. Occasionally, up ahead, she thought she caught glimpses of a flashlight, throwing brightness over and back, as if rooting through the landscape for an elusive treasure. Iris steadied her course so she was moving towards the beam, only too well aware that it might be extinguished suddenly. By her crude reckoning it was at least another fifteen minutes on foot, but now the wind was driving rain into her face and her clothes were strapped soaked to her body, she was not able to move at a brisk pace; sheer desperation drove her on.

The light went out once more and she cursed, realising that she hadn't been looking where she was going, not really. She'd only been watching that beacon in the distance and now she had come to the end of the stony plate and she was knee deep in mud and rushes. The water and soil squelched, horrible and cold, around her legs, icing her feet and she cursed, but managed to do so under her breath. She waded out to the side, she would have to keep going, just head for the mountains' peak – with a little luck, the beam would surface again and she could steer herself back on course.

The clouds overhead rumbled forebodingly now and she counted the seconds after a loud boom. Ten. Ten long, cold, wet and frightening seconds and then the sky lit up – a long sheet of electrifying whiteness that brought a pristine, if somewhat weird brightness to the vista ahead of her. Iris had been counting the seconds to figure out how far away the storm was; her father, well, Jack Locke, would have said that meant it was about ten miles away. That didn't matter now. All that mattered was that she moved fast. She was very close. She'd seen a flash of someone, caught in a stream of brightness from what looked like a moving flashlight, arms and legs and hair trailing behind, running wildly down the mountain.

Eleanor was coming straight for her. The only problem was, Susan was right behind her.

CHAPTER 34

Eleanor's body ached as it never had before. She ran, blindly, drunkenly, knowing only that she had to run. It was all she could do to stay in front, the leaves had ambushed her, the trees made her dizzy, their trunks passing by her, arms outstretched. She thought they were her allies, until she needed them. Would she never learn?

Her mind was clearing. Thoughts were rushing through her, racing, faster, faster and her feet kept hitting the damp ground, keeping up. Where was she going? West, towards the evening sun? Running away from morning light? It was foolish. Should she just stop now? And if she got there, what would she do? Throw her arms around her mother? No. Susan had never been her mother and Susan had killed Rachel, she'd seen her, she remembered now. There was no taking back those moments. She had forgotten that.

It seemed to her now – with the clarity these last days had given her – that she had forgotten far more than she really remembered in those moments after Rachel died. Must be the pills, they took so much away. The memories had become soft focus, evolving into a lifetime of days in the garden, on the beach, helping her forget a lot of the other. Not a bad thing, maybe. Maybe she should turn back now, before it was too late. She couldn't, and she only half knew it. There was something after her, chasing her down like a wild animal. When she saw that face earlier, intent on her plan, she knew she had to run.

A low rumble of thunder overhead made her jump. The sleepy veil that had cloaked her senses thanks to the scores of antidepressants was beginning to lift. What a wonderful gift secreted below. Beyond it, all her memories were safely stored, like hidden treasure. Pandora's box? She longed to sit, just for a while, and delve into them. Taking them out, turning them over in her brain, remembering, feeling the warmth, feeling what it was to be loved.

Then Susan was behind her, it was becoming a muddle. She dived over, hard and far, falling for long seconds into what felt like a watery eternity. In that minute, she looked at her: terror. Susan's face was filled with it. Was she afraid of the water? After everything she'd done to Eleanor, was she afraid to get wet? Eleanor laughed hysterically as she hit the icy palms of water that waited for her. She drifted easily downstream. It would take her some time to catch up on foot. Now she was behind her and somehow, bad and all as Curlew Hall was, she knew without doubt, it was better than what her stepmother had in mind for her. A shiver ran through her floating body, she would catch up, of that she was certain. Above her head, grey clouds rallied to cut the moon from her eyes. Would she make it home before Susan found her? She was determined to try; she had another score to settle before she rested.

The water was cold, it flooded into her wellington boots, and she stifled a scream, too late to turn back. She was a good swimmer, she'd learned in the sea. The memories rushed back to her now. The sun shone, scarcely warming the ice-cold west of Ireland waters that lapped from the depths of the Atlantic Ocean. There were screams of delight, were they hers? Her father had been there, he'd held Eleanor gently in the water, floating her on her back, carrying her over the waves, smiling each time he lifted her over the swelling water, helping her feel the rhythm of the sea. They were like any other family on the beach, their little family, just the three of them. Their picnic discarded until they were so tired and famished that warm egg sandwiches and flat lemonade tasted like the greatest treat ever. They ate hungrily, wolfing down the sandy food, Eleanor and Karena laughing, enjoying the summer sun, the lapping water, childhood.

She stopped a tear cascading down her cold cheek. Those days were gone. *Where are you now?* A tear plopped into the water. She turned, pushing the thoughts from her mind. She couldn't think of that now. Oh, how she'd love to turn back the clock to those happy days. Surely, they were just a dream.

She was swimming now, the water icy through her hair, the current dragging her away from the banks. She lay on her back, floating, her eyes open, and the black sky overhead rumbling through the uneven ceiling of thickly whipped grey clouds. She lay there for some time, enjoying the sensation, floating along, to she knew not where. Ophelia, in her watery bed: *goodnight sweet one.*

The sweep of the foliage on both sides and the heavens opening over her head welcomed her while she glided further away from the world as she knew it. Then something snagged her, she felt her wellington pull her up. The sensation scared her; she was no longer floating across a galaxy of water. Now the rush of the current was battling against her and she was stuck. She began to struggle, the water covering her face, surging up her nose, into her mouth, her head dragging beneath the level of the water. The force of the torrent against her was becoming too strong to turn. She raised her head once more. On her right, the bank was only feet away. She surged her body across, hoping to grapple some piece of stray foliage. She tried to make contact with the roots of a tree or even some abandoned branch, cast aside on one of the many windy nights she heard howl outside her window. She managed to bend across almost in half. She felt the action crippling her stomach, the unnatural force of the river against her; too much for muscles so unused to any physical exercise beyond walking. The effort was draining her.

She felt the water pound her body further down into the river. *Was this a seizure? Was this the end? Oh, not here, not now.*

She wanted to live another day. She wanted to go home to her father. Once more, she pulled her head above the water, gasping in fresh breath, snatching the view of the banks on either side. She lowered her head, right down, as far as she could to reach to the bed of the river. It was no good; all she could see was darkness, extending down, down, down. Eleanor felt her blood drain from her body. She was stuck, the water greedily sucking her down. The landscape above was fast disappearing – dark green merging into murky grey. Soon it would be little more than a hazy utopia, hardly discovered – the lost hope of what might have been. The moonlight, what there'd been of it, was vanishing fast behind scudding watery clouds. She closed her eyes. Accepting this was it. Her life, for what it was, at an end.

Then something happened. At her back, an almighty crash; a huge log was thrashing downstream. It heaved her forward, throwing every thought of giving up from her mind. With a surge, she raised her body once more towards the left, her arms outstretched, ready to grab anything protruding through her watery jail. The force was unbearable; she heaved with every ounce of strength she could muster, pushed using every grain of energy. And then she could see light, she was coming up, up towards the top of the water, her body twisted, something snapped, she didn't know what, couldn't think about it now.

She vaguely realised she'd heard the sound before, somewhere in her memory, it lurked, waiting to come back to her. For now, all of her effort – all of her mind and body – were pushing through the water, her arms stretching out further than ever before. Just then a lightning flash, enough to pick out the land around her, showing Eleanor where she needed to go next.

Across the bank, she saw her. She was just a figure, crouched in the gorse, she hadn't spotted Eleanor, but she was waiting for her, to take her to safety. She cried, and laughed and somehow, she was free, the tangle of branches had released her. Calm descended on her, wafted towards her, she could smell lavender, bluebells, daisies and freshly cut grass. The smells of childhood, of walking across neglected fields, often barefoot, all of it meshed into one hope, one memory.

Eleanor floated to the top of the water, turned onto her stomach and crossed to the side of the bank. She pulled herself out, grabbing the undergrowth of tree roots she'd eyed enviously only seconds earlier. She tugged herself to the relative safety and seclusion of a thickly growing mass of rhododendron. Once inside she lay on her back, feeling safe, away from the possible prying eyes of Susan. She'd rest here for a second, her breath was loud and ragged in her chest, God, she couldn't have a seizure now, not now.

Then the pounding footsteps of her stepmother on the ground above her ears knocked her quickly from her rest. She was almost here. Overhead, the thunder began to crank itself into a groaning frenzy once more and Eleanor knew she stood no chance against Susan in this state. She'd have to keep on running, run towards the foliage where she'd seen the woman hunching earlier.

CHAPTER 35

Slattery lay back against what he presumed was a tree stump – he didn't have much of a choice, the pain in his leg was searing through him in lancing stabs. When it happened, he'd felt hot salty tears leave his eyes – and he was not a crier, far from it, but the physical reaction to the blow had been so enormous that it seemed to rattle him to his very core. Well, he thought to himself now as he heard the low rumble of thunder overhead, there'd be no more of that carry-on.

He had watched as Iris ran out of sight – to be honest, he'd have given anything to trade places with her, the last thing that girl needed was more emotional baggage after their last case. He cursed. You never get to choose, wasn't that half the problem? He shifted awkwardly, hoping that the fresh darts of pain up his leg and into his stomach would be worth it for a cigarette; he wasn't sure. He felt a wave of nausea surge over him and then it was too late, he'd thrown up all over himself. He cursed again, lit the damned cigarette and regretted that he no longer carried a small bottle of Jimmy in the inside pocket of his jacket. At a time like this, whiskey could be the saving of a man.

He shook his head, stopped, suddenly his senses on high alert. Something had moved, not far away, in the undergrowth. It had been a rustle, more than a hedgehog – didn't they hibernate? Could be a fox? That was no harm. Slattery had always liked foxes, if anything he felt a bit of a kinship to them. Why on earth would anyone want to badmouth a fox, or worse send a pack of dogs to pull it apart? Another rustle and this time he decided to ignore the sounds. He was trespassing, perhaps sitting right in the centre of some forager's route to feed a family.

He smoked his cigarette, but it was still there and no matter how he tried to shake it off, there was no getting away from the fact that the hairs on the back of his neck had risen to a point of high alert. There was something close by and it or they were dangerous. Slattery thought for a moment about Susan Marshall – she'd have no reason to attack him here. A policeman she had little respect for, someone who she thought she was so superior to, if anything she'd walk around him and hope the elements took care of him.

He reached into his jacket, slid his hand along his chest, pulling out the standard-issue Sig Sauer. God, he hoped he could keep at least this perfect record. He'd never killed anyone – it was something to stand over, for Slattery it might be the best they could say about him. It slipped easily from the holster, its metal warm from lying against his body. He took the cigarette from his mouth, threw it down towards the drain beneath him. He didn't dare breathe, as he could feel the thing coming closer, inching towards him, a living, breathing animosity – he wasn't sure if he should call out. Perhaps if he remained silent whoever was there would pass by, unaware that they'd almost crossed paths? Then he thought of Iris and he felt the blood drain from his head, he couldn't let this horror follow her into that no man's land.

Without saying a word, he reached towards the ground beside him, pulled up his Maglite and switched on the beam at full light. Out of the pitch black, it pulled trees first and then it halted on the most remarkable sight Slattery had ever seen: a full-grown male grey wolf. The creature stood for what seemed like an eternity, considering what his best option was – fight or flight, presumably. Slattery tried to think of all those pub quizzes, but he couldn't figure out if this majestic animal was considering him for dinner or if he preferred more vegetable-based produce.

The wolf watched him with the curiosity one might expect a seven-year-old to display at the zoo, their silent communication only broken by a loud volleying in the clouds – thunder, long and low – it surprised him, making him jump, as if he'd reacted to something deep within his nature, and then he was gone, racing back into the woods and towards the emergency services Slattery could hear on the trail behind him.

'Christ.' It was as much as he could manage before he lit another fag and prayed to whoever Maureen had on call that Iris Locke would come out of there in one piece.

CHAPTER 36

Iris narrowed her eyes, hoped for another roll of thunder, another flash of lightning to bring into focus what she needed. She had two choices: she could hunker down here, where there was some coverage from briars and gorse, or she could begin to make her way to them. She had a feeling that if the lightning should pick her out, Eleanor would probably turn and run back into Susan's path.

There wasn't time to think. Iris felt her pulse thump in her veins. It was pushing a viral beat up to her brain, as if the pressure of what might happen next could somehow force an explosion inside her head. Then, she heard it, a soft rumble, low and steady – a long way off, or perhaps just warming up for the main curtain call. She dropped, as if pulled down by some invisible weight into the thorny wild shrubs that she'd so often admired from the roadside. Not so bloody lovely now that she'd be picking thorns from every inch of her at the end of this. Maybe, she thought, for one cynical moment, just maybe, a broken ankle would be easier.

She crouched down, her whole body on high alert, her eyes trained on the vista ahead. Come on. *Come on*, she willed Eleanor forward, *just come on, let's get this over with*. She wanted to call her, put her hand across her own mouth to stop shouting out. The one thing she had, apart from the Glock pistol in her holster, was the element of surprise. That was the only thing she hoped to use with a wild card like Eleanor to fight for – she had a feeling it could go either way.

And then, before she had time to think another thought, the thunder erupted like a symphony above her head. The sky had opened to let a massive groan out onto the land below and Iris shook with the ferocity of it, bent down further within the scrub, her eyes the only part of her venturing above the level of the bushes. It yawned out incessantly, so Iris forgot to breathe for what seemed like too long, then there was the most abrupt and total silence that she'd ever experienced and a second later, as if to punctuate the noiselessness, the sound of breathing, hard and fast, and boots squelching through the mud.

Iris still couldn't make out a shape; she couldn't be sure who was running towards her first. She stared, trying hard to see through the pitch black, counting the seconds off in her head. It seemed that each one was taking an eternity, then the pounding steps again. It felt as if her heart was hammering with each depression in the sodden earth. And then, on five – as if this place couldn't take it any longer, as much as Iris couldn't – a long narrow sheet of silver raced across the sky. At first it dazzled so bright, it almost knocked Iris back into the mud, but she steadied herself and searched out the land ahead and there, only feet from her was Eleanor, running alone, no sign of Susan.

Iris didn't dare move for a second, she wished she knew what to do – would calling out frighten her or would she now be happy to be led back to some kind of safety.

'Eleanor.' She felt the name drop in a whisper from her lips, she hardly heard it herself, but the girl spun around, as if she'd been called on a loudhailer. Iris found herself rising slowly, showing herself, hoping that having fallen in mud and run through the woods in the pelting rain she didn't look like the one to run from. 'It's okay, I'm Iris, I'm a policewoman, and I'm here to help you to safety.' It was too many words, she knew that, but it was nerves and exhaustion and, yes, she could admit it out here on her own, it was fear too.

And then it happened, a huge blinding blow from behind. Iris hardly registered it happening. It struck her low on her back.

Perhaps, if Susan had struck earlier, she might not have missed her footing. She might have hit her target instead of falling as she aimed the mighty blow. It still winded Iris, having Susan fall in on top of her didn't help either. Iris did her best to wriggle out as quickly as she could, but it was not easy, it was hard to catch her breath, never mind gain purchase on the slippery ground below. They were bordering on swamp here and she knew that if Susan didn't manage to finish her off one way, she'd surely try another. Then she felt those strong hands about her neck, pushing her forward into the mud, Susan holding her down as much with the full weight of her body as the strength of her hands. She was shouting, screaming, beside herself with rage, but Iris couldn't make out a word of it. Instead, she focussed on keeping her mouth and nose off to the side, avoiding the water, gasping. Susan was weighing her down and then she felt her face submerge into the mucky water.

Panic overtook her, she flailed and thrashed about, but the other woman was on her back, she had pinned her down, there was no getting away, the mud in her shoes from earlier was just another leverage keeping her low. Still, the ranting over her head, she could hear it, loud and angry – Susan was screaming at Eleanor. She was screaming that she hated her, that she should never have been born. She wanted nothing to do with Kit Marshall's daughter.

And then it felt as if the lights went out – not that it had grown darker, it couldn't possibly, but rather, Iris had the sensation that for the first time in her life she was alone. Really alone. Slattery was too far away and too injured anyway to help. June and Westmont were in the Ship's Inn at this point, probably wondering where she and Slattery had disappeared to now. Her mother, well, if that was what she wanted to be called these days, was tucked up in a convalescence home on the far side of Limerick – and everyone who really belonged to her was dead. The darkness was swallowing her now, but perhaps… she stopped fighting, stopped flailing, perhaps the darkness might not be such a bad thing.

And then, everything stopped.

Silence.

Until a low howl began to rumble just above Iris's head. She felt the force of Susan's weight suddenly shift; the hands behind her head relax. Then she was pushed heavily forward as the other woman jumped away from her. Iris didn't need to look up, wasn't sure she had the energy to manage it anyway.

It was a huge grey wolf standing over them, baring long teeth from behind his dark muzzle. His presence was a stirring, stupefying thing. It halted everything around them to a full stop. In her haste to pull away from him, Susan managed to fall backwards, into the water, stunned for one precious moment, before the wolf took off into the blackness of the mountain ahead.

The swoop when it came was frightening and delicious all at once. It felt at first as if Iris had been lifted high by an angel, but of course, she didn't believe in angels anymore, how could she? It had landed her on her back, against the soft turf that lay just feet above another gushing drain. Someone was wiping the hair back from her face, looking with concern into her half-open eyes. Iris realised it was Eleanor. Eleanor had pulled Susan off her, just as the wolf had appeared. She must have pulled her out of the water and dragged her away from the thorns and swamp.

'Thank you,' she murmured softly, raising her filthy hands up to her eyes. She could feel the mud everywhere. Her face and clothes had become drenched in it, so it was drying uncomfortably into her eyes – if she didn't get it out now, they would close up and there would be no way she could fight off another attack if Susan rallied. 'Where's Susan?' she whispered, then looked at Eleanor – but the girl just returned her stare before pointing at the bank below where a sodden, miserable heap of a woman was gasping for breath in the freezing waters.

Far down the mountain, Iris could see that the emergency services had arrived. She fished in her pocket for her phone and rang Slattery.

'You all right, partner?' she asked.

'Never better,' he groaned.

'Don't take up too much of their time, will you, we have a few more passengers looking for lifts up here too,' she said softly, and then she switched on her Maglite and aimed it high in the air. 'Not long now,' she said softly to Eleanor. 'Not long now.'

She watched the figure opposite, who was trying her best to get up and probably would have if Eleanor hadn't run at her with such ferocity that Susan hunkered down into a shuddering ball. This was how the emergency services found them ten minutes later.

CHAPTER 37

They kept Slattery in for a night. Somehow, even with the trolley crisis and a lack of X-ray services, they managed to volley him through, patch him up and dispatch him the following day. Iris had a feeling it had as much to do with wanting to get rid of him as it did with any kind of attention to bed blocking numbers. A broken ankle had done little to lighten his mood and when Iris went to collect him, he barked at her for parking in the disabled bay when there was plenty of space available on the double yellows.

'Watch yourself or I'll leave you here – I'll tell them I think you must have got concussion,' she threatened as she heaved his unstable wheelchair out the door.

Her own recovery had been swift – mostly she was thorn-free now, there was bruising where Susan had tried to finish her off but a hot shower had taken care of the mud that had settled hard and thick on her skin. Of course, she knew a shower wouldn't sort out everything, but she'd managed to sleep well after the ordeal – not surprising when she'd only had roughly three to four hours sleep a night for the past week. They wanted her to go see a shrink after it all; she didn't like to mention that after what happened with Jack Locke, really, Susan Marshall would have to stand in line if she was planning to keep her awake at night.

The case conference earlier that morning had been jubilant. They'd managed to save Eleanor and she was resting in hospital now with Kit at her side. Susan, thanks to one of the best solicitors in the country, was being surprisingly helpful.

'Diminished responsibility?' Slattery repeated gruffly. He stood for a moment, lit a cigarette beneath the NO SMOKING sign while he waited for her to move the passenger seat back and open the boot for the wheelchair the ward sister insisted he bring home with him. 'Who's going to find her capable of anything that takes reason?' he asked, plopping into the chair again so she could wheel him next to the car. 'She's as mad as a bag of weasels. He'll have told her to help us all the way. Later, they'll run a couple of psychiatric tests on her. Let's face it, Marshall's going to know the judge and prosecutor well enough to know how to swing things her way.'

'Well, he's seen through her, at least,' Iris said. She was disappointed. After all they'd seen, she knew that Susan Marshall had set out to murder Rachel McDermott. She had created an unforgivable wedge between Kit and Eleanor and if she'd had a chance, she'd probably have murdered her too. She was motivated not by the kind of madness she'd have a judge believe, rather she was driven by blind greed because she believed Rachel might mean trouble to her marriage to a wealthy man. They could talk all they wanted about the years of self-harm and the fact that she'd suffered several breakdowns, but at the end of the day, there's a big difference between being unwell and being a murderer.

'And you know that might hurt her most, when she's locked up in the central mental hospital, than any kind of therapy they offer her. Probably be an even bigger blow than being locked up.'

'How does a woman turn out like that?' Iris said as she pulled the car out onto the main road.

'Hasn't it dawned on you yet?' Slattery shook his head, smiling that wry, infuriating smile that just made her want to shake him. 'Eleanor's not her daughter. She was bloody screaming it up on that mountain for us all to hear. Eleanor is Marshall's daughter, not Susan's. She's spent most of her marriage jealous of the relationship he had with his daughters, tried to get between them at every turn.

I'd bet my lunch money that she was responsible for most of what Eleanor's been blamed for over the years.'

'It doesn't bear thinking about, does it? Poor Eleanor, she had no chance, no matter which way she turned.' Iris wanted to stop the car to take it in. The injustice of it was almost too much to take.

'Yep. I asked Susan about it, before they took her away. They gave her a quick examination in the ambulance before taking her to the hospital. The way she was screaming you'd have heard her over in Boston.'

'I heard her screaming, she'd done that earlier too, but… she had my head under water, I couldn't hear anything.'

'Yeah, well, she probably didn't think anyone else could either. It seems that Susan couldn't have children, but that wasn't the case with Kit, he had two children, both before he'd married Susan. In the beginning, he'd employed her to take care of them before his first wife died.' Slattery tossed the fag aside thoughtfully. 'You'd know straight off, even with all the fancy elocution, that she came from nowhere and nothing. Being married to Kit Marshall was her ticket to the kind of life she could only have dreamed of, she wasn't letting anything come between them, not even his daughters.'

'She told you all this sitting in the back of an ambulance?' Iris looked at him, and then remembered she was driving and looked back at the road in time to stop the car swerving off to the left.

'And that's not all. Rachel McDermott never wanted a penny from Marshall – all she'd ever wanted was to have a relationship with her two sisters and her father. But it turned out, that was another thing Susan couldn't tolerate. Susan never even asked Marshall if Rachel could have been his daughter, instead she took matters into her own hands. She went out to Curlew Hall that night to kill her and she would have killed Eleanor too, but the girl managed to slip away from her. Once Eleanor knew what she'd done, it was only a matter of time until Karena found out and so Susan followed her that night into the woods, hoping to clear up the remaining loose ends. Karena had gone to look for Eleanor, but she never arrived, instead she confronted Susan and…'

'God and all because of a stupid mix-up,' Iris said, thinking of the sheet of paper that they'd tracked down earlier. She also had a feeling that Slattery hadn't quite reached his trump card yet. 'There's something else, isn't there?'

'Kit's wife, the way she died, there were always questions…'

'So, Susan may have been responsible for that too?'

'We'll have to look into it, but well, if she's capable of murdering twice…'

'Wonderful, it won't do a lot to bring any of them comfort now though, will it?'

'No, but I'll bet it could be enough to make Marshall cut ties with her for good,' Slattery said and they both knew this meant that there would be no fancy legal team – which would be good for their case – good for justice.

They were speeding back into the city. Slattery had to be dropped off at home but then Iris was heading into the station to read back over the case file and put in additional notes that still lay on her desk. They had more questions for Susan, there were loose ends that Iris knew couldn't be left untied. Everyone was due at least a day or two off then, otherwise, the overtime bill would be astronomical. No one was going to argue with the order to stay at home for a long weekend in the middle of the week. This case had wiped them all out.

'What the—?' Slattery yelled at her as she turned into his street. 'I can't stay here, my flat is on the first floor. Do you know how many steps I have to get up and down every time I want to go and get a bottle of milk?'

'So, where to?' Iris pulled in on the path while he thought.

'I suppose…' he was angling.

'No way, you're not staying with me, Slattery. I'm staying in a bloody boarding house and lucky to have found a place at such short notice. The last thing I want is you upsetting Mrs Leddy with your cantankerous ways. No, Slattery, you'll have to go to Maureen.'

'No, I can't… not there, please.' He sounded like a child, pleading with her and if she didn't know him as well as she did, she might have given in to him.

'From what I hear, she'll spoil you rotten. You won't have to lift anything heavier than a teacup and she'll pray for your soul as well, what more could you want?' she asked, turning the car around and heading for the opposite side of town.

There was a certain sense of satisfaction, dropping Slattery off with Maureen that afternoon. The house was an average, everyday detached bungalow, tucked away in the centre of a horseshoe-shaped estate. The houses, all built in the 1980s, were probably homes to second families now, with the first generation of child-rearing having moved on, only Maureen and one or two more remaining.

'Oh, that's right, bring him in here,' Maureen said and she bustled about with great energy and enthusiasm for her uninvited guest. 'Of course, I'll look after him, it's what I promised the day I married him, for better or for worse. Mind you, if I'd known then…' she said ruefully, her cracking voice gave way the disease that lurked behind her bustling manner and Iris couldn't help but wonder, exactly who would be looking after whom. Then Maureen looked at Iris, with genuine concern in her eyes. 'You poor girl, you don't mean to tell me you have to put up with him all the time?' She shook her head, as if she could hardly take in the hardship of it all.

'Well, Slattery, I think you're in safe hands here,' Iris said, smiling at him, though she caught that unspoken word between them. He'd get her back for this, one day soon; he'd make sure he'd have the last laugh. Iris bent down, squeezed his shoulder. 'Try to behave,' she said to his cross snarl, but she still remembered the look in his eyes from that night in the woods, it had been as plain to see as if he'd uttered the words. He cared about what happened to her and that made him the closest thing to family she had these days – whether either of them liked it or not.

EPILOGUE

Five bells rang out across the river. Iris still hadn't succumbed to the urge to take out her semi-automatic and sort out their melodious intrusion. Funny, but she always woke at the same hour. This morning, she even welcomed the reminder that life was going on beyond the four walls of her cramped room. She switched on the kettle and dropped a peppermint teabag into a dark mug – all the better to hide the inevitable caffeine rings that surely loitered in its depths.

A few days earlier a letter had arrived; it sat unopened by the kettle on the chest of drawers. The handwriting was so familiar it still made her gasp. Her father. Reaching out to her from beyond the grave. She knew what it would say, Jack Locke would have sewn together the words he needed to exonerate his wife and shoulder the burden of guilt and blame. She knew, because the DPP had already been in touch. It seemed, that even in death, old Nessie was taking care of Theodora. For now, at least, it looked as if no one would pay for the crimes that had turned her world upside down and engineered the deaths of her sister Anna and Anna's two small kids. Iris couldn't bring herself to open that envelope and so she'd left it there to taunt her instead. She figured she could always burn it, cut it out as she was slowly cutting out Theodora – but she didn't think she truly had the heart for either.

She turned away from the recriminating envelope, she would think of something else. She sighed deeply in the empty darkness. She had to give some sort of shape to her life, even if she wasn't sure how to do that. She imagined Grady whispering in her ear: *One day at a time, just take whatever comes your way and make the most of it.*

Byrne had phoned earlier in the week. He cleared his throat, congratulated her on the closing of the case and then, as though he might choke, wondered if she'd be interested in applying for Grady's old post. The interviews were in two weeks' time. Detective *Inspector* Iris Locke. It had a nice ring to it, she thought. *Interested? Of course, she was interested.*

A LETTER FROM GERALDINE

Dear Reader,

I wanted to say a huge thank you for choosing to read *Why She Ran*, the second in the new Corbally Crime series. I've so enjoyed writing this book and, as you might imagine, there are many more stories waiting to unfold around this pair. Already, I'm plotting away at their next case and I promise it's as full of twists and turns as this one, but also filled with familiar faces from Corbally! If you would like to keep up to date with the latest news on my new releases, click on the link below to sign up to my mailing list. I promise to only contact you when I have a new book out and I'll never share your email with anyone else.

www.bookouture.com/geraldine-hogan

Writing a new book is both thrilling and scary. Really, my place in its creation is almost at an end by the time it arrives in your hands. At this stage, the thing I look forward to most is hearing how it's received, so if you have time, please do post a short review or share it on social media. There is nothing like word of mouth to help new readers discover my books! I'm always up for a bookish chat on Twitter or find me on Instagram or Facebook. There's something very moving about reading a review that really 'gets' a book!

If you enjoyed this book and you want to keep an eye on what I'm up to next, you can follow me on Amazon or Bookbub where I'll let you in on what's going on in my world of books!

Happy reading,
Geraldine Hogan

@GerHogan

faithhoganauthor

GeraldineHoganAuthor

www.geraldine-hogan.com

ACKNOWLEDGEMENTS

To you my reader – thank you for picking up my book – I do hope you enjoyed it and you'll come back for more…

In becoming the story in your hands today, I want to thank most sincerely the following people.

I count myself as very lucky to be a J girl – thanks to Judith Murdoch, my agent, who is kind, witty, savvy and very, very wise!

Thank you to Lydia Vasser-Smith, for putting in so much thought, energy and genius on my behalf! Thank you to team Bookouture – especially Jon Appleton, Leodora Darlington, Lauren Finger and Alexandra Holmes for their ace editing skills and to Kim Nash and Noelle Holten – publicity wizards!

A big thank you to all of my author friends across the Lounge, the Savvies and on Twitter – you make coffee break even better!

Since I began to write, I've been lucky to fall into a community of book bloggers – too many to mention and much too generous to forget. They share a love of books, generously and enthusiastically – you are a rare gift!

Thank you to Silke, Michelle, Olivia and Mairead, and all the Scannan–Beehive Team who have kept the show on the road, giving me a chance to write and to breathe!

Thank you to Bernadine Cafferkey – I wouldn't have written this without you.

Thank you to Christine Cafferkey who is always there and gave me the gift of time when this book was just a flicker of possibility.

To my wonderful family, Seán, Roisín, Tomás, Cristín – I count my blessings every day!

And finally, to James, for more than I can possibly begin to put into words. xx